ALEX'S ATONEMENT

Midnight Sons – Book Two

Carmen DeSousa

A Romantic Suspense Series

Alex's Atonement
A Midnight Sons Novel

Copyright© 2019 by Carmen DeSousa

ISBN: 9798620648269

www.CarmenDeSousaBooks.com
www.WrittenMusings.com

Cover Design: www.AustinWalp.com

U.S.A.

For any other permission, please visit
www.WrittenMusings.com for contact links.

THE MIDNIGHT SONS

Men as Wild and Rugged as The Last Frontier Itself

Five brothers risk their lives to rescue those caught in the death grip of the Alaska wilderness … and risk losing their hearts to women as tough as the Land of the Midnight Sun.

SERIES DESCRIPTION

The siren call of Alaska's untamed wilderness draws thrill-seekers from around the globe. But with more unsolved missing-person cases than anywhere else in the world, the Alaska Triangle has an ominous reputation. Enter SAR Team Alaska, five brothers who risk their lives to rescue those in peril.

Being a hero isn't all it's cracked up to be, though. The pay sucks, as does the fact that the team leaders have to be ready to spring into action 24/7, 365 days a year — a lifestyle not conducive to a healthy love life. Worse, while the brothers are experts in their individual fields, they each harbor inner demons and secrets that threaten to tear their family apart … and jeopardize any chance of finding the women who could complete them.

CHAPTER 1

~ Alex ~

Alex watched his brother Sam stroll toward the elevator with his bride. The newly wedded couple giggled and snuggled as they tottered inside. Sam had lifted his champagne flute a few too many times in response to umpteen toasts. But he was in his wife's arms. No condemnation. No fears.

Sam and Nora had each other, and that was all that mattered. For the time being, Nora's troubled past didn't matter, and their family's struggling business wasn't a concern. And after a night of bliss in their newlywed suite, they'd take off for their two-week honeymoon in Argentina.

Alex hadn't even felt the familiar waves of animosity from his brother that usually hovered over them like dense Denali cloud cover. He had been shocked that Sam had asked him to be his best man. Had Sam finally stopped blaming him for their father's death? About the part Alex had played?

Didn't matter. Even if Alex couldn't admit it to anyone, he knew the truth. His soul suffered daily from his actions. If it hadn't been for his immaturity, he wouldn't have forgotten his critical gear, and his father wouldn't have insisted that Alex take his ice ax. And his father, one of the greatest men who'd ever walked the earth, wouldn't have died in the avalanche. No, Alex would have died instead.

Alex had cheated death. Because his father had been a better man than he was, Alex had lived.

He exhaled loudly, his breath steaming up the window of the hotel bar. Outside, across the frozen lake, sat a row of seaplanes. One of them was his. Tomorrow, he'd set things right. For Sam, for his family ... for his father.

He'd had to wait two long years after he'd taken out the life insurance policy, after the company's contestability period. Even though he was certain his death would look like an accident, he couldn't take any chances that Sam wouldn't receive the nearly two-million-dollar policy — 1.8 million, to be exact. The company had maxed out his policy at thirty times his annual salary.

Nora showing up in their lives had delayed his plans another eight months. But it was for the best, and a part of him felt better that she was in Sam's life — and his mother's life.

He'd taken care of every contingency. He'd written a will, leaving everything to Sam, so the proceeds wouldn't end up in probate. His life wasn't worth much, but what he did have would assure that the Midnight Sons would continue saving lives long after his death. And wasn't that what made a man a hero ... the willingness to lay down his life for others? In a sense, his death would save others by saving the company that saved so many people every year.

"Beautiful in a weird kind of way, isn't it?" The woman's voice that came from behind him was low and raspy, almost secretive.

Had he spoken his plans aloud, initiating her odd question?

Alex turned to take in the woman, ready to defend his actions. Others wouldn't understand his decision, he knew. Wouldn't understand that every night when he tried to sleep he saw his father smothered to death by snow ... and knew that he'd been responsible. He'd spent the last ten years drowning himself in carnal pleasures, anything to take away the nightmare he relived nightly. Nothing had worked.

To his surprise, the female voice belonged to the auburn-haired beauty who'd been sitting in the back row at his brother's wedding. They'd shared a moment together from across the room, but when he'd looked for her at the reception, he hadn't been able to find her. He'd been tempted to look for a glass slipper, wondering why the mystery woman had disappeared. Now, here she stood.

He cocked his head, wondering why she was here now. Promptly at midnight, right after the open bar closed, all the guests from the wedding reception had staggered to their rooms. Sam and Nora were the last to leave. Most of his family's friends were first responders, so they had to make the drive back to Falcon Run early tomorrow.

"Excuse me?" he said, ready to tell her that what he did with his life was none of her business. Yeah, she looked good, but he'd already decided that he wouldn't ruin Sam's night by seducing one of the women at his wedding party.

The woman waved her hand at the glass windows. "The snow blankets even the ugliest trash and somehow makes it beautiful."

"Oh, yeah ... I agree," he said, shaking off his unfounded irritation. "It is beautiful in a weird kind of way. A little cold for my taste, but that's one of the downsides of living in Alaska. You have to deal with six months of dark and bitter cold to appreciate nearly round-the-clock sunshine during the remaining six months."

The woman strolled past him, leaving a hint of vanilla in her wake. She approached the bank of windows that surrounded the closed bar & grill. Her slender fingers splayed against the glass, the heat of her hands causing an immediate reaction on the icy pane. "Winter or summer, I never used to appreciate the beauty. I couldn't wait to escape."

Alex scrubbed at his five o'clock shadow and closed his eyes. The look the woman had flashed him earlier at the wedding had been an invitation if he ever saw one. And he'd seen plenty. *Not tonight,* he reminded himself. *Why not?* insisted his less-noble self. *She's not Evie. You don't even know her. Sam's night is over. Why shouldn't you have one final fling?*

He shook his head at his crazy thoughts but found he wanted to listen to them. After all, what difference *did* it make? He had lived a high-octane life. If he was going to go down in flames, might as well enjoy his last night. Without his permission, his legs propelled him toward the glass wall, to the beautiful woman.

Her auburn hair was a little shorter than he preferred, but it suited her. Her body, while shapely, was a tad skinny. He'd always preferred athletic types. Still, she was a woman, and he loved women. He hoped whatever realm he ended up in tomorrow had women.

He couldn't imagine spending eternity without a soft body next to him.

He stepped next to the woman, but his eyes remained focused on the line of seaplanes again. Actually, as she'd indicated, all he really saw was the snow as it fell beneath the lights of the marina, and the outline of the seaplanes swathed in a blanket of white. "Ever been on a seaplane?"

"Mm-hm."

Not many women had answered yes to that question. One of his best pickup lines was relating to a woman that he was a pilot. He wasn't sure why, but most women cooed at the idea of him taking them up in one of his three aircrafts. Technically, the airplanes and helicopter weren't his; they belonged to the family business.

He lowered his head to take in the woman up close. She was a good head shorter than his six-two. Petite and delicate. Even her skin looked so pale and soft that he feared she might shatter if he touched her. Her auburn hair was what initially caught his eye. The color reminded him of Alaska blueberry leaves, right before the season ended. When the fruit was the sweetest, the leaves turned to a dark reddish brown. The way her dark hair contrasted with her light skin made his hands ache to touch her. He imagined running his fingers through the loose waves.

Give it a rest, he ordered his libido again. Instead of fantasizing about how silky her skin would feel against his, he moistened his dry lips. "So, you're from here?"

She pointed southwest. "Saint Paul Island."

"You're kidding!" The burst of laughter that escaped his throat snapped him out of his meandering fantasies.

And based on her furrowed brows, if she'd been fantasizing about him, she'd stopped the moment he'd lost all sense of decorum by guffawing at her answer.

"Why is that funny?"

"I'm sorry. That was rude." He pinched his temple. "I don't know why I found that so funny. Maybe because, like … what, five hundred people live there? And most are native, right? Honestly, I thought only Aleuts and fur seals lived on Saint Paul Island."

She twisted her mouth and shook her head. "Yes, fur seals definitely dominate the beaches. Not all the human population is Aleut, though, obviously. But as I said, I couldn't wait to leave. I think the hottest it ever got in the summer was sixty. And the winters are brutal."

Alex forced a smile, the one his mother had always claimed would get him anything he wanted. "Again, sorry. I'm a bit slaphappy. It's been a long day. Also, one of the things I noticed about Alaska is that practically no one is from here — except my family, it seems — so I definitely didn't expect you to say Saint Paul Island. Is that why you're in Anchorage, are you running away from home?" He flashed another smile, hoping the crease between her brows would let up.

The woman's lips quirked upward, but then she closed her eyes, shaking her head again. "No, I left for college seventeen years ago and never looked back. Oddly enough, I ended up in San Francisco. Fog City, as I call it. Imagine my surprise when I ended up in a city with year-round temps like the summers on Saint Paul Island. Whereas most can't take the daily fog and damp weather of San Fran, it reminded me of home, only without the negative-zero winters."

"I've never been to San Francisco." He'd always wanted to go to California, but now he never would. He shrugged off his pathetic thoughts and focused on her. "So, you're going home? Booked a ride on one of those seaplanes, I take it?"

Her lips twisted again. "Yeah ... something like that. I doubt I'll stay long, though."

Seemed there was more to this woman's story, but as much as he'd like to get to know her, he couldn't. No strings. No attachments. He'd had to live by that motto ever since he decided his fate. Still, a name wouldn't hurt. It'd be nice to talk to someone, since he knew there was no chance he'd be able to sleep tonight.

He extended his hand. "I'm Alex."

The woman's hazel eyes held his. The brownish-red color closest to the irises nearly matched her hair. She smiled but didn't accept his hand. "I already knew your name, Alex. The maid of honor whispered it to me, along with a couple other tidbits."

He'd forgotten that Evie had bent down and whispered something in her ear. Since the woman wasn't going to take his hand, he dropped it. "What tidbits did she mention? Nothing bad, I hope."

The woman shrugged. "Bad is relative. I don't judge insider information as good or bad. I prefer to take the info and figure out the facts myself."

He raised the hand she'd rejected. "Hmm ... maybe I'm better off not knowing what Evie said. I would like to know your name, though."

A smile tugged up those apricot-stained lips. "Irene."

"Irene," he heard himself whisper back. *Damn, why was he letting this woman intrigue him?*

Irene turned from the window, strolling toward the row of high-top tables that lined the seldom-used dance floor. Even in season, most people just drank, watched sports, and of course, watched the outside show. The bar overlooked Lake Hood, the world's busiest seaplane base. Often, after a rescue, he'd end up at the bar … and then the hotel when he'd downed one too many drafts.

She kicked off her shoes and tossed a look over her shoulder. "Don't they play music here? It's only midnight, for Pete's sake."

"Not in January." For no reason he could fathom, he found himself following her. "I think my brother's wedding is the only reason the hotel's nearly full."

Irene toured the wood floor, stopping and spinning every few feet. "I want to dance." She pulled out her phone, tapped on a few keys. An Abba song started. She set the phone on one of the high tops, then reached for his hand. "Dance with me, Alex."

"Here?" He didn't dance. Not anywhere. With his trim frame and long legs, he always felt like a daddy long legs springing across the floor. Sam was the dancer. Even in high school, Sam would cut loose on the back of his pickup. The girls loved it.

She tugged on his arm. "Why not here? No one can see us."

He spied the doors that led to the lobby. "I don't know how to dance."

"Everyone knows how to dance. It's as natural as walking." When he didn't budge, she released his hand and planted her fists on her hips. "Life's too short not to dance, Alex." Instead of continuing to coax him, she twirled away as if she were the dancing queen looking for her king.

Her comment stabbed him deeply. Life *was* too short. His would be shorter than many. Why shouldn't he dance? He tentatively stepped on the floor as *Dancing Queen* streamed from the woman's phone. He'd never hear the end of it if his brothers or any of the first responders saw him dancing to *Dancing Queen*, of all things. Hell, after tomorrow morning, he'd never see them again, so what did it matter?

Nothing mattered anymore. Life *was* too short. Maybe spending his last night dancing would give this stranger something to smile about in the future. If she read about his death, she might say something like: *He didn't seem suicidal. He danced with me ...*

After all, he wasn't suicidal. Not in the least. The last thing he wanted was to die. He was just setting right a wrong. Maybe if Irene told his mother and brothers he'd been dancing with her the night before his death, they'd know he'd been happy. Maybe they would assume he'd just crashed accidentally. And if they did suspect anything, hopefully, they'd know that what he'd done, he'd done for them.

~ Irene ~

A haptic tap from her iWatch woke Irene with a start. Her eyes snapped open.

The alarm. The chartered plane.

She hadn't had to set the alarm in so long that the old familiar warning surprised her. She hadn't been on a schedule for nearly a year. Not since her surgery.

She blinked, trying to make out her surroundings. A streak of light streaming through the hotel curtains slashed a bare back. Alex Belgarde. A pilot.

Why was that so damn sexy?

Who was she kidding? When she'd spotted Alex the previous evening, she wouldn't have cared if he were an out-of-work deadbeat. She'd wanted him the moment she'd seen him standing at the front of the room as best man. He'd been staring out the windows as if he'd wanted to be anywhere other than where he was. Then, when the preacher asked for the ring, and the groom had turned to Alex with a look of fear, she'd found herself laughing for the first time in months.

Their eyes had met. She'd done her utmost to convey in those few seconds that she found him attractive. He'd shrugged off her laugh and returned her smile.

She'd flown into Anchorage the day before yesterday, and after she'd found a pilot who was willing to fly her to the island of her birth, she'd gone looking for fun. Except nothing had been going on at the hotel. The online pics she'd seen when she reserved the room had made the place look so lively. Supposedly, the hotel sat next to the most extensive collection of seaplanes in the world — and the website had boasted that the planes ran year-round. She hadn't hesitated to reserve a room. But then, nothing had been happening inside the lounge, and it was too freaking cold to leave the property.

Just as she'd been heading to her room, she'd heard the Wagner's *Bridal Chorus* streaming from the banquet room and decided to mark off one of her bucket-list items. Never in her life had she crashed a wedding.

She stretched her arm up, blinked a couple times to clear her mascara-caked eyes, and focused on the time. Five a.m.

Her gaze roamed over Alex, at the blanket that lay across his hips. As tempting as Alex looked, she didn't have time to wake him up for round two. 'Course, he had said he was a pilot, so maybe she could ask him to take her to Saint Paul Island.

No, if he'd wanted to take her, he would have offered. The last thing she planned to do with the rest of her short life was to chase anything. Not a career. Not a man.

She'd decided six months ago that she wouldn't waste one minute of her precious life. That was the only reason she was in Alaska. She'd lost too many hours — years — being angry. If she couldn't forgive and forget — and be forgiven — fine, but at least she would try. That way she wouldn't waste another minute thinking about the past.

The future wasn't a guarantee. All she had was now.

She gathered up her clothes, slipped into the bathroom, dressed, and then left Alex's room with one brief look. Damn, he was cute — and good. A tickle ran through her as she remembered how he'd made her feel last night. That Evie woman had been right. Well, she knew Alex's name and what he did for a living, so if she wanted, she could look him up when she returned to the mainland.

But that would mean she'd have to erase a check mark from her bucket list.

The previous night with Alex had been another first. She'd never had a one-night stand. Even in college, she'd been more concerned about her studies and her internship. While many of her classmates were reveling in the college life, she'd been studying or following mentors around the newsroom.

She should feel guilty for sleeping with Alex, but she didn't. She'd needed it. Desperately. Still, as she rode the elevator to the third floor, wearing the same outfit she'd worn last night, with her strappy heels dangling from her outstretched fingers, she couldn't help but feel a teensy-weensy bit trashy.

"Okay, a lot trashy," she giggled. "Who knew dying could make me feel so alive?"

The elevator dinged its arrival, and she hustled down the hall barefoot. She dug inside her clutch for the keycard and swiped it. It took all of ten minutes to pack her things and head downstairs for the shuttle.

In a few hours, she'd be with her family. Maybe. They might toss her out on her ass. They'd definitely toss her out in the snow if they knew what she'd done during her layover in Anchorage.

That thought made her smile. She had to put an end to the secrets. Forever. She would clean the slate with her family and accept whatever happened.

Thirty minutes later, Irene pulled her faux-fur-lined coat tighter around her neck, doing her best to block the harsh wind. Why hadn't she decided to return home in May?

"Oh yeah, because if the cancer returns," she spoke into her hands, trying to warm them, "you might not be alive in four months. That's why you're freezing your knickers off, Irene, remember?"

Teeth chattering and knees knocking, she waited in the hangar where the pilot had instructed. He'd been clear. If she wanted to go to Saint Paul Island, she had to be ready and waiting by six a.m. sharp. So where was the pilot? Had he taken her thousand dollars and run? He was the only pilot she'd found on such short notice who'd fly the eight hundred miles in January. The reputable company she'd used in the past didn't fly to Saint Paul until the end of March.

A loud crunch caught her attention. A nondescript Ford Taurus pulled into the snow-covered gravel lot and parked. A man hopped out, then hustled to the trunk. He slammed the lid closed and headed her way, pulling two wheeled duffle bags.

Like Alex, the man stood tall and trim. Was there a law that all pilots had to be tall, lean, and handsome? Maybe they needed to be tall to see out the window.

She glanced down at the duffel bags. Then again, maybe the man was another passenger. After all, why would the pilot need two stuffed-to-the-zipper duffle bags? Her gaze traveled back to the man's clothes. Simple, but expensive. Just the thick leather coat with the double collar and front placket probably went for a couple thousand dollars. What business would he have on Saint Paul Island? He certainly didn't look like a crabber or fisherman. And he certainly didn't look like a man who'd take her father's place as pastor.

And she highly doubted a man who dressed like that would stay at the only lodging on Saint Paul Island; he didn't look like the type to share bathroom facilities with other guests.

The man scanned the area, then jutted his chin at her. "You Irene Rose?"

"I am."

"You ready?"

Even though his question was curt and he hadn't had the decency to apologize for making her wait in the arctic weather, she smiled. "Been ready for fifteen minutes." It wasn't the first time she'd had to force a friendly smile. Hell, it was a job requirement.

The man's mouth lifted in a tight-lipped smile — rather, a smirk. Apparently, his job didn't require such niceties.

With an attitude like his, at least there's no chance of another slutty one-night stand anyway. Even if they were the only eligible singletons on an island of five hundred.

Although she'd written *one-night stand* on her bucket list, she'd never really intended to carry it out. She hadn't planned the previous night's fling, but Alex had been charming and funny. He'd danced with her even though she knew it challenged his manhood. This guy, though, was a tool. She didn't need to spend three hours on a plane to realize it. There was something to be said for first impressions; they weren't usually wrong.

The pilot eyed her two bags. "Those over a hundred pounds?"

"Fifty pounds on the nose each, according to the airlines I flew in on."

"You need help?" A huff made visible by his heated breath in the cold air followed his question.

"I'm fine. Thank you for your concern." Truly, she could use help. She was still recovering her strength after the long months of radiation therapy. From the time she'd left the baggage claim, the Uber, and even the shuttle, each of the drivers had assisted her. She hadn't had to ask. Not this man, though.

"Follow me." The man walked toward a gold-and-white seaplane with the word *Kodiak* written along the nose.

At least the plane looked reliable, even if the pilot

was a jerk. She'd get to Saint Paul Island in one piece, and that would be the end of their dealings. She had a good mind to head back to the hotel and pay Alex to take her. But no, her new life code was *Never look back*.

She'd just let this man do his job. She didn't need to talk to him or even tell him how much more business he could get by being pleasant — and punctual.

It wouldn't kill her to keep her thoughts to herself for three hours.

CHAPTER 2

~ Alex ~

Alex sat with his back to the wall. The floor-to-ceiling windows allowed cloud-diffused sunlight to brighten the restaurant. From his vantage point, he could see the seaplane port to his left and the double doors that led to the lobby on his right.

While he ate and offered a word or two to the breakfast conversation, his mind was on Irene. Why had she left his bed without saying goodbye? Had she already checked out, or would he see her as she tried to slip by the massive doors? Had her plane already left for Saint Paul Island?

He should have offered to take her — no, he shouldn't have. What was he thinking? He didn't have a future to — A clap on the table, which made the silverware and glasses rattle, cut off his thoughts. Vince had slapped his massive hands on the table and thrown his head back. Laughing, as usual. Telling another tale, no doubt. The man was a born storyteller.

Vince brought his head forward and wiped his eyes. Although he spoke loud enough for the entire restaurant and half of Anchorage to hear, it was clear he was talking to Nora. "Then, Sam jumps in that icy water and comes up with a kicking calf. Don't know where the mother was — thank God — 'cause that wee moose was screaming like Sam was gonna eat it. Sam had one arm latched around its belly and tried to cover its muzzle with the other. But the thing just kept crying 'til he shoved it up on shore."

Alex smiled but kept his mouth shut. It didn't matter if anyone knew the truth.

Sam smacked Vince's back. "You must have been on one of your binges, man. That wasn't me. I didn't jump in the river to save a moose. That was Alex."

The eight other heads at the table turned to look at Alex, then back to Vince.

"I thought that was you, Sam," Vince said, but then followed everyone else's dumbfounded looks. "Alex, that was you who jumped in to save that drowning calf, not Sam?"

Alex shrugged.

Sam smiled. "Of course it was Alex. You know I love animals, Vince, but unless it's one of my pups, I'm not risking my life to save it. That was a suicide mission. If Alex had missed that safety line, he would have slipped under that ice, and it would have been bye-bye Alex." Sam's regard moved to their youngest brother, Daire, who often pulled stunts befitting his name. "Sure, we put our lives on the line, but we have to be smart. Doesn't do any good to die without a cause."

Suddenly parched, Alex reached for his water glass. Sam was right. It'd been a foolish thing to do at the time. But Alex couldn't watch anything drown. He'd been upside down in his kayak enough times to know that it wasn't a pleasant way to die, no matter what people claimed. Nope, he planned to go out fast … and preferably unconscious.

Nora smiled at Sam and then nodded to Alex. "I think it was a noble thing to do, and Alex didn't die, so he obviously knew what he was doing."

"Thanks, Nora," Alex said with a smile. "I appreciate your vote of confidence, but Sam's right. I'd been young and dumb. Thought I was invincible back then. I should have planned instead of just jumping. I've definitely learned my lesson over the years."

Again, he hoped that when the family found the wreckage, they'd know he hadn't done anything without thinking ahead. Even though Sam didn't trust him with the business, Alex wasn't the same irresponsible idiot he used to be. Well, not when it came to rescues. He still tended to be a bit reckless when it came to women.

Like last night …

His gaze flicked to the doors again, hoping Irene had just gone back to her room and might show up for breakfast.

What was he doing? Why couldn't he stop thinking about her? Maybe because she'd gotten him to dance. Or perhaps it'd been their kiss — kisses. He hadn't intended to ask her back to his room. They'd just headed to the elevator together, and then she'd stepped out on his floor. He'd assumed she was heading to her room, but then she followed him —

"So, Alex," Erik broke him from his thoughts. "Any plans today?"

Alex tilted his head. "Uh, not really. I was just going to work on the plane. Maybe take it out for a short flight. Why?"

Erik shrugged. "Since we hardly get a free day in Anchorage, Vince and I are heading to Portage Pass Trail, just for something to do."

"Oh," Alex said. "That's all right. I'll pass. Thanks, though."

Erik didn't waste a moment turning to Daire.

Once again, Alex felt alone among the ten other people at the table. Not looping in Nora's mother and grandmother, of course, who spoke very little English.

Even though Erik had invited him, Alex knew Erik and Vince would have more fun without him, especially in his current mood. They'd been best friends since grade school, and both were a lot younger than Alex.

Daire was twenty-one, so the last thing he wanted was to hang around his thirty-three-year-old brother. His mother was, well, his mother. As much as he liked playing cards with her, she had her life. Evie hadn't missed a beat; she'd spent the previous evening dancing with a new firefighter who'd recently moved to the area, and now they were sitting awfully close to each other.

Even though Alex and Sam were five years apart in age, they'd mostly gotten along. Sam hadn't even minded when Alex hung out with him when he was in eighth grade, and Sam had been a senior. But Sam had Nora now.

Alex hadn't realized how much he would miss Sam. Hadn't realized how much he relied on him. In a way, Sam had taken the place of their father.

Shaking his head, Alex looked to the lake. What he could see of it anyway. The cloud cover hung low. The wind was also cranking, whooshing white mist across the water's surface. Looked like one of those nature shows where they sped up the film to show the time passing.

Not caring about what the day had in store, he'd only glanced at the weather. He had to make sure that he could at least get safely into the air. After that, he had planned to let nature take its course. According to the AccuWeather app, though, the cloud cover would burn off by midday. Temps would be in the teens, not too cold. It would be a beautiful flight. Nature wouldn't do the trick. He'd have to conveniently *forget* to fill up his gas tanks.

The server started clearing the dishes, so Alex motioned her over. He slipped two hundred-dollar bills into her hand. "This should cover the bill. Keep the change."

"But, sir …" said the young woman. "The bill isn't even close to —"

"It's okay." He offered her a smile, and her face lit up.

Sam caught his eye, and Alex waved him off too, mouthing, *My treat.*

At that, Sam scooted back his chair. "I guess we have a plane to catch."

"You need a lift, Sam?" Alex asked, but his mother stood.

"I'm going to take them, Alex," she said, "then head back home. Unless you want to come with me."

"Nah. I'll say my goodbyes here." Alex walked to Sam and pulled him into a hug. "I love you, brother. Be safe."

Sam returned the hug. "Aren't I always?"

Alex leaned back. "Yeah, you always are." He sighed and walked around the table, walking up to his mother. Alex pulled her against him.

"Oh!" Claire Belgarde laughed. "Thank you for that,

sweetheart." She pulled back and looked up at him. "You okay, Alex?"

"Yeah, Mom. Just be careful driving home, okay? The roads are a bit icy. I love you."

She smiled, showing off the crinkles that fanned out at the edges of her eyes. The wispy lines hinted of a life well lived, the maturity of her fifty-some years, the happy times … and the sad moments that had plagued her. He hoped his death wouldn't add more.

His mother touched his cheek as she stared up at him. "Of course, honey. I'll drive slowly. You be careful if you take out that old seaplane. We should probably think about upgrading Old Betsy soon."

Alex huffed out a nervous laugh. "Yeah. Probably need to." He released his mother and walked up behind Erik and Vince, draping his arms over their shoulders. "Since we're all hugging …"

The pair laughed, but then turned and returned his embrace one by one.

"You two be safe out there today," Alex said. "Don't wake up any bears."

Vince laughed. "What's the fun in that?"

Alex stepped away and caught Daire as Sam was saying goodbye to him. "What are you up to today, Daire?"

His baby brother smiled. "If I don't get a call, I'll be studying for the upcoming exam. I really hope to be on the force before summer."

"Good move!" Alex pulled him into a hug. "Love you, man."

Like his mother, Daire leaned back and stared at him. Unlike his mother, Daire was eye-to-eye with him. "You okay, bro?"

"Sure. Just feeling a bit nostalgic with Sam getting married and all. Soon you'll be leaving the family home."

Daire laughed. "Not too soon. I don't plan to settle down for a long while. I saw what Vince went through with his wife. No thanks! Not many women like Nora around."

Alex squeezed Daire's shoulders. "You're only twenty-one, and you're a hell of a catch, Daire. Don't hide from it. Let whatever happens happen."

A snort came out of Daire's mouth. "Like you, dude? I don't see you running out and buying a ring. Hell, you don't even go out with a woman long enough for us to learn her name."

Alex released a long breath. "Yeah, that's what I'm saying. Run from it long enough, and you might outrun it."

"Okay, man. I gotcha. Love ya too. I'll see ya later." Daire pulled back, then stopped. "Oh, and thanks for breakfast."

Alex nodded and watched Daire jog off. When had he stopped being in a hurry? Even now, especially now, he felt like a sloth. While his family was hustling around, running off to their next appointment, flight, or adventure, his feet felt planted to the floor.

Then again, he had nothing to rush off to. While his mind was made up, he wasn't in a hurry. He knew it wouldn't be painful. The impact would knock him out, and he wouldn't feel a thing. *Still…*

Sam wrapped an arm around Nora, and they headed to the elevators, with her mother and grandmother trailing them.

His mother walked toward the parking lot. Knowing her, she'd already packed and carried her stuff to her

SUV before breakfast.

The others left the restaurant in twos, chatting amongst each other.

Alex inhaled deeply then let it out. "Well, I guess that's it. Time to fly." Like his mother, he'd packed his carry-on bag and checked out before breakfast.

He walked to his truck and drove the short distance to the hangar.

When he arrived, he was surprised to see only one other car in the parking lot, a black Taurus. The Kodiak he'd been ogling yesterday was gone, already flying in this overcast. Not smart.

Had that been Irene's ride? Was she flying in this weather?

Alex scanned the base. No other cars were there, just tire tracks from two vehicles, so the shuttle probably dropped her off.

"What's wrong with you, man? You're never going to see her again. You're never going to see anyone again."

With that thought, he headed to his plane. He took his luggage just so no one would break into the truck. He wanted to leave Sam with the most assets he could, so he'd added life insurance to his truck too. Wrecking the plane wouldn't hurt the business. As his mother had said, they needed a new one anyway.

He opened the door to the cockpit, tossed his luggage between the seats, and hopped in.

"Well, Alex, this is it. Your last flight. Not how you thought your life would go, but hey, you should have died ten years ago at twenty-three."

He pulled out the screwdriver he'd stowed in his carry-on. Systematically, he unscrewed each of the bolts that held the radio. He tossed the screws and radio on the co-pilot's seat. FAA regulations didn't require a plane of this size have a black box. After a few days, Vince would send out a search party, and they'd find the wreckage so that the business would receive the life insurance payout and reimbursement for the seaplane.

"At least I get to choose my last act on earth." Alex turned the ignition. A small part of him had hoped it wouldn't start. But it did. Another sign this was his destiny. He smiled as the plane parted the mist and lifted into the air. "Today, I'll be the hero I set out to be, Dad."

~ Irene ~

The plane lifted, and Irene gripped the armrests. Her freshly manicured nails dug into the soft leather as the plane jogged higher and higher. All she saw was white stuff rushing past the side window.

Fog? Snow? Probably a mixture of both. How could pilots see in this dense haze?

As the plane lifted and banked left, some of the cloud cover dissipated, allowing her to appreciate the Kenai Peninsula in all its glory. The way the mountains rose up right next to the Gulf of Alaska was breathtaking. There simply wasn't a better word to describe it. Sure, she'd enjoyed California. But Alaska was majestic. Why hadn't she realized how beautiful life was, before she was faced with losing it?

She gazed down at the glaciers and the snow-capped Kenai Mountains. Shook her head at the crab boats that were heading out into the icy waters. Her father had counseled many a parent or wife after losing a child or husband to the dangerous job.

Wait a second … Why was the plane heading south-east? Saint Paul was southwest, in the Bering Sea. She clicked the intercom on her headset. "Excuse me … Umm … I'm sorry. I didn't catch your name."

"Kevin," the pilot said curtly.

She resisted laughing. Man, this guy was a jerk. *Maybe I remind him of an old girlfriend or something.* "Did I do something to upset you, Kevin?"

He tossed a look over his shoulder and actually smiled — well, grimaced would be a more accurate description. The plane wasn't the least bit warm, and yet, a bead of sweat dotted his forehead. "No, you're fine. I'm just really tired. It's been a long week."

"No problem. I understand bad days." He hadn't offered an apology, but at least she could let him know that she understood things not going well. She'd certainly had her share of bad days on the job. On occasion, she had taken her frustrations out on an innocent intern or two, since that's how she'd been treated when she was interning. "But I do have a question, Kevin. Aren't we supposed to be heading southwest?"

He turned and glared at her, the full weight of his aggravation seemingly bubbling to the surface again. "I wasn't aware that you were a pilot." He didn't smile off his comment, just furrowed his brows.

Of all the nerve, she growled internally. Bad week or not, there was no need to be all snippy just because she'd asked a question. "I'm not a pilot, obviously, or I wouldn't have paid you a thousand dollars to fly me to Saint Paul Island." She furrowed her brows, giving him her best I'm-the-customer look. "If you don't want to take me, you can turn around right now, and I'll find someone else."

Alex's broad smile popped into her mind. She was sure he would be happy to fly her home. Who knew … if she'd chosen Alex to fly her, they might have been able to put the plane on autopilot, and she could have actually *added* an adventure to her bucket list. Her anger dissipated slightly with that thought … and flashbacks of the previous evening. Just the thought of his large hands had her body heating up, which was nice since it was so flipping cold.

Kevin faced forward without any reaction to her statement. Good. She didn't need his sourpuss face ruining her memories.

A second later, Kevin's voice came over the headset. "There's a storm brewing over the Alaska Peninsula. I'm heading south a ways, then I'll circle back."

Was that so hard? He still hadn't apologized for being such a jerk, but maybe she'd been wrong to question him. "Thank you, Kevin."

No response.

Remembering that she'd decided never to waste time on idiots again, Irene redirected her thoughts and eyes to the churning waters of the North Pacific. The plane was flying low, so near to the ocean that she was able to spot a pod of whales. As much as she wanted to ask why, she decided not to question him again. Maybe he was trying to avoid the cloud cover. Although, now that they were off the coast, she couldn't see any sign of a storm.

So why is the plane still heading southeast? Her career as a journalist had taught her to ask questions, but she didn't want to upset him further.

Deciding to hold her tongue, she pulled out her phone. No signal, of course. If he'd flown over the peninsula, there would have been. She opened her *Words2* app and started a practice game. She'd become an expert over the last six months. After all, what else is there to do when you're too sick to get out of bed?

Irene lifted her hand to block a glint of light that nearly blinded her.

"Wait." The plane hadn't turned, so what could have reflected that light? She stared out the window again, then blinked. She clicked the intercom. "What the heck is that?" The pilot ignored her, but yes, they were clearly dropping altitude, and there was a tower of some sort. "What the hell are you doing? You're going to crash us!"

"Shut up!" he shouted.

Irene gripped the armrests again. He was trying to land. She peered out the window, looking for smoke or fire ... a missing wing ... any signs there was something wrong with the plane.

Seagulls, millions of them, parted as the plane careened toward the island. Below them, seals fled the snow-covered beach for the open water. There were no trees, but the island was dotted with plenty of cliffs, a rusted ship, and crumbling metal buildings. None of which she wanted to hit.

And waves. Giant waves. And this son of a bitch was trying to land.

Irene released her death grip long enough to click the mic again. "I don't understand. Are we in trouble?" The plane banked sideways, and Irene was sure she was going to lose the contents of her stomach as she stared straight down at the monstrous waves crashing against the rocky beach. "Oh, my God! What's happening?"

The pilot tore off his headset. His hands gripped the

yoke. She couldn't tell if he was pulling, pushing, or turning, but his knuckles were white as he struggled to maintain control. An artery bulged at his temple that matched her heartbeat.

She was going to die ... not of cancer, as she'd fretted for the last year, but in a fireball. At least it'd be quick. Better than throwing up all day, losing all her hair, and withering away to nothing if the cancer returned.

But I don't want to die. Not when I've just learned to live.

She stared down at the raging waters again, not sure if she should hope for the plane to hit the water or land. If they hit the water, they wouldn't last long in the icy seawater. If they hit the beach, there were sure to be rocks beneath the snow. Which death would be the least painful? Which one did she have a better chance of surviving?

Not that it mattered what she hoped for, Kevin was going to do whatever he damn well pleased.

Of all the stinking luck! She tore off her headset too. "Damn you, Kevin! I didn't survive a cancer diagnosis to die in an airplane crash! I thought you came this way to avoid the storm!"

"Pipe down, lady!"

He was right. She shouldn't distract him. She squeezed her eyes shut, but the phosphenes caused bright white streaks to stab her brain. Not liking the sensation and unable to take not knowing how she would die, she snapped her lids open again.

The view was all wrong. What was she looking at? Fog? Whitecaps? No! Ice!

The plane was heading straight toward a cliff!

"Oh, God!" A shrill scratch and snap drowned out her screams. The seatbelt strained to hold her in place. Her stomach plunged as the plane dropped, then twisted, as if some gigantic hand had picked it up and propelled it in the opposite direction.

She no longer saw blue sky or white-capped waves rushing past the side window. Instead, she saw nothing. Blackness.

Rocks or ice, she wasn't sure, clawed at the window, begging to enter the plane like a stray pup. They were no longer flying. The plane was falling … or rather, sliding.

Around her, metal shook and rattled. High-pitched screeching sounds pierced the air as a biting wind chilled her to the bone. She lifted her hands to her ears to shield them, but then remembered all the occasions flight attendants had demonstrated what to do in the event of a crash. How many times had she tuned out their rote emergency procedures? Hundreds?

No overhead compartments had dropped oxygen masks, and she hadn't seen any flotation devices, so the only thing left to do was bend over and cover her head.

Just as she bent forward, the plane slammed to a stop. The seatbelt felt like it had slashed her in two. Something hard knocked her arm, then another flying missile soared past her, scraping the side of her head as it rushed toward the front of the plane. Before she could determine if she was bleeding or in one piece, the plane jolted, then soared backward.

She felt like she was riding one of those roller coasters that come to a fake stop, then started up again, only to thrust you into another loop-de-loop. Through the cockpit window, she watched the blue sky fade away as mud and rocks battered the nose of the aircraft. Up and down, the plane jostled her as it bounced.

Without warning, the plane came to another full stop with a boom. Her body rocketed forward and back, and then her world went black.

CHAPTER 3

~ Alex ~

As soon as Alex left the coast, he unlatched the side window and tossed out the radio. He didn't want to leave himself an opportunity to call for help.

Typically when he was in the air, he had a voice in his ear, or his attention had to be on finding wreckage or a lost soul.

Not today. Today, he'd enjoy his last flight. Until he ran out of fuel, that is. It would take every bit of courage he could muster not to bring the seaplane down safely once he ran out of gas. He would have to force himself to override his preservation instincts and let the plane drop from the sky.

He flew south, avoiding the more trafficked area over the Alaska Peninsula. As much as another night with Irene appealed to him, she obviously wasn't interested. And even if she was, he couldn't do that to her. Instead of heading southwest, the way she'd pointed, he set his course for open water. After Cordova, he pretty much had wide-open space. He'd fly low and enjoy the sights for once.

Only one island sat below Cordova: Middleton. But he'd steer far from it this time of the year. He didn't intend to wash up on a deserted isle.

Unlike the island in *Castaway*, Alaska's uninhabited islands were deadly. If you didn't die from lack of food, exposure would kill you. Although the mean temperatures hovered in the forties, it wasn't uncommon to drop into the single digits overnight. The wind was the worst though; gusts from 75 to 145 mph weren't unusual.

"Nope, no *Survivor Man* for me. I'd rather be knocked out from hitting the water. I may be willing to die, but I don't want to be in pain."

Just as he said the words, a flash of light glinted across his windshield.

"Oh, for God's sake. It can't be. It's just that shipwreck from 1919," he said aloud, hoping to convince himself. The reef-lined waters around Middleton Island were deadly. With all the technical gadgets, though, ships rarely beached anymore unless they had to.

He failed at his attempt to convince himself; the rescuer in him couldn't fly by without checking. Knowing how deadly the waves and winds were south of the island, he headed for the west side, but then he got a better look at what had caught his eye.

"Damn! Double damn!"

He banked east. It was dangerous, but he didn't have a choice.

"What on God's great earth would possess a pilot to attempt to land in the winter?"

Thankfully, no smoke poured from the plane, but there was no doubt it was a fresh wreck. The cliff face that had torn off the wing was devoid of snow where the plane had slid down the fifty-foot cliff and landed on the beach. The pilot must have been attempting to find the runway, but then a gust of wind swept the plane into the cliff.

Alex searched for a section of beach without tumultuous waves. There weren't many choices. One small bay behind the wreckage looked promising. He'd have a short hike, but better to live long enough to offer help than to die trying to land.

He glanced up at the sky, where Sam's plane was probably flying overhead at this moment. "See, Sam, I think before I leap now."

Alex reached for his radio to call in his coordinates, then stopped when his hand reached nothing but air. "Oh, that's right. I'm supposed to be killing myself, not rescuing someone. And what if no one's in the wreckage? What if you're wrong?" He shook his head at his idiocy. "If you land, you won't have enough fuel to take off again, and then you'll be stuck on this godforsaken island."

He released a long exhale, trying to convince himself that he was wrong, that it wasn't a recent crash. But he could lie to others; he couldn't lie to himself. The crash was new.

And since he hadn't received a search-and-rescue call this morning, more than likely he was the only one who knew about it. So he had to help.

As he neared the wreck, he blinked a couple of times, hoping his eyes were betraying him. But no, he had perfect vision. The damn plane was sinking.

He didn't have time to overthink the rescue. If there were any survivors, they wouldn't last long in the icy water.

"Dear God, are you punishing me? Couldn't let me have an easy death, could you?"

Thankfully, he'd already been flying low. He made a wide arc, then brought the plane down as close to the wreckage as was possible.

Only a few hundred feet offshore, he looked left and right repeatedly, watching for rogue waves as he taxied toward the beach.

"Please, God, just don't let there be exposed reefs. I don't want to be sliced alive and end up shark food. I was willing to die for my sins, but is there something wrong with wanting to go silently … unconsciously?" The back of the plane lifted as a wave moved toward the shore. "It's now or never, Alex! You don't want a wave to throw you on shore." He pushed forward, literally surfing onto the shore. "Hang ten!" he shouted. "I might not get to Cali, but I can surf!"

The wave propelled the plane onto the beach, and Alex hopped out, immediately anchoring it down. No trees were available, but a large boulder on the beach wasn't going anywhere. He darted back inside for another safety line, ax, and his rescue pack, which held his first-aid kit and other critical gear, then took off toward the downed plane.

Had to be a top-of-the-line Kodiak. Big sucker. Heavy.

"Hello!" he shouted over the din of seagulls and fur seals. Between the squawking and barking, he couldn't have heard if ten people were screaming. Still, he knew that in life-and-death situations, people panicked. Hearing there was help on the way would give them hope. "Hang on! I'm on my way."

No one answered, but he had no doubt it was a fresh wreck. The strong scent of gasoline and oil filled the air.

He pushed his legs, but the soft sand made him feel

like he was running in a dream, like the nightmares he'd had about his father's death. No matter how many times he'd tried to rewrite the past, every night he tried to move through the waist-deep snow. He'd dig and dig and dig until his hands stung so severely from the cold he couldn't feel them.

Now he was digging through seaweed, rocks, and sticks. He hadn't dressed for a rescue, so he wasn't wearing his boots or waders. His feet were numb, but he persisted.

A few yards from the plane, his fears were confirmed. It was slow, but the liquefaction was causing the aircraft to sink. One large wave would knock it loose, sending it out to sea.

He glanced up and down the beach for something to use as an anchor. No trees or large enough boulders were within reach. The plane had created a wide trough as it slid down the embankment.

Alex glanced skyward. "Really? This is how you want me to go?" No way did he want to crawl inside a sinking plane. Crashing and being knocked out was one thing, drowning in sand and water was an entirely different story. Talk about nightmares.

The cliff face had shredded the wing, creating a hole in the fuselage, which unfortunately wasn't large enough to crawl through.

"Anyone inside?" he called, making sure no one was on the other side trying to get out before he axed his way inside. "What are you doing, Alex?" he berated himself again. He seemed to be doing that a lot lately, but Sam wasn't here, so who else would tell him he was putting his life in danger?

"If that plane shifts, it'll pull you in with it," he mimicked Sam.

He hopped up on the skid and swung the pick edge of the fireman's ax into the seam of the door and pried open a gap.

"Hello!" He swung again, pried again. The words *Heeere's Johnny* threatened to pop out of his mouth, but if there were any survivors inside, he didn't want them to think he was some deranged psycho and shoot him.

Repeatedly, he clawed at the hatch until the door broke free. He popped his head inside. The pilot was on his back. The seat had bent backward, and the innards and controls of the cockpit had him pinned. Blood trickled down the man's face. That was a good sign. If he was still bleeding, his heart was more than likely still pumping.

The contents of the cargo hold looked to have piled up in the front of the plane.

Alex pulled himself up further to check for passengers. They would be his first concern; the pilot would be last.

He saw only one arm flung over an armrest. "At least I don't have to drag ten people out." He carefully pulled himself into the plane, trying not to jostle it.

Before he could take a step toward the passenger, the plane shifted, causing one of the suitcases to fall in the cockpit.

"Oh!" cried a woman in response to the loud bang. "Oh, God! Help!"

The sound of the woman clawing at the seatbelt tore at his heart. It amazed him how often people couldn't think in life-threatening situations. Something as simple as unlatching a seatbelt was nearly impossible. "I'm coming, ma'am, but the plane is —" Her head popped up, and Alex gasped. "Irene." The missing Kodiak he'd been eyeing. How the hell had the pilot ended up in the middle of the gulf? Irene had said she was heading to Saint Paul.

Irene blinked, confused. "I don't understand. Why are you —" She shook her head, fumbled with the seatbelt again. "I can't unlatch this blasted thing — I can't get out!"

Alex lifted his hands. "It's okay, Irene. I'm coming." He took another tentative step, thankful the plane held its position.

She stopped fumbling with the latch and just stared up. Tears streamed down her face. Black stained her cheeks where her mascara had run. Scratches lined her face and arms, but he couldn't see any blood — thank God.

He took another cautious step, praying that the plane would hold as he bent down toward her.

With one click, he easily unhooked the latch.

She soared out of the seat before he could stop her, and the plane pitched again, this time backward. Her body slammed against his. "Oh, Alex! What's happening?"

With one swift move, Alex pulled Irene to his side and escorted her to the hatch he'd pried open. Outside, it was clear how far the plane had drifted. Waves crashed over the skids, leaving behind long strands of seaweed.

"Out you go!" He lifted her, and she yelped. He'd learned not to ask questions in a rescue. People tended to be unreasonable. If he'd told her to step out, she more than likely would have argued. He set her down on the skid. "Go! Now! Head to shore!"

"But my —"

"Go, dammit! The plane is sinking."

Irene's eyes widened, but instead of arguing further, she hopped off the skid and tottered toward shore.

Alex turned for the pilot. Maybe it was better the man hadn't come to. He leaned down and checked for a pulse. Alive. He was thankful and upset at the same time. Every second he remained inside the plane increased the likelihood that he'd drown. Once the thing broke free from shore, it'd go straight down.

He unlatched the pilot's belt and attempted to pull him from the seat. Normally he wouldn't move someone if the plane wasn't on fire, but he didn't have a choice. And it wasn't like an ambulance would be showing up.

Alex looked at the buckled dash. Why wasn't a rescue team showing up? Hadn't the pilot called for help as soon as he knew there was trouble? Few crashes happened so quickly that a pilot didn't have time to send out an SOS.

An eerie squeak reminded Alex that he needed to get a move on. He stood and pulled up on the control panel, but it was no use. Even if he pried up the dash, he needed a second person to pull the pilot from beneath it. He should have thought about that before sending Irene to shore. Still, he wouldn't have kept her here.

Outside, a wave crashed against the side. The tide was coming in. "Can anything else go wrong?" Alex bent down and smacked the pilot's cheek. "Hey, man, you gotta wake up."

Nothing.

"Dude, the plane is going down. If you don't wake up, you're going down with it."

The man's eyes moved beneath his closed lids, but he didn't stir.

Alex stood again, doing his best to pull the control panel up and push at the man with one foot.

Splashing came from outside. Had a rescue team arrived? Odd that he hadn't heard it.

A red head popped up, and before Alex could scream *No*, Irene crawled back inside. She immediately shoved her hands beneath the pilot's armpits and pulled. She managed to drag him to the open hatch before the plane bucked again.

"Get out!" Alex screamed. "Now!"

Irene hopped down, but stayed on the skid, waiting.

"I said go, Irene."

"Not until you're out!" she shouted back. "I'm not an invalid; I can help."

Alex latched an arm around the pilot's body and under his arms. He slid the man forward, then moved his own legs out the opening.

Irene immediately positioned her body under one of the man's arms as Alex stepped out. Together the two of them hopped into the knee-deep water and dragged the man onshore. Alex bent down and checked for a pulse. Still beating, but the man needed an emergency blanket. And God knows what else, which meant he had to go back inside that sinking ship. Most of the luggage had soared to the cockpit, so he could easily throw them out now that there weren't three people weighing down the plane.

"Stay here. I'll be right back." Alex dropped his emergency pack on the beach and headed back into the icy surf.

Water splashed behind him. "Where are you going,

Alex? Are you crazy?"

Alex smiled but didn't turn or respond. He'd been called worse.

At the plane, he realized he *was* crazy. Now that he'd rescued Irene and the pilot, he didn't fear dying again. Had it only been the thought of someone else dying that had scared him?

He climbed back inside and pulled two duffle bags from the cockpit. Since Irene refused to stay on shore as he'd requested, he tossed them as close to her as possible.

Next, he hefted two heavy purple suitcases, which must be hers. Hopefully, she had something other than shoes and clothes in them.

Irene sloshed through the water, snatched the handles of her suitcases with a vicious tug, then shoved them toward the shoreline. "Now get out of there, Alex!"

Alex shook his head and went back inside. He had his first-aid kit, but you could never have enough medical supplies. He stepped back toward the cabin, but this time his foot landed in ice-cold water. He snapped the latches on the overhead bins, searching for the vital kit and anything else they'd need to survive. He took another step, and the water came up to his knee. "Damn. Where is it?"

He flicked open bin after bin, finally breathing a sigh of relief when he found a blue plastic crate filled with supplies. He pulled it down and headed back to the hatch.

Irene stood just outside the opening again. "Alex, get out of there."

He smiled at her concern as he handed her the crate.

"Here. Take this. I need to get the radio."

"*Ugh!* All men suffer from *macho-itis!*" She grabbed the plastic crate and waded through waist-deep sea-water. "This water is freakin' freezing, and you're screwing around."

"You won't be saying that when the rest of my team shows up." He laughed and headed back toward the cockpit. The plane dipped forward, tossing him into the rutted dashboard. "Crap!" The plane was loose. He'd hoped that without all the weight, it wouldn't slip deeper into the ocean, but evidently, all the weight he'd tossed out had been anchoring the plane from the inside.

Too late to pry the radio free … or even to attempt an SOS. He righted himself and shuffled back to the hatch as water surged inside the cabin.

"Alex!" Irene's scream sounded too far away.

Unfortunately, the beach had a short shelf. An earthquake in the sixties had caused a sudden uplift of twelve feet. If he was still inside the plane as it slipped off the wave-cut platform, it would be *Bye-bye Alex*, as Sam liked to tease. Next stop: 26,000 feet under the sea.

He gripped the seats, hanging on as the plane lurched backward. He gasped in a breath and held it as white foam from a crashing wave filled the cabin, making it impossible to see. He forced his way through the incoming water. He felt for the opening he'd created and held himself upright as a flood of water surged in, struggling to free himself as the plane threatened to take him under.

His foot found purchase on a solid object, and he pushed off, sending himself through the hatch as the plane disappeared beneath him.

Seconds felt like minutes as he held his breath. The outflow pulled him down. He just needed to fight until another incoming surge. Just a few more seconds. Hang on for a few more seconds.

It wasn't the first time he'd had to hold his breath under water. He could do it. He'd practiced rolling his kayak enough times.

His lungs burned, and his limbs felt like lead weights. The salt water stung his eyes, so he squeezed them shut. Not that there was anything to see but white foam. He kicked, or at least he thought he kicked.

Something gripped his arm. Had the devil decided drowning wasn't enough? Had he sent a shark to finish him off? He opened his eyes and realized he must be hallucinating. A redheaded beauty was swimming next to him.

The surf switched, propelling him forward. The grip on his arm tightened, and he tried to kick again.

He didn't want to die, he realized. He wanted to live.

I don't want to die! he screamed in his mind. Still, he couldn't breathe, so more than likely, he was going to die. Right now. From drowning, of all things.

At least his last act had been a noble one.

His ears strained from the pressure. The icy water numbed his entire body. He was going to die whether he wanted to or not.

He no longer felt his heavy weighted legs. He no longer felt the pressure on his wrist. He no longer saw the red hair of his own personal mermaid.

He *had* imagined her. Somewhere in the depths of his mind, he remembered that drowning became euphoric in the final seconds. It was supposed to be peaceful, so of course, he would imagine a woman.

He didn't feel euphoric, though. He was mad, mad that he'd planned to throw away his life over money, and now his life was being stolen from him. And Irene ... Irene might die on this island if he didn't make it. The tide will come in, and she'll drown ... Blackness engulfed him.

He no longer felt the pain in his lungs.

At least his father's legacy would live.

But I don't want to die.

~ Irene ~

Irene gasped as she broke the surface.

She latched an arm around Alex and kicked toward the beach. How had they been swept out so quickly?

A wave crashed over them, and she squeezed her eyes and mouth tight, gripping hard against Alex's chest. The salt scorched her throat, stung her eyes.

Worse, Alex had become dead weight beneath her arm. "Alex! Wake up!" She stopped shouting as another wave broke against her face.

Instead of screaming, she tried to ride the wave. She kicked as the next wave swelled beneath her, letting it propel her forward.

Please don't die, Alex, she thought without shouting, so she didn't swallow even more salt water than she already had. She didn't really know Alex, but the thought that she'd never see him again tore at her heart. If he hadn't found the crash, she would be the one dead right now.

Another wave pushed her forward, and she nearly cried for joy when she realized she could finally stand. She gathered a handful of Alex's jacket and dragged him to the beach.

On land, she lowered her ear to his mouth, but it was impossible to hear with the cacophony of seals and birds. She didn't have time to second-guess; she tore open his shirt and layered one hand on top of the other. She used her body weight — what little she had — and pressed, hard and fast. She stopped long enough to tilt his head back, squeeze his nose, cover his mouth, and deliver two full breaths. Then she returned to the compressions, which she'd heard were more important anyway.

"Alex! Damn you, you stupid macho maniac!" *Press. Press.* She hit his chest. One because she'd seen it work in a movie, and two because she was so damn angry. She was on some God-forsaken deserted island with two dead pilots and a million and one seals. Not to mention some God-awful stench combination of bird poop, rotten eggs, and ammonia made her want to puke. "Wake up!" she screamed as she forced her hands harder against his chest. "Wake up!"

Water spurted out of Alex's mouth, so she quickly pulled him to his side. He slowly moved to his knees.

Aack. Aack. He spewed liquid, heaving until he collapsed.

Tears burst to Irene's eyes. "Thank God!" Then she smacked him on the arm. "You idiot!"

He slowly turned his head and blinked, coughed again, then his light golden eyes locked on her. He coughed and gripped his chest. "Damn that hurts."

Irene stood and stared down at him. "Not as much as dying, I'm sure."

"Probably not," he choked out and rolled to his back, one arm stretched above him. "How the hell did you end up on Middleton?"

Her eyes traveled the length of the rocky beach, then she jutted her chin at the prone pilot. "Not sure. I guess something happened to the plane. I think he was trying to land." She walked toward Kevin to make sure he was still alive. She knelt, felt one of his carotid arteries. Now that Alex was breathing, she had to attend to Kevin.

Since when did I become Florence Nightingale?

She headed for her luggage, hoping the hard-shell cases she'd sprung for had kept at least some of her clothes dry. She unlatched a suitcase and heaved a sigh of relief when the inside was dry. She rummaged through the contents for the long overcoat she'd brought. She should put it on herself, but it was the only article of clothing large enough to cover him. Hopefully one of the bags Alex risked his life for held the pilot's clothes, then she could get her coat back. She pulled out a lighter and yet still water-and-windproof jacket and tossed it over her shoulder. She snapped the lock closed on her luggage, then tucked the long jacket around Kevin.

Irene walked back and stared down at the man she'd never expected to see again. "He's still out, so I have no idea why I'm here. Why are you here, Alex?"

Alex propped himself up on his elbows, cleared his throat again. "To save you, obviously."

Irene sighed and knelt beside him. "Thank you." She smacked his arm again. "But you almost killed me with that stunt. I could have drowned. You almost died. And now I'm freezing worse than I was." She pulled away when he reached for her. "I said I'm freezing. I need to put on some dry clothes."

"I was reaching for you to keep you warm," Alex called out behind her.

She turned and flashed him a scowl. "My jacket will do a much better job than you. You look like a drowned rat."

He clutched his chest. "Ouch! That hurts worse than the bruised ribs you gave me. That's the thanks I get for saving you?"

"It's an expression, Alex." She rolled her eyes. "And you haven't saved me yet. I would have managed to get myself out of the plane; you just confused me. You were the last thing I expected to see when I came to." She started to pull on the jacket then realized she needed to change all her clothes first. No sense in putting a dry jacket over wet clothes. She opened her suitcase again and pulled out a thick sweatshirt and jeans, socks and hiking boots. She turned back to Alex, then glared at the unconscious Kevin. There was nowhere to change. No trees. No boulders. "Close your eyes and turn away."

Alex laughed. "Why?"

"Because I need to change."

He shook his head. "You're kidding, right? I saw every inch of you this morning. You're not going to pull one of those 'I was too drunk to remember' lines, are you?"

Just her luck to screw up a perfectly good one-night stand.

Irene dropped her head and scratched her forehead. "Nope. I knew exactly what I was doing. I hadn't even had a sip of wine. I didn't expect to ever see you again, which means I don't expect you to ever see me naked again either." She raised a hand, dropped the pointer finger, and gave him the universal sign to turn around.

Alex rolled his eyes but obeyed and turned.

Crouched, she quickly shed her wet zippered jacket and long-sleeve shirt and pulled on the sweatshirt, which fell over her hips, so it wasn't as though he would have seen anything except her bra anyway. Next, she tugged at her wet jeans, clenching her teeth when a grunt slipped out. Removing skinny jeans was always a workout, but doing it while they were wet, and directly after performing a water rescue, was akin to cardio training.

"Need some help?" Alex shouted.

"No ... thank you ..." she huffed out. She toed off her sneakers, then rolled the wet denim off her feet. The sun was shining, but the wind whipped cold air against her bare ass. At least it might dry her off enough to make getting into a dry pair of jeans easier. Chilled to the bone, she slipped a sand-covered foot into one leg, then repeated the process. She hopped up, shimmying into the tight denim. She collapsed onto her luggage and quickly pulled on the dry pair of socks and hiking boots.

The only good thing about being sick was that she'd lost all the weight she'd gained over the last ten years. When she'd started feeling better, she donated all her large clothes and bought herself a new wardrobe, determined not to gain back the unneeded weight. Although, she could stand to gain a few more pounds.

She slipped into the dry jacket, then walked toward Alex, who was sitting up and fishing in his side pocket. "Hey, pilot, why don't you start really saving me by bringing that plane over here and flying me to Saint Paul?"

Alex reached into his other pocket, then stood up,

smacking his legs. "Damn."

She stepped next to him. "What happened?"

"My phone."

She shrugged. "It's not like you'd get a signal anyway."

He turned to her, and his eyes were wild. His expression mirrored the look his brother the groom had the previous evening when he thought Alex had forgotten the wedding ring.

"No," Alex grumbled, "but my family could have used it to see my trek. They would at least know the direction I headed. I can't remember if I brought it on the plane with me."

Irene narrowed her eyes. "What do you mean? Why does your family need to follow your trek? Isn't that your plane?" She pointed to the red seaplane a few hundred yards down the beach. "Can't you just fly us out?"

Alex dropped his head. "No, it … ummm … took a lot of gas to land against the heavy winds. If I tried to fly us out, we wouldn't get far, and then we'd be in a worse predicament than we are now."

"The radio! You have a radio, right? You can call for help …" Her words faltered at the look in his eyes. "You were looking for Kevin's radio … because yours …"

"Broke," Alex finished. "I tried to call in the coordinates as soon as I spotted your wreck, but I wasn't able to …"

Irene ran her fingers through her damp hair, paced back and forth on the beach. "So … no one knows we're here?"

Alex rested a hand on her shoulder. "The pilot, Kevin you called him, certainly he called in an SOS, right?"

Irene shook her head. "Not that I heard. He was trying to land, but I wasn't sure why. I hadn't heard or seen anything. No smoke. No bang. One minute we were flying, and the next thing I knew, we were heading straight for a cliff." She lifted her head skyward. The sun would set in a few hours, and the temperature would drop. She moved from beneath his touch, walked a few paces, then stopped. There was no place to go. Even the cliff face looked impassable. What if the water came in farther? "What are we going to do? We can't stay here." She struggled to keep her tone light, to not let him know how freaked out she was.

"It's okay," Alex said, lifting his hands to her shoulders. "First things first, I need to do what you did: I need to put on some dry clothes, and then we need to find shelter and start a fire. Someone is bound to fly this path, so they'll see the smoke. We just need to let them know we're here. Wanna wait here while I grab some clothes?"

"Uh, no …" She scanned the shoreline again, eyeing some of the seals that were darned near as big as she was. The seagulls weren't so small either. The way they were circling overhead reminded her of a horror movie she'd seen as a child. Were they hungry? Would they attack?

Alex tilted his head. "Are you okay? There's no reason to panic yet. We have warm clothes. We'll find food. We'll be fine."

She straightened her spine. "I'm … not … panicking," she said each word slowly, convincingly. "I'm just pointing out that we need a plan," she continued in a lackluster tone. The last thing she wanted was for Alex to think she needed him to calm her down. She'd put herself in scarier situations than this when she was trying to prove herself as a journalist.

"All righty then." Alex turned and headed toward his plane, but then stopped when he reached the unconscious pilot. "He's about my size. One of these duffle bags must be his, right?"

She shrugged. "I would think so. He carried them from his car to the plane, and I was the only passenger."

As Alex hauled one of the black bags away from the encroaching tide, Irene dug inside her luggage for the lighter she always carried in her makeup case. She flicked the lighter, then turned to Alex, smiling at the fact that she was prepared ... to build a fire anyway.

Alex flashed a wide grin. "Great. The more light sources we have the better, but don't waste the fuel." Standing next to the cliff face, he unzipped the bag and stared inside. A second later, his head popped up. He stared up and down the beach, then jogged to the second bag.

She was ready to growl at him for his comment, since at least she had a lighter, but his sudden nervous actions confused her. "What's going on, Alex?" She gathered up driftwood pieces as she walked toward him.

Alex ignored her, dragged the second bag next to the other one, then carefully unzipped it. He pulled out a couple articles of clothing, then plopped down onto the snow-covered sand.

His hand over his mouth, Alex stared up at her. "Don't light a fire, Irene. The pilot's friends will be looking for us very soon, and we can't let them find us."

CHAPTER 4

~ Alex ~

Alex dropped his hand from his mouth and ventured back into the duffle bag. Maybe he was wrong. Maybe he'd misconstrued what he'd seen in the pilot's bag. But what else would someone wrap in thick brown paper ... and wrap again with plastic and duct tape? And the sheer number of identical packages. Other than a few articles of clothing, nothing else was in the canvas bags. The seams were nearly bursting from the sheer volume of paper-covered blocks.

Irene dropped the wood shards she had gathered next to his feet. "What's going on, Alex? Of course, we need a fire. I'm freaking freezing. And why in the world wouldn't we want someone to find us?" She crossed her arms, staring at him as if he'd not only dropped out of the sky to rescue her, but had also grown two heads.

He rubbed his eyes, as if doing so might change his view. Of all the stupid, idiotic, senseless, unthinking, ridiculous things he'd done in his life, today's decision — decisions — definitely topped the list. Not only had he screwed up his best chance to right the wrong he'd done to his father and family, but now he was sitting on an abandoned beach with a pissed-off woman and drugs ... lots and lots of drugs. More drugs than he'd ever seen. Drugs that someone would be looking for real soon. Sam wouldn't just be laughing if he were here; he'd be doubled over, howling so violently his insides would nearly split in two. Alex could just imagine his brother taunting, *You can't even kill yourself properly.*

Then again, if he hadn't made the decision to try to off himself today ... If he hadn't made the second decision to land, Irene might be dead right now. Even though he would be dead and never would have known about her death ... the idea of her dying troubled him more than any other issues he was dealing with. The thought of never seeing those arresting eyes again —

Irene squatted in front of him. "Are you okay? What happened?"

"Do you know him?" Alex jutted his chin at the prone pilot. Was it possible Irene had known there were drugs?

She pulled back as if he'd accused her of sleeping with the man. "No ... I chartered the plane online. Not many flights heading to Saint Paul Island this time of year." She flicked her eyes to where the pilot still lay unconscious. "He's a pill, though. Cranky as all get out. I must look like someone who jilted him. He didn't like me from the moment he spotted me."

Suddenly aware his teeth were chattering, Alex just grunted at her answer and pulled off his jacket and shirt. He pulled the pilot's clothes out of the duffle bag with shaking fingers. Adrenaline was something else. Keyed up as he was from the rescue and then the drug discovery, he hadn't even noticed his body trembling.

Icy wind whipped at his back as he pulled the long-sleeve shirt over his head. Thank God, he and the pilot were similar in size. As soon as he unbuttoned his jeans, Irene hopped up.

She waved her hands. "I'll umm … see to the pilot again." She hustled off, sending sand and ice in his direction.

"Oh, for crying out loud," Alex grumbled, irritation overtaking him. "You didn't have any issue stripping me out of my tux within seconds of entering my hotel room."

Irene kept her head turned away as she bent over the pilot. "One-night stand, Alex, remember?"

"Is he still alive?" Alex called out. "If not, I might just kill him." He pushed off one sneaker with the toe of the other shoe, then the second one with his freezing toes, then peeled off his jeans. Rid of his wet clothes, he quickly pulled on the dry pair of jeans and stepped back into his wet tennis shoes. He purposely stomped to where Irene knelt next to the pilot, ready to clobber the man into consciousness.

When he reached Irene, he realized his annoyance was unfounded. It wasn't her fault. He inhaled deeply and let the breath out slowly. At least all the plastic-covered blocks of drugs had caused the duffel bag to stay afloat, keeping the clothes dry. His mother had always told him to be thankful for what they had. So here he was, stuck on a deserted island in the middle of winter, and he was thankful for dry clothes.

Irene tilted her head up and then stood, apparently relieved to see that he was dressed. "You didn't answer me, Alex. What the hell's going on? Do *you* know Kevin?"

"No." Alex leaned over the pilot. He didn't want to mention his drug theory aloud if the man was merely faking unconsciousness, which was highly unlikely. "Hey!" he shouted into the man's ear. No response. Not even a flicker of his eyelids, as he'd gotten earlier. Alex quickly lifted the man's hand and dropped it over his face.

Irene shoved him so hard he fell backward. "What the hell are you doing to him?"

Frustrated again, Alex stood and brushed the snow off his dry clothes. "That little tap didn't hurt him. It just so happens to be one of the best ways to find out if someone is faking unconsciousness."

Irene's hazel eyes darkened. "Why would he be faking? He probably has internal bleeding, and you try to break his nose!"

"I wasn't trying to break his nose. I was trying to see if he was really unconscious." He reached out, took her hand, and urged her down the beach to no avail.

Instead of walking with him, she reared back. "What are you—"

He raised the hand not latched around her wrist to her lips. "Shh ... Just walk with me, okay?"

"The hell I will." She groped at his hand. "Let go of me!"

"Irene, I just need you to walk with me."

"I'm not going anywhere with you!" She kicked snow at him. "Help! Kevin! Wake up!"

"Dammit, Irene!" he growled. "I'm not abducting you; I'm trying to talk to you."

She yanked her hand back. "Talk here!"

"You have to trust me," he muttered, then wrapped his arms around her waist and pulled her backward until they were out of earshot.

Instead of trusting him, she dug her heels into the

sand and snow the entire way.

Alex stopped when he made it to the bed of seaweed he'd plowed through earlier to save her life. He released his grip from her waist but held onto her wrist again.

As soon as she was upright, she took a defensive stance.

He positioned his body so she couldn't kick him in the balls, which looked like her next move. "Irene, listen to me!"

She fixed him with a wide-eyed stare, apparently realizing that she couldn't over-power him and that he was serious.

"I'm not trying to hurt you. I'm trying to tell you something. And I can't take the chance he's not faking." He released his grip when she stopped struggling. "I'm going to ask you again … Do you know the pilot? Personally?"

"No!" she spat. "I told you. I chartered the plane online. I only met him a few hours ago."

Alex leaned toward her. "Those black duffle bags … They're his, you said, right?"

"Yes." She crossed her arms, apparently discarding the thought of pulling self-defense moves on him, but still a million miles away from the woman he'd spent a glorious evening with. "Why?"

"They're stuffed with what I believe are drugs."

Irene jerked her head back in the direction of the pilot. "Are you sure? He didn't look like … He doesn't look like he does drugs."

"Most mules don't look like they do drugs … That's why dealers use them. If the people who transported the illegal drugs were addicts, the drug dealers wouldn't be able to trust them. No, the dealers usually get their transporters in other ways. People who owe them money or a favor."

"So that's why he was trying to land here? He was trying to drop off drugs?"

Alex nodded. "Probably not to land. I'm guessing he just dropped off the packages. There *is* an airstrip in the middle of the island. Middleton used to be an Air Force station, but it closed in the sixties. It's mostly unin- habited, especially this time of the year. In the summer months, birdwatchers and rabbit hunters might visit —

She held up her hand. "Rabbit hunters?"

"Yeah ... Umm ... apparently there's an abundance of wild rabbits on the island, which earlier residents brought to feed the foxes. I guess there used to be a fox farm here. The rabbits are now all feral, and from what I understand, the only land animal that remains." He shook his head. "Anyway, that's not the point. The point is your pilot friend there was probably dropping a shipment of drugs."

It was Irene's turn to shake her head. "Not my friend. And dropping off drugs for whom? The rabbits?"

Alex scratched his forehead then peeked over Irene's shoulder to make sure the pilot hadn't moved. If he was a drug dealer, he might be dangerous. He should have searched deeper in the bag for a weapon. "Not rabbits obviously, and not even for anyone here. My guess is that the pilot brings the drugs here from Alaska, then goes about his business of dropping passengers off at Sitka or, an unusual situation like yours, to Saint Paul Island. Then another mule picks up the drugs and heads to Vancouver or Seattle."

Her thin brows lowered. "That doesn't make any sense."

"Why doesn't it make sense?"

"The cost? Who would pay to fly drugs from Alaska to Seattle?"

"God, woman, you're unbelievable. I tell you the pilot is delivering drugs, and you argue over the logistics of whether drug running from Alaska to the Lower 48 is a financially viable business." Not believing they were having this conversation, he lifted his eyes. "When does the drug-dealing trade make sense? But in this case, it does. It's probably meth. Cooking meth smells. In Alaska, there's a lot of land and, mostly, if you stay out of trouble, the cops don't mess with you. So, it makes perfect sense that the drug dealers would cook meth here and ship the stuff to the Lower 48." He waved his hands when she opened her mouth to ask another question. "Enough arguing already. I just needed you to know what's going on. Now, we need to find shelter. We'll worry about what to do with him later."

Irene nodded, but her pursed lips made it clear she still wasn't pleased with him. "Of course, that's the first item on Maslow's hierarchy of needs: warmth and shelter." She looked down. "Obviously water isn't an issue; we just need to figure out how to melt what's all around us. When the plane was going down, I saw some buildings."

"Yeah, most of the buildings are piles of rubble now, but there's a research station on the other side. There has to be food and heat, and if we're lucky, fuel for the plane." He rested his hands on her shoulders. "You're not going to scream and try to kick me again, right?"

She lowered her eyelids in a slow blink. "That depends. As long as you don't try anything, I won't have any reason to hurt you."

He sighed. "I wasn't trying anything a few minutes ago."

She fisted her hands and rested them on her narrow hips. "How was I supposed to know that? Far as I knew, you were dragging me off to rape me."

He huffed out an unbelieving chuckle. "Rape you? Where the hell did that come from?"

"I don't know. I'm upset." She stepped back, causing his hands to fall from her shoulders. "I know one thing. You have a lot to learn about women, Alex. Next time, maybe try whispering to me, giving me a hand signal or something. Don't manhandle me and expect me to be okay with it. Then, I won't have to scream."

He wanted to point out that she hadn't minded a little *manhandling* in his hotel room, but now wasn't the time. Instead of arguing, he dropped his head. He'd already told her that he didn't want to talk in front of the drug-dealing pilot, in the event that he was faking or came to.

"Let's go," he said. "We need to get your pilot on my plane and use the meager fuel remaining to motor to the other side of the island. God help us if we run out of gas. If we do, we'll either be carried out to sea or thrown against the rocky shoreline."

As cold as it was, her face flushed as if she'd just run a marathon. "We have to get inside … a plane again? Can't we just … you know … hike around the island? Or climb the cliff?"

Seconds ago, she was acting all tough, ready to take him out with a kick to the groin. Now she was afraid to get in a plane?

He shook his head, resisting the urge to laugh. "The cliff's impassable without gear. More than likely, we'd only cause a rockslide. And even if it were possible to travel around the island via the shoreline, which it isn't, it would take all night. We'd freeze to death before morning." He looked behind him, to where his ancient floatplane sat on the beach. "Sorry, honey, Old Betsy's our only chance at making it through the night."

~ Irene ~

Honey? Irene didn't feel like arguing over how demeaning it sounded to call a woman *honey* when you weren't even in a relationship. She had bigger concerns.

She followed Alex's gaze to the faded red seaplane that was less than half the size of Kevin's plane. If Kevin's plane hadn't been able to manage the gusts and land, then how was that tiny plane going to handle the winds? Then again, Alex had made it sound as if they weren't going to fly, but "motor" around the island. How did that even work?

Alex turned and headed back to Kevin.

"Wait ..." Irene ran up behind him and latched onto the sleeve of his jacket. "I don't understand. If Kevin couldn't land, how are you going to get to the runway when you don't even have enough fuel to fly?"

Alex looked down at her hand clutching his jacket. She'd just berated him for *manhandling* her, and here she was doing the same thing.

She released her grip. "Sorry. It's just ... One second we were flying, and the next instance a cliff was ripping the plane to shreds."

Alex straightened the jacket sleeve and stared at her with a cocky tilt of his head. "That's because *your* pilot didn't know what he was doing."

She clutched her elbows, anything to keep her hands from reaching out and smacking him upside the head. "He's not *my* pilot. I don't own him. I simply chartered his plane. He has a name. Kevin. Use it, all right?"

Alex ran his hand over his mouth. "Okay … *Kevin* didn't know what he was doing. If he knew anything about Alaska, he'd know that the only safe way to enter Middleton is from the western side, which protects the plane from the strong east wind. I'm not going to attempt to get in the air and land on the runway. The tide is coming in, so it should be easy to motor right next to a small gravel spit of land. The area bares at low tide, so we need to get a move on while it's still shallow." He stopped talking and just stared at her.

She blinked, not sure why he stopped talking or what he expected her to do. "What?"

"Do you have any more questions, Irene, or can we get a move on?"

She waved him forward.

Back in front of Kevin, Alex stooped down again. "Yo, Kevin!" He tapped his right cheek. "Kevin, I'm not looking forward to carrying your ass. Wake up, dude!"

Nothing. Irene wasn't looking forward to carrying him either, but she couldn't help but smile. Kevin was just irritable enough that he might be faking. Maybe he didn't want to have to explain himself to some guy he didn't know who kept yelling at him.

"Would you stop already?" Irene stepped to Kevin's other side and stooped. She tossed the trench coat she'd covered him with over one arm, then draped the man's arm over her shoulders.

Thankfully, Alex stopped his interrogation and

wrapped Kevin's other arm over his shoulders and lifted. Together, they dragged the unconscious pilot across sand and seaweed the couple hundred yards to Alex's plane.

At the plane, Alex motioned her to open the door. "I got him."

She untucked herself from beneath Kevin's dead weight and stared up at the seagulls that covered the cliffs, boulders, and every inch of sand beyond twenty feet of wherever she stood. "Do they ever stop?"

Alex lifted his free arm. "Who?"

"Them ..." She waved a hand at the millions of white birds. "Those nonstop-squawking feathered things. Ugh! I might go insane." Yeah, she was used to them on Saint Paul and the beaches surrounding San Fran. But never so many in one spot.

"Probably not." Alex shook his head. "This is their home, after all. We're the invaders here. This guy's a bit heavy. Do you mind grabbing the door?"

Irene ran to the rear passenger door of the plane and unlatched it. Then ran back to help heft Kevin into the back seat.

After Alex buckled him in, she nudged him aside so she could tuck the trench coat around him.

Alex shook his head, as if he couldn't believe she cared about keeping the man warm, but then opened the front passenger door for her. She almost made a wisecrack about his courteous action after he'd been so gruff, but she held her riposte and simply said, "Thank you."

He responded with a grunt, then ran back in the direction they'd come from. Before she could decide whether she'd be of any help, he'd already reached the bags.

Minutes later, he was stuffing the black bags in the back, and then he ran back for her purple suitcases, and then the blue crate.

He opened the back door, and she turned in her seat. "I'm sorry my bags are so heavy. I would have offered to help, but I figured I'd be in the way."

He offered her another grunt, then trotted to a thick rope latched around a boulder.

The feathered onlookers flapped their wings, flying only feet away before landing again, and then proceeding to squawk louder, as if miffed by the intrusion.

Alex wound the rope into a circle and draped it over one shoulder, then proceeded to push the plane backward.

"Do you need me to help —"

He waved off her question. "Stay where you are."

What did I see in him last night? He's awfully snippy today. She tried to conjure up physical images of their evening together. That wasn't so hard to do, not with watching him push the front of the plane. The wide smile he'd flashed her several times joined the image of his unbuttoned shirt.

The plane bobbed and, within seconds, Alex was splashing through the surf and entering via the pilot's door. His eyebrows lowered, but then a smile accompanied his quizzical brow. "What's funny?"

"Umm ..." she stuttered. "I wasn't laughing."

He buckled himself in. "You were smiling."

"I was?"

He nodded and then reached for the key on the dash. "You were. Now, how 'bout saying a prayer?"

"A prayer?"

"Yeah, that Old Betsy starts." He paused a couple seconds, looked up at the roof, then turned the key.

CLICK.

He turned the key back, then tried again.

CLICK. Nothing. Dead air.

He stroked the dashboard. "Please, baby, one more time. For me."

Irene gulped, then realized he was talking to the plane. *Pray?* she silently questioned his request. She hadn't prayed since she received the cancer diagnosis. Not that her prayers had done any good. Well, that wasn't completely true. The cancer had been operable, and she'd woken up from the operation, so at least something had gone well. She wasn't convinced she could give the prayer credit, since she'd begged for the biopsy to come back benign.

But okay ... *Dear God, please ...*

"Please, baby," Alex said again and turned the key. A high whine sounded, then the propeller slowly started to turn. "Thank you! Good girl, Betsy!"

Irene smiled again. There was the Alex she couldn't keep her hands off at the hotel. And more importantly, the plane was moving. She watched as Alex worked the different controls.

Her heartrate sped up as they left the shoreline. In front of them was wide-open sea. Alex navigated away from the island and headed north. She looked out the window at the waves crashing over the skids — or floats, she guessed. Dozens of seals barked as they bounded from rocks, crisscrossing one another in their haste to reach open water.

She found herself looking from window to window, wary — and excited — about what she might see. The farther they moved from land, the more anxious she felt. At least on land they had snow as a water source, and possibly eggs to eat — She jumped when something touched her leg, but looked down to see Alex's large hand on her knee.

"Relax, Irene. It's a beautiful day. We'll be fine. The gust that took down your plane must have been a fluke. It's quite common here, especially in the winter months."

Fine? She wasn't accustomed to things going fine. She'd had to work for everything in her life; things didn't just fall in her lap. If anything, hurdles always seemed to pop up. So, sitting in a plane with zero control over her surroundings didn't offer her much confidence that things would be *fine*. She looked over her shoulder, expecting something to go awry. A great white shark maybe? That'd be her luck. Still, she'd promised herself not to worry about the things she couldn't control. She needed to let go.

She pulled her gaze from the windows and stared into Alex's golden-brown eyes. "Are you sure?"

He moved his hand from her knee to the grip. "I'm sure. There's a bay around the other side of the island. We'll be fine."

The occasional wave rolled beneath them, pushing them forward. At the end of the island, he made a wide arc and headed south, staying far enough offshore to avoid the crashing waves. A quarter of the way down the coastline, he turned east again, approaching the shore from the west.

She saw the area he'd described, a bay created by a naturally formed jetty of rocks, which protected the beach from the crashing waves. He centered the plane and motored right up on shore.

As soon as the plane beached, she jumped out, thrilled to be back on solid ground. "You did it!" She ran around the back of the plane and embraced Alex.

He stepped back and flashed a quick smile. "It was nothing. Just had to know it was here. I've flown all the waters of Alaska. I'm guessing Kevin is new to the area …" Alex trailed off as he turned away and walked toward the end of the beach, to where high reeds of golden grass and sand dunes replaced the soft sand. As she stepped beside him, he nodded to the plane where Kevin hadn't moved. "Maybe new to the drug-running trade too. That plane of his was brand-spanking new."

Irene bit her lip as she scanned the dunes. "Yeah, he did seem nervous."

With the excitement, she'd momentarily forgotten their predicament. They were still on a deserted island with no radio, no plane, no food, and illegal drugs that someone would probably be looking for soon. And they had to somehow manage to climb these dunes, she guessed, the reason Alex was scouting the area. Or maybe he just wanted to put distance between them and Kevin before speaking, since she could see a structure at the far end of the jetty. At least they would have shelter.

"We better get going," Alex said. "We have a long walk, especially since we have to haul him."

"Long walk? What's wrong with seeking shelter there?" She pointed to the behemoth structure on the cliff.

"We can't camp in that rust bucket; it's completely open on the top. That's the S.S. Colebrook, a cargo ship. Only birds live there. Too dangerous. One scratch on the rusted metal would quickly turn into a nasty STAPH infection."

Irene stared at the rusted structure, which now she could clearly see was the ship she'd spotted from the air. But it didn't compute. "How did the ship get all the way up there?"

"When the captain beached the ship, it was in water. But in 1964, an earthquake caused the island to uplift twelve feet. The only shelter will be in the middle of the island, about two miles away."

She shook her head. "You're like a walking version of Wikipedia, you know that?"

Alex shrugged and strolled back toward the plane. "It's just stuff you pick up when you work search and rescue. Little tidbits here and there that come in handy in a situation like we're in."

Irene ran to catch up. The man had such long legs. And when he moved, he moved quickly, as if he were always in a hurry. "Alex, do you really think there will be shelter and food … and fuel?"

He stopped and stared down at her. His eyes were soft, but his stance was all business. "We'll be fine, Irene. If we're lucky, there might even be a working radio, but …"

"But what?" she filled in his empty air.

"But … we have an unconscious drug runner we need to attend to, and his colleagues will obviously be here eventually. Maybe he was supposed to radio them after he dropped the shipment. If that's the case, we might have some time to figure out our situation." He started walking again.

"Alex," she said, and he stopped again. "No matter what happens, thank you for landing and saving me."

He nodded, then dropped his head, but not before she saw sadness in his eyes. Yes, they were on a mostly deserted island and out of fuel, but he rescued people for a living. He knew what to do in an emergency. Finding a way home should be a challenge for him, a chance to flex those macho-itis muscles, as he'd done earlier.

So why did Alex seem more upset than she felt. What was she missing?

CHAPTER 5

~ Alex ~

Alex glanced at his watch, then the sun. They had less than two hours to carry a two-hundred-pound man up an embankment, over unstable dunes, and then nearly two miles up an unkempt road to shelter.

No way would he have time to come back and get their luggage ... or the drugs. Not that he wanted to haul around two duffle bags of drugs, but if he could stash them away, he might have leverage when the owners showed up. Not happening, though, so better to let the incoming surf crash the plane against the rocks and carry the pieces out to sea. With any luck, if he stuffed the bags deep beneath the seats, they'd go down with the fuselage instead of ending up on some beach.

He grabbed his emergency pack and a back-up pack out of the cargo area.

He handed one to Irene. "Stuff this with any life-saving gear or food and the warmest clothes you have."

She offered him a slow blink, her way of telling him she didn't want to comply, he'd noticed. "You expect me to leave all my things here?"

He shrugged. "It's either your luggage or your pilot; take your pick. Don't take too long to decide, though.

The tide is coming in, which means this beach will be covered by eleven feet of seawater in the next few hours. He might be okay in the plane, but if the winds pick up, I doubt —"

"Oh, cut it out!" she barked. "Obviously I'm not going to choose my clothes over a human being, even if he is a drug-running P.O.S." She opened the latches on one of her purple suitcases. "Can't we at least take them up to where they'll stay dry? Those dunes don't look as impassable as the cliff on the other side did."

"Be my guest. But not until we find shelter. The closest building is nearly two miles away ... and then we have to break in ... find a generator —"

She raised her hand to stop him. "I get it. Survival mode."

"Exactly." Alex sifted through his own luggage. A lot of good a tux would do him here. And now that he wasn't dead, he'd have a hefty sum to pay if — when ... he returned to the mainland. Thankfully, he had been wearing a sweatshirt the previous day.

He pulled out several pairs of socks and undergarments, and then checked the side pockets for anything he might have left from a previous trip. His fingers found plastic. Ooh ... food. He always kept a few protein bars in his emergency pack, but he doubted Irene had brought anything, so the more the better.

He peered down at the plastic-wrapped squares. Not food, but if they were going to be stuck on the island alone for a few nights, they might come in handy.

Hopefully, Vince wouldn't wait more than three days to send a search team.

Alex stuffed all the items in the backpack, then sifted through each of the duffle bags before shoving them under the seats. "Damn."

Irene looked up at him, each of her hands full, as if she were weighing different articles of clothing. "What happened?"

"I was hoping there might be a weapon in his bags."

Instead of one slow blink, she blinked rapidly. "As in a gun? I thought there wasn't anything but rabbits and seals on the island."

He nodded to the unconscious pilot, still not wanting to mention his suspicions in the event the man was faking.

Ohhh … she mouthed.

At least Irene understood simple gestures. As a rescuer, he was accustomed to his team knowing what he needed without having to spell out demands. When he'd spoken with Irene at the bar, she told him she was a journalist. When he'd mentioned only life-saving gear, food, and warm clothes, she'd responded with *survival mode*, which made him wonder what type of journalist she was.

Later, he thought. If they made it to shelter, they'd have plenty of time to talk. Maybe then he could figure out why this woman intrigued him so. Was it just the fact that he'd thought it was his last night on earth, or was there something else about Irene that he found hard to resist? *Great timing, Alex. Now you think about more than a one-night stand.*

"Ready!" Irene sounded chipper, as if she were going off on an adventure.

He looked up to see that she had strapped on the pack, covered her head with a knit hat, and for whatever reason, had a smile on her face. She *was* ready for an adventure.

Oddly enough, her attitude directly affected his. Since they were here, they might as well enjoy it. If only Kevin weren't here ...

And just that quickly, his mood turned again.

He stared up at the embankment and then at the incoming tide. "We need to go!"

Irene crawled back into the plane, reaching beneath one of the rear seats, as if she'd spotted something. "I said I was ready, sourpuss! What happened to that fun guy I met?"

Alex pulled on his pack. "I just want to get up that embankment before a rogue wave drenches us. Thanks for getting ready and understanding the need to limit what we bring."

Irene peeked up at him from the floor. "They're only things, Alex. Things are replaceable; our lives aren't." Crinkling sounded from beneath the seat. "Ahh ... I found a hidden treasure." She lifted her bounty, showing off her find. "Protein bars! These will definitely come in handy."

"Definitely. Every nugget of food will make three days — or more — bearable," he said solemnly, thinking about her ... *They're only things* statement. Her comment had stabbed him in the gut. Hours ago, he'd been prepared to give away his life. Not over things, but over integrity ... and pride ... and if he were honest with himself, guilt.

Things ... Was his life just a *thing*? Was his life replaceable with money?

As Irene dug into the pockets behind the co-pilot's seat, Alex sighed and reached for the buckle that held the pilot.

He gasped and then stared up wide-eyed when he

realized the buckle wasn't latched. He hadn't been paying attention to Kevin because his mind had been on Irene.

Instead of seeing the closed eyes of an unconscious pilot, Alex saw a fist heading right toward —

Alex fell back, his head connecting with something hard. He blinked, but the asshole had hit him so hard he saw nothing but stars. Blinded and pissed, Alex struggled to his feet. It wasn't the first time he'd received a sucker punch. Hell, he'd upset a few men when their ladies had preferred his company. Sam and he had tangoed a few times too. But with Sam, there'd never been anything at stake other than his pride. He knew Sam would never really hurt him. All he could think about now was what Kevin might do to Irene if he lost this battle.

"I ... rene, run —" Something hard hit his chest. He tried to blink away jagged stripes of gray and white that flashed in front of his face. His vision finally cleared enough to see Kevin throwing a purple suitcase in his direction while his other arm was wrapped around Irene's neck.

Alex pushed off in the soft sand, dodging the second purple missile by mere inches. "Let her go, Kevin!"

Kevin pulled Irene to the cockpit the same time he pulled a gun from inside his jacket. "Get back."

Irene, her skin paler than usual, clawed at Kevin's hands, but to no avail. Her attacker had at least a hundred pounds on her.

Pissed that he hadn't checked the man's coat, Alex lifted his hands.

Kevin released Irene long enough to shove her into the co-pilot's seat.

She gasped for air, then groped for the door handle.

Kevin elbowed her back. "Move from that seat and I'll shoot him, Irene!" The whine of the engine started the moment he turned the key.

Figures Old Betsy would start when Alex didn't want her to start. "Kevin," Alex said calmly, "you won't make it —"

"Shut up! One more word and I'll shoot you right now!"

Alex splayed his hands in front of him, palms down, a gesture that usually worked on humans and animals alike. "You can take the plane, Kevin. I don't care. Just let Irene —"

The hand that Kevin was using to hold the gun shook, and Alex realized talking was no longer an option. The guy was probably hypothermic and scared. Scared or cornered people and animals did irrational things.

Since the gun was trained on him, not Irene, Alex lunged forward as the plane started to move. He bounded into the rear compartment. Kevin attempted to whip his arm around, but Alex drove the man's head past the yoke, directly into the instrument panel.

Without waiting to see if Kevin would come to, Alex reached across Irene and shoved open the door, pushing her out at the same time.

Irene fell with a grunt, and Alex toppled out after her. Scrambling to his feet, he ran to the back of the plane and shoved. Seeing what he was doing, Irene followed his lead, and together, the two of them pushed through the incoming surf.

Kevin groaned from the cockpit, so Alex gripped onto Irene's wrist and tugged her toward the dunes.

The whine of the engine increased and wind from the propeller battered Alex's face. Kevin had obviously come to and decided flying away with his stash was a better decision than fighting again.

"Oh, no!" Irene whimpered beside him. "You said ..."

Alex glared at her. "I tried to reason with the man, and he pointed a gun at me ... and you. What was I supposed to do? If I'd shouted that the plane didn't have fuel, he might have chosen to kill us both and stay here instead of flying away." He shook his head. "I was right. This is a new gig for him. No seasoned pilot would take off without checking his gauges."

They stood for a few minutes, watching the red plane fade to nothing but a dot above the horizon.

"How far will he get?" Irene finally asked.

"Not far." Just as Alex said the words, the red dot lowered in the sky. From where they stood, Alex couldn't be certain if Kevin was bringing the plane down, or if the old girl was finally breathing her last wind. He'd miss her. She'd been a good plane.

"Oh, no!" Irene cried.

Alex wrapped his arms around Irene and pulled her head to his chest so she didn't watch. Irene was worried that Kevin was going to crash, even after he'd pulled a gun and nearly choked her to death, but all Alex found himself hoping for was that the man *did* crash.

After all, if Kevin brought the plane down safely, he and the drugs would end up right back on Middleton.

"Let's go!" he said, snatching up her suitcases since he didn't have to haul a two-hundred-pound man through soft sand.

"But, shouldn't we —"

"Get out of here before his friends show up or before

the sun goes down? Yes, we should."

She stared at the purple suitcases. "You don't have to bring those … it's mostly just clothes."

He plodded toward the dunes. "Yeah, I do. Who knows what we'll need? Plus, I don't want to leave any evidence that we're here. I was actually hoping the outgoing tide would erase all evidence of the plane and drugs … and us." He tossed a look over his shoulder. "But now … who knows what will happen? More than likely, that damn plane's gonna wash back up on shore."

Irene slogged toward him, her boots sinking in the soft sand. "Do you think he might still be alive?"

Alex turned back toward the dunes. "Yeah …"

"Are you just saying that to make me feel better?"

He turned around and dropped the fifty-pound weights. "Why would that make you feel better? That *drug-dealing loser*, as you called him, nearly choked you to death and was about to pull the trigger on me."

She caught up with him. "He's still a person, Alex."

"He's a drug runner, Irene, who nearly killed you by taking you on a drug drop, and then tried to kidnap you."

Instead of agreeing with him, her eyes stayed locked on his. She reached for one of the purple bags, so he pushed her hand away.

"I got them." He snatched up the bag and started walking again.

She ran to catch up. "I'm sorry, Alex. I never would have wished this on you …" She heaved a sigh. "But I'm glad you're here."

He stopped and looked at her. Her eyes were glassy. Alex dropped his head. They didn't have time for this. But he'd spent his thirty-three years living under the same roof as his mother. As tough as Claire Belgarde was, she was also a woman ... a loving and sensitive woman.

He heaved a long sigh, knowing he'd have to shove his macho-itis, as Irene had called it, aside. "I'm not upset with you, Irene. None of what has happened is your fault. You had no way of knowing what Kevin was up to." He brushed his fingers along her cheek. "I know it won't make any sense, and you probably won't believe me ... but I'm glad I'm here too."

And he was ... As sad as it was that she was going through this, if he hadn't spotted the plane wreckage, he never would have landed and tried to rescue passengers.

Nope, he'd be the one crashed or floating in open sea right now instead of Kevin.

~ Irene ~

Irene's chest warmed at Alex's words: *I'm glad I'm here too.*

But how could he possibly be glad that he was stuck on a deserted island with no food and no chance of flying out? Previously, she'd thought they'd find fuel and be able to fly back to the coast. Now they didn't even have a plane.

Irene pulled the straps on the backpack, which had come loose when Kevin whipped her around the plane as if she were a ragdoll. The first thing she planned to do when she made it home was gain twenty pounds and start up her self-defense classes again.

When he'd had his arm around her neck, she'd gone blank. Instead of gouging out his eyes or kneeing him in

the balls, she'd scratched at his arm. Rookie mistake …
and she wasn't a rookie. Kevin wasn't the first loser to
take her hostage.

When she'd walked the streets in San Francisco, her
hand had always been latched around her Vipertek. She
hadn't been allowed to take the Taser through TSA,
though, so she'd tucked the 230,000,000-volt stun gun
that looked like a flashlight away in her luggage. Now it
was at the bottom of the backpack. First opportunity,
she'd fish it out and keep it close. If she'd had the Taser
in her hand when Kevin attacked her …

Alex turned to her as they made it to the start of the
dunes. He nodded to the purple fifty-pound weights he
carried. "Anything in these breakable?"

She shook her head, wondering if he was going to
leave them — nope, not leaving them. She watched in
horror as he dropped one of her new Tumi suitcases,
and then pulled back and swung the other one up the
embankment.

She sighed. "I guess that's better than letting the
ocean take them out to sea."

Alex grinned and picked up the other one. "Are you
kidding, these babies are made for this. What do you
think the luggage handlers do with them at the airport?"

"I suppose, but I don't witness their attack on such
beautiful luggage."

Alex tossed the second suitcase, and then moved to
her. "Turn around."

She pulled back. "You're not throwing me up there!"

He shook his head. "No, but it'll be easier if I lift you
to the first ledge, then crawl up myself."

Irene stared at the ledge that looked to have been

cut away by the surf. She could probably do it. Of course, that would be the end of her beautiful manicure.

"Ready?" Alex moved behind her again.

She inhaled a deep breath and released a long exhale slowly, then nodded, allowing him to pick her up by her calves.

She started to grip onto a plant with long reeds, and Alex shouted, "Not those. Those will slice your hand right open. Just dig into the ground while I boost you up."

Irene dug as he instructed, cringing when tiny crabs skittered to and fro. "Ewww ..."

"Probably not as *ewww* as drowning," he mimicked a line similar to her earlier words.

"Probably not." She clawed her way up the edge as Alex pushed beneath her feet. She stood up, shooing away all the creepy crawly things.

Alex gripped onto a rock and pulled his entire body weight up the ridge.

Yep, as soon as I make it home, it's back to the gym. While she'd been withering away on the couch in her apartment, she'd watched every movie on Netflix and Amazon Video. One of them had been G.I. Jane. In fact, she'd watched it several times, dreaming of the day she'd be strong again, determined to look like Demi Moore after she beat the cancer monster.

Alex brushed off his jeans and trotted to the luggage. "That was the hardest part. Now, it'll mostly be a calf workout. Let's go!"

Irene did her best to keep up, but Alex was right. The ground was so soft in spots that the sand literally poured into her boots. Around her, seagulls remained her constant companions, always waiting for something. "Shoo … Go away!" Next to her feet, reeds of grass rustled constantly. "There aren't any snakes here, are there?"

"I doubt it," Alex called over his shoulder. "Too cold. Not enough spaces to hide either. If there were, the birds would pick them off."

Irene jumped as something fluttered beside her. "What are those things, then?"

Alex stopped, then stooped down next to her, gesturing that she should squat too. He raised his hand to his lips and pointed. *Watch*, he mouthed.

A few seconds later, a white rabbit skittered from beneath one reedy shrub to another.

"Oh … there really are rabbits here. I thought you were kidding."

Alex pointed to the sky, where a wide-winged bird circled. "They're trying to stay hidden from him."

"Is that …"

Alex nodded. "A bald eagle. Last count there were seven nesting pairs. The entire island is a bird sanctuary."

"Oh, wow!" She scanned the area with fresh eyes, gazed at the tower in the distance that seemed to have been made for the gulls. Not just gulls, but other birds too. More than she'd ever seen in one area.

Alex smiled and helped her up. He picked up her suitcases and continued trudging over the dunes.

After nearly an hour of sloshing through calf-deep sand, they crossed another dune, and Irene almost cried when she saw a road. "Oh, thank God!" Well, sort of a road. The mostly crushed sand and rock had divots and potholes deeper than California roads, and that was saying a lot. Still, it was a road. Anything was better than trying to trudge through soft sand.

Alex turned and smiled. "Told you it was here. Now, we have about another thirty-minute walk to the nearest inhabitable building."

Irene glanced at the horizon. "Will we make it before the sun sets?"

Alex set down one of the cases and stretched out his arm, bending his hand back to him at the wrist. "With fifteen minutes to spare if we keep a good pace."

She'd been trying to step in his steps across the dunes, but now that they were on flat ground, she ran up next to him. "How did you just measure that?"

He stopped and laughed. "You are inquisitive, aren't you?"

"Very!"

He lowered the luggage and held up her right arm. "Stretch out your arm and bend your hand back like this." He gently pulled back on her fingers. "It's not an exact science, but however many fingers you can put between the sun and the horizon is about fifteen minutes. Three fingers, forty-five minutes, give or take."

"Cool!"

He laughed. "Glad I could show you something. Now, let's go."

Alex hefted the cases and his long legs quickly carried him away from her.

"Well," Irene said below her breath, "I might be stuck on a deserted island, but I can't imagine being stuck with anyone other than Alex Belgarde. Good pick for a one-night stand, Irene," she giggled to herself, then ran to catch up.

Maybe her one-night stand wouldn't be a one-night stand after all.

CHAPTER 6

~ Alex ~

As they crested the last dune, the incessant cries of thousands of kittiwakes drowned out all other sounds. Even the relentless yelps of the seals dulled in comparison to the black-legged seabirds.

"Oh, God! What's that smell?" Irene groaned behind him. "It's worse than the beach."

"Kittiwakes." Alex turned with a laugh. "Can't you hear them shouting their name? *Kitte-wa-aaake! Kitte-wa-aaake! Kitte-wa-aaake!*" he mimicked their squawk the best he could. "Or, does *E-E-Eh,*" he attempted a half-dolphin, half-seagull shrill, "sound more like them?"

"Stop! Stop! For all that's holy, please stop!" she screeched, hands over her ears. "It's like a nightmare. And it smells like a chicken farm."

"That may be, but look, Irene." Over the ridge now, he pointed to a rickety one-story building in the distance. "It may not be a chateau, but it's dry shelter."

"Oh! Thank you! How would I ever have found this without you, Alex?" She swung her arms up and around his neck, kissing his cheek. She shook her head and stepped back, her cheeks a bright pink. "I wouldn't have. I would have drowned on that beach when the tide came in."

Alex stepped forward. "I doubt that. You would have come up with something. You're a survivor. I can tell."

She huffed, then shook her head, mumbling something below her breath that he couldn't hear with all the squawking.

He lowered his head. "What did you say?"

"Nothing." Irene peeked up at the twilight sky. "Let's go. As long as that shack has four walls and a roof, I'm good. I've stayed in worse."

Alex doubted that, but he hefted the suitcases again. His arms felt like jelly. Curling a fifty-pound dumbbell was nothing. But carrying fifty pounds in each arm for miles through soft sand was an intense workout. But he'd been right to bring her luggage. Not only didn't he want to leave evidence of their arrival on the island, but he was also certain that they'd want all the clothes they could get, for warmth. He assumed there'd be blankets in the shelter, but he doubted they'd be clean.

As they got closer, the birdsong diminished. Not because there were fewer birds. In fact, there were more. In every window of the rotted-out barracks they walked past, birds nested, roosted, perched … whatever they did at night. There were occasional squawks where one bird was apparently angry at another bird. But for the most part, they seemed to be settling down for the evening, which is exactly what Alex and Irene needed to do before the sun melted away, and he had no light to find wood for a fire.

Irene ran ahead of him and knocked. "Hello?"

"No one's home, Irene. Believe me. In the summertime, sure, but not in January. I'm sure that's why Kevin's drug dealers chose Middleton."

She tested the doorknob, then peeked over her shoulder. "It's unlocked."

"Who'd break in? The rabbits?"

Irene furrowed her brow. "Smartass."

"Irene, open the door, please. Your bags weigh a ton."

"So snippy!" She opened the door and turned to him, her nose and brow all crinkly again. "I told you to leave them."

Alex moved past her and dropped the purple weights within inches of the entry. He shook out his arms and rolled his shoulders. "It's not a Motel 6 even, but it's shelter."

Irene followed him inside, her gaze drifting over the four recliners and sofa all huddled in the center of the small space next to a wood-burning stove. Her attention then went to a fridge and washer and dryer. "Is there electric?"

"Nah. There should be a generator, though. Let's hope the researchers that spent the summer here didn't bring just enough to last them."

Irene opened the fridge first. Empty. Then she checked the stove, turning the knob. No *click, click, click* sounded.

Alex stepped up behind her. "Look in all the cubbies and cabinets for supplies, especially food, candles, and fuel before it gets dark. I'll go search for wood."

She whirled around. "Don't go far."

Alex tilted his head. Was she worried about him? "Nothing scary out there other than the cold."

She blinked a few times, something he noticed she did when she was nervous. "You said Kevin's friends would be looking for the drugs."

"I'm sure of it, but I think we have a little time before we have to worry about them, since you said he didn't call in an SOS. My guess is that he was supposed to make his drop today, and someone would pick up the batch tomorrow. Doubtful they'd take a chance of breaking down in these waters at night."

Irene nodded. "Okay. But ... be careful, okay? I don't want to be here alone."

He offered her a nod and left the shelter without a word. So she wasn't concerned with his welfare as much as she was her own. Made sense. She'd said she was glad that he was here, but she'd meant because he was a rescue worker. They'd shared a bed together, but that was it. Just sex. Just a one-night stand, as she'd so eloquently put it.

"Serves you right, Alex!" he scolded himself as he walked the rough road. How many times had he slept with a woman, knowing he'd only wanted one night? But in his defense, he'd never wanted more than one night with any woman because he knew his days were numbered. Why take the chance of falling in love when he'd already decided his destiny? "And you couldn't even do that right."

He heaved a long sigh and scoured the area for wood. The day was bearable; he'd only been shivering because he'd gotten wet. Survival 101: don't get wet. But the night would be painful if they didn't have heat.

He couldn't help but smile, as he thought about what they could do to stay warm. Irene had been hot. Scorching hot. That's all it was. That's why he couldn't stop thinking about her at breakfast ... on the plane ... fighting Kevin.

"Yep, keep telling yourself that, Alex."

Alex peeked into the dilapidated barracks, hoping for spare pieces of wood. He covered his mouth and nose at the stench. The area had been cleared out of any scrap wood anyway. That was probably the first spot the research team had scavenged.

He scanned the sky for aircraft. Not that he didn't believe what he'd told Irene, but he figured why take a chance. The good thing was … he'd be able to hear a plane approach. His largest concern was Kevin washing back up on shore. The man would be pissed. And he had a gun. If Kevin had been able to bring down Old Betsy in one piece — and he was pretty sure he had — he would have enough survival equipment to last a few days. The plane was stocked with a life raft and emergency blankets. If Alex had had time, he would have emptied it.

"Stop thinking about the what-ifs!" he admonished himself. "Your number one concern is staying warm! Think, Alex. Where would there be wood?" There were plenty of shrubs, but they were too moist. He needed old, dried-out wood. "That's right!"

He turned directly to the setting sun to get his co-ordinates. It was a bit of a hike, but when he was looking for a place to land, he'd seen an old wooden boat that had washed up on shore. He took off in a jog, heading due east.

He needed to hurry. He didn't want to be out too long after twilight. If Irene didn't find a lantern or candles, he'd have a difficult time finding his way back to the cabin.

~ **Irene** ~

While there was still light, Irene quickly scavenged the shack for anything of use. She'd pulled back the plain dark-blue curtains, but already it was hard to see.

She searched the darkest spots first — under the bed and other pieces of furniture — and then she sifted through drawers and a closet, pulling out anything they could use.

She piled her finds on a small dinette. A flashlight she hadn't checked. Batteries she hoped would fit the flashlight she hadn't checked. A lighter she didn't try. Matches. A vacuum-sealed bag with sheets and another with a blanket. She was certain that visitors were supposed to wash the linens before they left the island, but she'd yet to find fuel. If — when ... they made it through this, she'd find out who owned the place, and she'd repay them for everything they used.

After her search of the closet, she headed to a set of cabinets with a countertop that served as a kitchen. She closed her eyes as she opened the cabinet beneath the sink — hoping — then opened the warped doors. She inspected every canister, but found mostly cleaning supplies. Nothing resembled fuel. She was happy to find a kettle, though. That would work to boil water for coffee.

She lifted a lantern from beneath the sink and was happy to discover it was full. At least they'd have a bit of light in an emergency.

Irene stood, hands on her hips. She turned, taking in the entire cabin again. "Oh, crap. No bathroom."

She sighed and headed for the front door. She stepped out and headed for a small shack behind the cabin. She lifted the wood latch and stepped inside. "Oh, goodie, an outhouse. It's official. This isn't the worst place I've stayed."

Across from the toilet — a hole with woodchips — sat a small alcove with a drain, which held nothing but an empty bucket. Well, not completely empty. Once upon a time, it appeared that a spider had used the metal bucket to catch bugs. She imagined that the bucket and stall were used to take sponge baths.

Again, not the worst place she'd ever spent a night.

Still, since there wasn't anything of use here, she needed to search some more, then return to the cabin before it got too cold and dark to find her way back.

Outside the tiny bathhouse, she raised her hand to the setting sun. Not even a finger remained between the sun and the horizon. Not that she needed to use her hand to figure out that she wouldn't have sunlight for much longer.

She jogged toward the crumbling building Alex had referred to as barracks. More like a henhouse. She stuck her head through the open doorway. Chitters and occasional squawks resounded, but it seemed the birds were settling down, which meant that she and Alex should too. Besides, she could see nothing of worth from the doorway, and she damn sure didn't intend to enter the coop. She'd let Alex do that if he wanted.

Speaking of Alex ... She turned and headed back to the cabin. They'd manage. They had a few cans of food, protein bars, and a kettle to boil water. Even if Alex didn't find wood, they'd make it through the night. It wasn't as if they'd starve in one night, and now that they had shelter, they wouldn't freeze.

Together, they'd be able to keep warm. Just thinking about his hands, she felt instant warmth. She'd been so hot this morning that she'd actually opened the hotel window.

Irene peered over the cabin's roof. The sun had already sunk behind it. She stepped to the side and watched as the sun seemingly melted into the ocean. She'd always marveled how fast it disappeared when it finally hit the horizon.

After she'd been diagnosed and before she'd gotten too ill, she'd spent time on Stinson Beach. In the weeks she was there, she never missed a sunset. She hadn't missed a chance to reflect on her life either. She'd spent her days walking the beach, and her nights deciding what she would do if she woke up from the operation.

All the years she'd lived in San Fran, she'd only gone to Stinson Beach once. She'd always wanted to return, but never made the time. More often than not, she'd end up in Carmel or Monterey ... because it was where a friend or significant other wanted to go. The people she hung out with didn't want to vacation in Stinson Beach because it wasn't a party town, and there was little shopping available. But she loved it. Without a doubt, it was one of the cleanest and sandiest beaches on the California coastline.

She closed her eyes and shook her head. Seventeen years of her life, gone. She'd done well financially, but she'd gone broke spiritually. She had no love life, no family, and no hope for anything except her career. And her illness had taken that away overnight.

A rush of wind battered her, sending shivers through her core. She gathered her jacket tighter around her and reached for the door handle. She pushed the door open as the wind lashed at her, threatening to carry her away.

Inside, she pushed against the door, fighting the wind that wanted to enter. She finally got the latch to click, then gasped. Alex was in that wind … in the dark. How would he find his way back?

She ran to the window. Peered in both directions. Already, it was nearly impossible to see. If only she'd found some wood or fuel, she could have set a fire.

She whipped around, feeling her way to the dinette where she'd stowed all her treasures.

The lantern. No. Too windy.

She felt for the flashlight. Her fingers gripped the cold metal, and she padded her way back to the door.

The wind howled, shaking the front door. She carefully unlatched the metal handle and held tightly as a gust threatened to slam the wood against the wall. She tugged it closed as she stepped out into the cold. The temperature felt like it had plummeted twenty degrees in mere seconds.

She pressed the button on the flashlight and heaved a sigh of relief when the bright beam shot from the top, blinding her. She whipped the stream of light forward, aiming it at the road, and then the spiny vegetation that covered nearly every exposed inch of the island.

Remembering that most flashlights had a strobe function, she clicked the button again. The flashing light would make a beacon for Alex to follow back.

Several thumps sounded in the sand beside her, and then a black mass charged her from the side, grabbing the metal from her hands.

"Are you crazy?" Alex yelled, extinguishing the light.

She collapsed into a squat, a yelp emitting from her throat. "Oh, God!" She thought she was dead. Thought that Kevin or one of his drug dealers had found her.

Alex draped his arms around her, pulling her to her

feet. "I'm sorry. I didn't mean to scare you." He opened the door and pulled her inside. "Irene ... I'm sorry."

She could feel his warm breath on her face, his hands on her arms as he tried to soothe her, but she couldn't stop herself from shaking. It was too much. Today had been too much.

"Irene, I'm sorry. I didn't mean to scare you. It's just ... that LED light is bright; it's made to be, so rescue teams can see it. My team won't be here for at least a day or two, so ... we can't take a chance. We need to lie low for a few days."

She covered her face, pressed on her eyes, tried to make everything go away. "I'm okay," she said in her hands, partly to assure him, but mostly to assure herself. "You just scared me. I thought Kevin ... or ... one of his men ... had found us. I just wanted to make sure you could find your way, Alex." Another hitch rose in her throat. "It's just been a long day."

It's been a long year, she cried within, not wanting him to hear her internal breakdown. It was bad enough that she'd fought for her life from an illness. But now she'd crashed in a plane, almost drowned, been nearly choked to death ... How much more could a woman take?

"Here ..." Alex ushered her from the door to the sofa. "Relax, honey. I'll make a fire. We'll be fine. No one's coming tonight."

Irene gulped in more oxygen, sniffed, and tried to relax her quivering limbs. "I'm fine," she choked out through shaky gasps.

You are *fine!* she screamed internally. *You've survived worse than this. You investigated and reported atrocities from the streets of San Francisco. You survived cancer, for*

God's sake. You can certainly handle a few days on an island.

But what if Alex was wrong? If they couldn't signal anyone, how would they notify a rescue team they were here? Or worse ... Alex had said, *No one's coming tonight* ...

What would happen when the drug runners showed up tomorrow?

CHAPTER 7

~ Alex ~

Alex hustled away from Irene, leaving the cabin to pick up the wood pieces he'd chucked.

What had she been thinking, flashing an SOS light?

He knew what she'd been thinking. He'd heard her call his name, and he was grateful. So why had he nearly tackled her instead of just explaining?

He smacked his head with his hand. He wasn't used to women, normal women that is. His mother would have known better. Nora would have known better.

He'd never welcomed a woman into his world, so other than his mother and Nora, he'd never had to deal with one while on a rescue. Irene wasn't like Nora and his mother. She was a city girl. A fragile city girl at that. And he'd nearly tackled her in his haste to turn off the flashlight.

No one would be here tonight, he was certain, so he could have just asked her to turn it off. Instead, he'd scared her.

He gathered up the scraps of wood and tossed them next to the door. As much as he didn't want to open the door in the night when he needed to add to the fire, he also didn't want to invite any fleas or critters in via the wood.

Before opening the door, he peered up at the darkened sky. It was a clear night, with the stars lighting up the heavens, which meant it'd be cold. He chose three logs and entered. A golden flame flickered on the table, casting flittering shadows across Irene.

"I figured it'd be okay to light the lantern since you found wood for a fire and said we wouldn't be here more than three days."

Embarrassed by his earlier actions, Alex simply nodded. "No, that's great. The light will make it easier for me to start a fire."

She walked toward him. "I'm sorry I freaked out … and that I used the flashlight. I should have known better."

He set the pieces of wood on top of the cast-iron furnace. "No need to be sorry. That was my fault. I shouldn't have stayed out past dark and, as I said, I don't expect anyone to show up tonight, so I was a bit melodramatic."

A smile tugged up her cheeks as she stopped in front of him. The candlelight flickered in her hazel eyes, making them dance.

A sharp pain stabbed Alex in the stomach as he stared at her. He moved forward, his fingers immediately finding her soft auburn curls. Without thinking or asking, he pulled her toward him. He dipped his head, finding her mouth. She opened for him, accepting him.

Her hands slid up his chest, and he moaned at the memory of how she'd unbuttoned his shirt and stripped him of the tux within seconds of following him into his room.

He pulled back from the kiss. "Irene …" He rested

his forehead against hers. "I don't want to stop, but we need a fire, honey." He hadn't wanted to light the fire in the daytime, as the smoke would easily be visible, so they needed to get it as hot as possible tonight. Not that they needed a fire to stay warm. Their two bodies entwined added up to 197.2 degrees. Not technically, but he liked the notion of her naked body pressed against his again.

She groaned quietly. "Yeah … and food. We might as well use the heat from the fire to cook. I found a few cans of food, and I tossed coffee in the backpack you gave me. You said only necessities, but coffee is a must-have for me."

Alex pulled her back to him. "Woman, you already know the way to my heart."

"Mine too … and my head. My head is throbbing, so it's either the lack of caffeine or water. I figure I'll kill two birds with one stone."

He peered down at her. "I *am* sorry I overreacted."

"I'm okay, Alex. I just needed a bit of a breakdown. Women do that, you know. It's our way of getting everything out so we can start afresh."

He backed away. "Okay. You get dinner started, and I'll make the fire."

Irene turned away, and he immediately wanted to pull her back, scoop her up, and carry her to the loveseat. They didn't need a fire to stay warm; his body was on fire.

But he refrained from drawing her back. That would be irresponsible. If he was wrong, and Vince didn't find them in the next three days, they'd get mighty hungry. They needed to keep food in their bellies so they didn't gorge all at once and run out. He'd heard of people eating the eggs of seabirds, but that prospect didn't appeal to him. And even if he could catch a rabbit, the meat was too lean to live off.

He knelt next to the stove, carefully opening the front, making sure an animal hadn't set up house inside the cast-iron block. He arranged the three logs upright, added some shards and paper, and then used one of the firestarter sticks from his emergency pack. No sense struggling to catch the fire when he had the right supplies.

In seconds, bright orange flames licked at the glass and heat poured through the vent.

"Fire's ready!" He stood, tossing a look over his shoulder. Not that he'd done anything spectacular, since he'd had the firestarter sticks, but Irene didn't know that.

"That was fast. I haven't even been able to get this blasted can opener to work. It works for about two turns and then stops. I wish all manufacturers would go to pop-top lids. According to a YouTube video I saw, some Millennials don't even know what a can opener is, let alone how to use one."

Alex stepped to the counter, retrieved the can opener and can of beans. "I'll get it. You can start the coffee." He opened the handle, releasing the catch, then leveled the blade on the edge again and squeezed, turning the handle. Irene just didn't have enough strength to use the cheap contraption. The rubber-handled one he used at home was smooth. "You're not serious about Millennials, are you?"

Irene lifted her head from the blue kettle she'd been inspecting. "Dead serious." She reached into her back pocket, then froze, laughing. "Oops! Where is my head?

I was actually going to show you the video on my phone."

He laughed, then set the can on the counter next to her. "Here. I'll go find some snow."

She wagged her head again. "I'm not accustomed to not having electricity and water at my command."

"That's just sad."

"Hey ..." She crinkled her nose. "Not everyone hikes and camps for a living."

Alex laughed. "I'm not talking about you. I'm talking about not knowing how to use a blasted can opener. And I thought I was a sorry-ass bachelor because I still live in the family home. At least I know how to use a can opener and build a fire."

Irene stared up at him, the question he'd seen hundreds of times lighting in her eyes.

He raised his gaze to the ceiling and shook his head. "Yes, I still live with my mother, but I have a very good reason."

She lifted her hands as if she hadn't been thinking, *What a loser*, and turned to retrieve the beans from the counter, but not before he saw the smirk.

"You could get your own snow, you know. I can live without coffee. I had a big breakfast with my family, since you left my bed before dawn."

She turned back to him. Her top teeth grazed her bottom lip, then she nodded to the fire. "That's a great fire, Alex. Would you be a dear and bring me some snow so I can make us coffee?"

He snatched up a bucket, exiting the cabin without comment. He pulled out the flashlight, but aimed it at the ground.

He understood why women reacted that way — out-of-towners anyway. The few local women he'd gone out with didn't have a problem with his homestead. Then again, most of them knew about the vacation rentals at the rear of the property, the ones his mother rented out from May through September. Off-season, though, he and his brothers staked out their favorites. His was the two-story closest to the lake, with a deck leading off the bedroom that overlooked the woods.

All his brothers lived at home; even Sam and Nora had said they wanted to live there after their honeymoon.

Since their father had died, the five of them had decided not to leave their mother to fend for herself in the wilderness. Except Vince. Vince's wife had insisted they buy their own house, and then she'd left him, so he'd moved back eight months ago. Even with the five of them still living there, there were many times when the house was empty.

His mother knew that one of them would always be home overnight, though. The five of them had a text chain they'd kept going for years, sharing things they didn't share with their mother and Nora. An unspoken rule was that their mother was never alone. When any one of them said, "I won't be home," one of the others would always ping back, "I'll be home."

Another stab to his gut nearly doubled him over as he realized he had planned to never text those words again by making the decision to end his life. What had he been thinking? There had to be another way.

He found a fresh mound of snow, far away from the bird barracks. He swiped off the top coat and then filled the bucket.

Once upon a time, there had been water on Middleton Island, before the uplift. He'd also heard stories of gold washing up on the shores, but that was a long time ago. Now, the island was really only livable in the warmer months. And even then, all supplies had to be brought in, which reminded him. Obviously, Irene hadn't found fuel, or she would have announced it, rather than apologizing that she was using the fuel in the lantern.

"Vince," he said aloud. "Please don't take too long to send out a team." Vince had been the one who'd insisted they look for Sam and Nora. Alex had been too pissed at Sam to care if he ended up caught in a storm.

Alex had also tried to soothe Irene, but truthfully, he was scared. He had no weapon, and he had a woman to look after. If Kevin or his associates showed up overnight, the cabin was the first place they'd look. But what else could they do? They needed shelter. Tomorrow, he'd have to head to the radar building at the far end of the island. There had to be a working radio there. Worst case, there was a weather cam. He could write an SOS message and post it in front of the camera, hoping that someone would be watching.

Until tomorrow, though, he had to figure out what to do. Not only for security, but also with Irene. The heat between them was undeniable, but was it right to go further with her? She'd said one-night stand ... But what would happen if they made it through this ordeal?

Would she want more from him than a few nights and safe passage home?

Could he give her more if she did?

~ **Irene** ~

As soon as Alex left the cabin, Irene berated herself. "What are you doing? One-night stand, remember? You don't have more to offer Alex than one night." *Not when, even if you do get off this island, there's still only a fifty percent chance that you'll live for more than five years.*

She stirred the navy beans, bending over them and sniffing, assuring herself they weren't spoiled. The expiration date was good, and there hadn't been any dents in the can, so they'd probably manage to escape getting botulism.

The wind howled, causing the door to rattle. Obviously the cabin had seen years of bad weather, so chances were it'd hold up for three more days, but the long wails were nerve-wracking. How could someone take them for nights on end?

The handle turned, and she braced herself. She should have already retrieved the stun gun from the pack, but she had felt safe when Alex was nearby.

The door opened, and the wind whipped through the cabin, along with Alex. He shoved his shoulder against the panel, securing it again.

"No wonder the plane crashed," Irene said. "Those gusts come out of nowhere."

"They do." Alex scooped snow into the kettle. "Looks good. No foreign objects anyway. Make sure it boils before you use it, though."

Irene stared up at him from beneath her lashes, resisting the impulse to tell him she understood basic food safety. Instead, she extended her hand and accepted the kettle. She replaced the bubbling pot of beans with the kettle, and then carried their meager meal to the counter. She poured equal servings into two bowls she'd wiped out the best she could. Most germs didn't grow or survive on dry areas, so they should be okay.

She carried her bowl to the dinette and plopped down.

Alex picked up the second bowl and sat across from her. "Not the prime rib we had last night, but it's food. Thanks!"

Irene scooped up a spoonful. "I didn't eat prime rib. I had pizza delivered."

Alex chewed his mouthful. "Are you a vegetarian?"

"No," she laughed. "I was a wedding crasher last night ... but then I returned to my room and ate pizza until the reception ended."

"I'm shocked. Can't say that I've ever crashed a wedding. Do you normally crash weddings? And if so, why wouldn't you crash the reception too?"

"No ... definitely a first, but then I chickened out at crashing the reception, especially after you made eye contact with me."

Alex shook his head and took another bite. "Which reminds me ... What exactly did Evie whisper in your ear?"

"Your name ... and that ..."

Alex cocked his head. "And that ...?"

"You were a great dancer."

He laughed. "No, she didn't. Evie and I have never *danced*."

"But you've done other things?"

Alex set down his spoon. "No ... She and my brother dated for a minute. I'll admit I was thinking about dancing a few steps with her, but she's my friend. I have to work with her on rescues on occasion, so I decided against it."

Irene stared across the tiny table. "Dancing is innocent enough ... I'm sure it wouldn't have affected your work relationship."

Alex licked his lips. "Hmm ... I suppose not. Evie found someone to dance with her quickly enough. They were enjoying each other's company over breakfast, too, unlike some people I know."

"I had an early flight, Alex."

Alex picked up his bowl and drained it, then stood. He tossed it in the sink, then carried the kettle and two mugs she'd left on the counter to the table.

He filled the two cups, then pushed one to her and lifted his, staring into it. He inhaled then chanced a sip. He lowered the cup and stared at her. "It's good."

"It's from Andytown in Outer Sunset."

"Outer Sunset?"

"Outer Sunset is on the Pacific side of San Fran. More family oriented than other areas in Fog City. Oddly enough, the local joke is 'Why did they name that section of San Fran *Sunset*?' "

Alex raised his cup to his lips as he raised his brow. "I'll bite. Why did they name it Sunset?"

"Because the *sun's* always *set* there. Truly, weeks could go by without seeing the sun. But I loved hearing the foghorns, and if the wind blew just right, I could even hear the sea lions, which reminded me of home. Seems I'm getting a bit too much of those lovely creatures now, though."

"True. The abundance of seals and gulls could drive a person mad. Hard to imagine that early settlers lived here year-round. I can't imagine." He shuddered. "Is that where you live in California ... Outer Sunset?"

"No, I live in Pacific Heights."

"I've heard of Pacific Heights." He looked up at the ceiling, as if trying to remember where he'd heard of the city.

"The movie," she offered, filling in the bubble over his head so he wouldn't strain himself.

"Oh, yeah. The couple invested everything in a high-priced neighborhood."

"Yep. That's Pacific Heights."

A furrow appeared between his eyebrows. "So ... you've done well as a journalist?"

"I did well." She shook her head. "You know what? Let's not fill the air with mundane chatter about work and other boring questions."

Alex leaned back in the chair, resting his cup on his chest. "I'm game. We have a long night. About sixteen hours of darkness before the sun rises, so we might as well fill them."

"Ugh ... I remember those long nights." She stood and stretched, then moved to the loveseat in the middle of the room. She sat down and patted the cushion next to her. "Okay ... I think I can come up with a few non-work-related questions."

Alex carried his cup over and sank into the loveseat, his back against the armrest so he was facing her. He pulled his knee up. "Ask away."

Irene stretched her neck, resting her head on the cushion and staring at the ceiling. "Hmm ..." She sat up. "Okay ... what's the best thing that has happened to you in the last year?"

Alex twisted his mouth, thinking only seconds before he said, "Nora."

His answer surprised her. "Nora? Isn't that the name of your brother's new bride?"

"Yes. But she brought life to my brother … to my mother. To the family. They all seem happier with her in our lives."

"And you, Alex? I asked what is the best thing that has happened to you?"

He rubbed one of his eyes, nodding. "My family's happiness is important to me."

"Okay. I can understand that. All right, another one. What do you do for fun?"

Alex brushed his hand along his five o'clock shadow. "Are we being honest? You won't hold my answers against me?"

"Yes, we're being honest."

"I live for my job, so I'd say search & rescue is the most fun I have in my life, but when I'm not working … I'm rather fond of women."

"That's definitely honest. I hadn't thought of myself as a *pastime*, but I can't say that I'm surprised. I think Evie's comment kind of alluded to your *hobby*."

He leaned forward, head cocked. "You said she mentioned my dancing."

Irene pushed him back to his side of the couch. "I'm not finished, and we all know dancing isn't your forte."

"No, I guess it's not." He sprawled back on the sofa, arms spreading out.

Alex looked to be in his comfort zone right now, so she decided she'd keep the questions light and fun. "Here's a fun one … Who's your favorite superhero?"

Alex rolled to a straight-back position and sighed. He looked up, his eyes holding some emotion she couldn't place … sadness, it seemed.

"My father," Alex said finally.

"Your father is your favorite superhero?" While

most men and women she'd posed that question to did, in fact, look up to their parents, most didn't call them superheroes. She'd had people say their grandparents were superheroes, though.

"Yeah ..." Alex relaxed just his shoulders as he released a long breath. "My father started the Midnight Sons, trained my mother, brothers and me, and countless others over the years. He saved more lives in his time than anyone I've ever met. I definitely think of him as a superhero."

Irene touched Alex's knee so he'd look at her before she asked her next question. "In his time?"

Alex gulped back his emotion, his Adam's apple bobbing in response. "Yes. My father died ten years ago."

"How did —"

"Irene," he cut off her question, his topaz eyes holding so much emotion that she wanted to unravel. "I'm sorry, but I really don't want to play this part of the game."

"Oh ... That's okay. It was supposed to be a fun question. I don't think I've ever met anyone who's said their father was a superhero."

Alex nodded and stared off again.

"Hey ..." She moved to his side of the tiny sofa. "It's okay. I don't like talking about my family either, and they're far from superheroes, and I've been lucky enough not to lose them before I could mend our differences." She hoped that opening her own emotions would help Alex to open up.

He turned to her, forced a smile. "Yeah ... you said you've been gone for seventeen years. What happened?"

It was Irene's turn to feel melancholy. After a rescue

team arrived, she would probably never see Alex again, so what difference did it make? After all, what had happened with her family wasn't a great secret. What had happened when she was seventeen was only a great secret on Saint Paul Island. At least, she assumed it was still a secret.

Yeah, it had to be. If her parents had heard the truth, she definitely would have heard from them. For that matter, the boy she had once loved would have probably called her too.

But worse, the fact that her sister had started the entire debacle made her loss even greater.

CHAPTER 8

~ Irene ~

As much as Irene wanted to curl up in Alex's arms, it was easier to talk from the opposite side of the loveseat. She plopped a pillow against the armrest and pulled up her knees, tucking her sock-covered toes under the seat cushion. For the most part, she'd come to grips with her personal losses. She'd thought that she'd even come to grips with her lack of family. But receiving a death sentence had put things into perspective.

Worse, waking up in the hospital to chattering reassurances and declarations of love that *weren't* directed at her had made her realize how empty her life was.

Alex draped his arm around her knees, and it felt so natural … as if they were a couple.

But they weren't. They couldn't be. Not when she knew she might be leaving this earth. Alex had choked up over his father's death, so no way would he want to sign up for a relationship with someone who might die before he's forty. How could anyone plan a future with that prognosis looming over them? You couldn't …

She had agreed that they should be honest, and she would. It wasn't as if he was going to ask if she might die in the next five years. She wouldn't have to relay how sad she'd felt when she'd thought someone from her work had come to the hospital to check on her, but that it had been the woman in the bed next to her who'd had a roomful of doting loved ones.

The wind howled and the door shook, forcing her mind to the present. She darted her gaze to Alex, whose attention had focused on the door. He'd barred it shut after he'd returned from his last run, but it seemed he was on edge too. He'd said he had no concern that anyone would show up tonight, but his eyes said otherwise.

He turned to her and smiled. His face held a relaxed natural expression that said without words, *Everything is all right.* "So, seventeen years ago ..." he prompted, obviously an attempt to get her mind off the fact that someone might be coming to kill them.

More than likely, he'd learned to perfect that mask. She imagined that with all the rescues he'd done, he must have had some life-threatening ones that he'd had to reassure a person that they weren't going to die. She remembered his actions after the plane crash. She'd been freaking out, not even able to unlatch the seatbelt, and he'd calmly told her, *It's okay, Irene. I'm coming.* And then had swiftly picked her up and set her outside with an, *Out you go!* as if she were a toddler. Alex might be a bit grumpy on occasion but, mostly, he seemed sweet and funny, a charmer, and a man who cared about people, his family ... his mother. A good combination.

Irene shot another glance at the entry. The door shook on the hinges, as if a ghostly being were attempting to escape from another realm and enter theirs. "Are you sure, Alex?"

He patted her leg. "I can promise you this ... I'll hear if anyone tries to break in. I won't let anyone hurt you."

She smiled softly. "Are you a superhero too, Alex?"

"Not even close, but I *do* take my job seriously. I'll make sure you get home safely." He smiled widely. "Now, tell me why you haven't been home to our beautiful state in seventeen years."

"Well, now it feels a bit anti-climactic, but if you understand my family, it will make sense." She took a sip of her coffee. "As you're probably familiar with small towns in Alaska, everyone knows everyone."

He nodded.

"Saint Paul is probably even worse. Like you said ... five hundred people. And with my father being the local pastor, everyone knew my sister and me ... And what we did, who we dated ..."

Alex laughed. "Understood."

"As a teenager, there weren't a lot of available boys. I was older — only by fifteen months — but that meant I was able to do everything before Kirsten, which drove her crazy. With all your brothers, I'm sure you get that."

Alex looked thoughtful, his thumb casually rubbing the seam of her jeans. "My older brother, Sam, the one who got married yesterday, is five years older. I think I grew up faster because of that. I always wanted to do whatever Sam was doing."

"Exactly." Irene laughed. "Obviously, you couldn't though. Five years apart is a lot. And your younger brothers?"

Alex shook his head. "I really am the middle child. Erik is adopted; and he's six years younger than I am. Vince, while not adopted, is quasi-adopted. He followed Erik home in grade school and practically never left. His parents didn't seem to mind having one less mouth to feed. And my youngest brother is twenty-one."

"Wow ..." Irene worked the math from the eldest to the youngest. "Seventeen years between your older brother and baby brother."

"Yeah ... And talk about growing up fast. Daire has lived up to his name in every way, shape, and form. Even his delivery was a death-defying feat. My mother had to go into Anchorage to have him. I was only twelve when he was born, but it seemed there was a lot of emotion surrounding his birth." Alex tapped her knee. "Hey, we were talking about you ... and your sister."

Irene smiled. Her job was to get other people to talk. "Long story short, Kirsten apparently didn't like any of the other boys, so she seduced mine."

Alex whipped back his head as if she'd slapped him.

"Yeah ... That's what it felt like for me too, but it gets worse."

Alex blew out a breath. "How can it get worse than that? I may be a dog, but I'd never go after one of my brother's girlfriends."

"She got pregnant."

Alex nodded for her to continue.

"And then had an abortion."

His mouth shaped into an O.

"Yeah ... but no one knew it was her. One of the parishioners saw her on the mainland ..." Irene took a large breath. "The woman told my father it was me."

"Damn ... Did she come clean?"

"No. I was leaving anyway. Heading off for college in San Fran in a few weeks, so she begged me not to tell them." Irene shook her head. "But you know what bugs me the most?" Alex nodded for her to continue without interrupting. "My parents are supposed to be all about forgiveness, and they've never once asked for any explanation. If they preach forgiveness, then why wouldn't they ever forgive me? For something I never even did! It got to the point that I didn't want to tell them the truth."

"And now you're going home to tell them?"

Irene sighed again. "I don't feel it's my position to ask them to forgive me, especially since that would be lying. The only thing I know for sure is that *I* must forgive the actions of a sixteen-year-old girl. I've been mad that my parents never tried to forgive me, and yet, I never tried to forgive my sister."

"That's a good thing, Irene. And not easy to do. We do make mistakes when we're young, and it's hard to own up to them. Your sister will appreciate your forgiveness." Alex ran his fingers over her knee, doodling again. The silent air caused him to look up. "What?"

"Nothing." She stared at him. "You put on a playboy vibe, but there's more to you than that, isn't there, Alex?"

He closed his eyes and shook his head. "Once upon a time maybe ... not now."

Irene pushed herself upright so she was right beside him. "What does that mean?"

"It means, I used to have dreams, but now I don't."

"Why? You're only thirty-three. Whatever you decide to do today, you could do for the next thirty years and still retire from it."

He crinkled his nose and huffed. "It's not that easy."

"Sure it is!" she snapped. "If you don't have a terminal disease, you might live for another sixty-some years, so how can it be too late for anything? Is it because your father died?"

He lifted his hands to her shoulders. "I told you ... I don't want to talk about my father."

Irene raised a hand to his cheek. "I'm a good listener, Alex."

He closed his eyes again, and when he opened them, there was fire in them. He pressed his lips to hers at the same time he pushed her to her back. His lips left hers for a second. He stared down, his lips parting, but then he shut them again.

Alex buried his head against her neck, his warm breath tickling her ear. "How sold are you on us being a one-night stand?"

Irene's heart leapt. Not that she'd thought she'd have to talk him into having sex, but she'd wanted him to try. Checking off her bucket list was one thing. Seducing a man she actually knew was different. Last night she'd been another person, a woman who crashes parties, dances in closed bars, and follows a man to his hotel room.

When she'd woken up this morning and got on that plane to return home, she'd been plain old Irene, the woman who hadn't slept with her boyfriend at seventeen, so he'd had sex with her willing sister. Then she'd had to deal with the accusations. Not only that she'd gotten pregnant and had an abortion, but that she'd cheated on the boy she'd been with for several years.

Alex pulled her upright and lifted her sweatshirt over her head and arms. "You know, you wouldn't even let me look at you earlier. Now you're letting me undress you."

"Careful, Alex, I'm slowly learning your secrets too.

You'd hate for it to get out that you're not the playboy you claim to be."

He pulled on her lip, talking through his kiss. "You sure about that, Irene?"

"I'm pretty sure I am." She moved to her knees, then worked her way onto his lap, settling down right where she wanted to be. She worked her fingers up his chest and around his neck.

His head rolled back as he released a groan.

She threaded her fingers behind his head and pulled him toward her so she could kiss him again. She kissed him long and deep, then pushed him back, waiting for his eyes to open. "I'm sure ... There's more to you than you let on, Alex, and I *will* find out what it is. It's what I do."

The question is ... *Will I lose another part of my heart in the process?*

~ Alex ~

For the first time since he could remember, Alex was scared. Not of dying or commitment — hell, he was good at committing; he'd committed his life to his family and career — but of losing the one part of himself he'd shut away: his heart.

How could he open up to someone? How could he open up to Irene? When she found out what he'd done, she certainly wouldn't look at him as if he were a superhero. No, he was the man who killed the superhero. He was the man who had diligently planned how to throw away his life because of the guilt that had ravaged his soul for ten long years.

But oh, how he wanted her. If they were making

love, she couldn't ask questions. She couldn't dig too deeply if his mouth was on hers.

Alex released the clasps on her bra, freeing her beautiful breasts.

Maybe he *had* died. Maybe he was in heaven. He couldn't imagine a better forever than being trapped with this amazing woman for all eternity.

Irene's cool fingers wandered beneath the hem of the sweatshirt he wore. He moved forward and up from the couch, allowing her to lift the thick fabric over his head.

The movement caused his hips to thrust upward, and he couldn't help but wonder if his lap wasn't the softest place to sit at the moment. Of course, how could she blame him? What man wouldn't get excited with a sexy woman on his lap, one he could still recall every inch of, every moan of pleasure?

As if on cue, she moaned. "Mmm …" He liked hearing her delightful sounds of approval. "I remember this."

"I would sure hope so." He chuckled. "It hasn't even been twenty-four hours. If you forgot me that quickly, I'd have to question my performance."

She nuzzled her face against his neck, dropping tiny kisses around his ear. "Yeah, but I hadn't planned to ever feel you again, so I was trying to forget how good that performance was."

Alex stood up with her straddling him. "For two bodies that fit so perfectly together to never join again … that would be a shame, Irene. A waste."

He carried her to the bed, which surprisingly, looked to have clean sheets. He lowered her to the cream-colored cotton. Her bronze waves shimmered like embers. Her pale skin, flawless and nearly translucent, glowed in the orange firelight filtering through the room.

As he gazed down at her body, hungry to consume her, but not wanting to rush as they had in his hotel room, she moved her hands to her waist. She deftly unfastened each metal button until the flaps fell open, forming a V that revealed white panties. She lifted her hips, shimmying out of the dark denim.

"God, you're beautiful, Irene."

She smiled up at him. "Thank you, Alex. So are you."

He lowered his body over hers to take her mouth again, and she reached for his jeans. Trying to ignore her cool fingers moving beneath his waistband, so he wouldn't explode, he concentrated on her mouth. Her tongue moved with his and it took everything he had to ignore the fact that he was still wearing jeans, that she was still wearing panties. He felt like he had when he was seventeen: raw carnal need. A desire to move forward without caution or concern. Without caring.

But no, Irene deserved more. Even if they could never be more, she *was* more, and she deserved more.

Without warning, Irene pushed his shoulders, and Alex immediately chastised himself. *Did I move too fast?*

But no ... she was still pushing him, directing him to his back. She tugged off his jeans the rest of the way. Then his boxers.

Alex lifted himself on his elbows so he could watch as she shed her white panties. "Come here, darlin'. How you could ever think once is enough is beyond me."

She moved toward him, straddling him again. He reached in the drawer next to the bed where he'd stashed his find. Irene snatched the plastic square from him, tore it open, and sheathed him with one swift move.

Then she took complete control of his body, rocking his world, physically and mentally.

Somewhere between her moans of total gratification and his need only to watch her pleasure as it spread across her face, he was pretty sure she was right: she was discovering a part of him that he never knew existed.

And yet, it couldn't last. They weren't in heaven, which meant that when they left this temporary paradise, all his problems would still be there, which meant he couldn't let her discover that hidden part of him.

CHAPTER 9

~ Alex ~

As Irene lay in his arms, Alex listened to the rain as it pelted the metal roof. The winds had calmed down, but a storm had moved in, hovering over them.

An omen?

Or … would the storm be a blessing? Would the retrieving drug-running plane put off picking up their cargo until the storm passed, which would give Vince an opportunity to get here first?

Or … would the storm cause Vince to wait longer? No, the first night Alex didn't check in with his family after telling them that he was taking out the seaplane, they'd get nervous.

And … would the storm cause Kevin to float further out to sea, or would the increased waves and tide throw the drug-running pilot onto Middleton?

The non-stop questions kept him awake while Irene slept. He wasn't jealous of her contentment, though … actually, just the opposite. The fact that she slept so soundly gave testament of her trust in him. Trust he shouldn't want, but nevertheless cherished.

"Irene," he whispered, nearly inaudible, "why did you have to *perfect* my *ruined* life?" He couldn't help swapping the words around. He could see how this woman could change his outlook.

He gently touched his lips to the back of her neck, then pulled back. He ran his free hand up the back of her neck, along the raised scar. The bright pink, almost-red color indicated the scar was a recent addition to her pale skin. A new scar. He had plenty of scars, which had faded into an off-white color paler than his tanned skin. The scar was also large, with tiny indentations where staples had been.

What could have happened to cause such a large scar? Had she been hit? The thought caused his heart to thump harder. The idea that anyone could have ever hurt her sent a roiling tide of emotions through him.

He sucked in a breath and cleared his head. If she wanted to tell him, she would. Her past wasn't his business. For that matter, her future wasn't either. But her present was his business, and he'd take it. He'd do everything he could to make sure that Irene made it home.

As much as he didn't want to move, the fire needed a few more logs if it were to last until sunrise.

He slowly pressed his arm deep into the mattress so he could pull it out from beneath her.

"Mmm …" Irene licked her lips, looking as if she would settle right back into a deep sleep, and then abruptly, she sat up, blinking. "Alex? What's … what's going on?"

He sat back down on his side of the mattress, touching her shoulder. "It's okay, honey. I'm right here."

She whipped around. "Oh … okay."

"Wow, you're a light sleeper. I barely moved."

"Yeah …" she mumbled sleepily. "Sorry." She settled

herself back on her side, pushing the pillow up beneath her neck where his arm had been only seconds ago.

"No worries. Go back to sleep. I just need to throw a few more logs on the fire. I was trying not to wake you, I swear." Even though he had thought about waking her for another go, since he'd just been staring up at the ceiling, a barrage of *what-ifs* pummeling his brain.

"Hmm ..." she groaned lightly. "Thank you."

Alex smiled, pulling on his jeans and shirt as he made his way to the door. Irene stirred easily, but it appeared she fell back to sleep just as quickly. He shook his head as he realized he was already getting to know her more than most women he'd ever been with. In the past, he'd barely taken the time to learn what a woman did for a living, let alone her sleeping habits.

Alex unbarred the door and stepped out. Might as well take care of nature's calling while he was out here. Thankfully, the rain had turned to snow, so he wouldn't get soaked. He walked to the outhouse, careful to stay close to the building.

While he could see the faint orange outline around the closed curtains, the light wouldn't travel far. A few yards away, and the shack would be invisible, as black as the surrounding night.

Alex felt his way to the small shed and stepped inside. Safe behind the closed door, he pulled out his flashlight and clicked the button. He made a swath with the bright beam, checking all four corners.

He breathed a sigh of relief.

Not that he wouldn't have known by now if Kevin had made it to the island, but still, there was something unnerving about not knowing if you're alone before pulling down your pants.

Whenever Alex or his brothers wandered away from camp, to take care of personal business, his father would warn, *Keep watch! Don't get caught with your pants down.*

Alex searched for the antibacterial gel he'd seen earlier, then hurried out, anxious to get back to Irene's side.

At the cabin door, he stooped down, tucked three logs under one arm, then reached for the latch with his other. He stepped in quietly, careful not to wake her again.

He added the logs to the fire, then settled on the loveseat. He glanced at his watch and groaned. Nine more hours of darkness.

He closed his eyes, but it was no use. Scenes and comments and equations rattled in his brain. Conversations from the wedding and breakfast table mixed with the words he'd uttered and heard while rescuing Irene and fighting with Kevin. More often than not, what went wrong on a rescue wasn't what haunted his nights, but what could have gone wrong.

Images of the snow covering his father melded with the water rising to swallow Irene. If he had hesitated minutes before deciding to land, Irene could have drowned inside the plane. If Irene hadn't helped him to the surface, he'd be the one dead right now.

What if? What if? What if?

His life was a series of *what-ifs* and *what had happened*. How had his entire life been changed by one event? How could he ever escape it?

"Oh, Dad," he whispered, "I'm so sorry." He pulled one of the throw pillows over his head to block the firelight, hoping it was the light and not the barrage of thoughts that kept his mind spinning.

I wish you could tell me what to do right now, Dad. I don't want to forget you, but I need to figure out how to forgive myself. You taught me how to handle every aspect of a rescue except one ... You never taught me how to handle being responsible for your death.

~ Irene ~

Irene blinked, trying to take in her surroundings. Bright light penetrated the cabin. The slim gaps bordering the curtains were no match for the sun. She could only imagine how difficult it would be to sleep in the summer months.

She slowly turned to the opposite side of the bed, but then bounded up when she saw it was vacant. "Alex?"

A crinkle of leather caught her attention, then Alex's head popped up. "Yeah?"

She blew out a breath. "Nothing. I was just ..."

He blinked. "Just what?"

"Why are you over there?"

Groaning, he shrugged and rolled his shoulders in the same move. "I couldn't sleep, and I didn't want to wake you." He cracked his neck one way, then the other. "Now I'm paying for sleeping on this tiny sofa."

"Want coffee?"

"Oh, God, do I!" He rolled off the loveseat and crawled toward the bed. "But first ..."

She giggled. "I have to brush my teeth first."

He blinked again, shaking his head. "I'm flattered, but I meant sleep a bit more."

Irene pulled back the cover and let him crawl in

next to her. He rolled over so his back was to her. "Don't let me sleep more than an hour, okay?"

"Okay," she said on a chuckle, then rolled out of the bed. Alex had pulled his boxers back on, but his bronzed back was open for inspection.

Even while he was resting, she could see the wide shoulders and sinewy muscle that lined nearly every inch of his body. She'd been looking forward to morning sex. It'd been forever since she'd had the pleasure. In her experience, men were usually ready and har —

"Irene," Alex groaned, cutting off perfectly delicious erotic thoughts. "In or out, please. It's freezing."

"Oh!" She covered her mouth to hold back a laugh. She tucked the sheet and blanket around him, then searched for her clothes. She hustled over to the smoldering embers, ready to stoke them, then remembered … smoke. At night, the smoke would be hard to see, but in the day, it'd be akin to sending out smoke signals.

She pulled on her clothes and coat, then stuffed her feet into her boots without lacing them. She wouldn't be outside long, she was certain. If it was this cold inside the cabin, she could only imagine how cold it was in the open. Lastly, she snatched up her toiletry kit and headed for the door.

Outside, she raised her hand to shield her eyes. With the sun blazing off the white sand and snow, it was nearly impossible to see, but she could hear. The seagulls scattered to and fro, squawking at one another as they scavenged their surroundings.

As her eyes adjusted, she scanned the area bordering the cabin for any indication that someone other than she or Alex had spent the night.

She laughed. "What am I looking for? Luggage?" As if

Kevin had tipped a bellhop and left his duffle bags outside the cabin, and then had strolled off to search the resort's facilities.

Still, she flicked her eyes from the bird barracks to the dunes bordering the road to the outhouse. In the event someone had tried the front door and found it locked and had decided to spend the night in the smaller cabin, she palmed her Taser, ready to strike.

The Taser would only incapacitate an attacker for a few seconds, a minute at best, but it was effective, leaving her enough time to escape.

She lifted the latch, allowing the door to swing open. She peeked inside to the left, then the right, assuring herself that the shed was empty.

She blew out a breath. "You're going to give yourself a heart attack."

A gust of wind spewed snow and sand across the floor, so she hustled in, pulling the door tightly closed behind her. Inside, she closed her eyes. "Yes, I'm definitely causing undue stress." Alex had been clear that they'd hear if anyone showed up.

Next to the sink sat a now-full bucket of water. Alex must have heated up more snow and brought it in for her. She smiled at his thoughtfulness. As she'd suspected last night, he wasn't the cold-hearted playboy he pretended to be. Somewhere deep down, there was a hurt little boy. Everything in her wanted to investigate, figure out what made him tick.

She splashed the cold water on her face, then pulled out a couple of her makeup cloths, using them to clean herself up from forehead to ankle. She applied lotion with sunscreen, deodorant, and then lined her eyes with waterproof eyeliner. She could go without makeup, but she insisted on applying eyeliner, since her lashes were so fair.

Irene gathered up her toiletries and headed back to the cabin. Back inside, she grabbed the kettle. She sloshed around the water. Alex had obviously filled it up again, too. Since they couldn't light a fire, she set up the propane burner she'd found yesterday. Just as it boiled, she turned off the burner to save fuel, then poured two cups of hot water, adding a packet of instant coffee to each.

She carried a cup over to the nightstand next to Alex, then made herself comfortable in one of the recliners.

It took only a few seconds and Alex stirred. He sniffed, then sniffed again. "Did you make flapjacks too?"

Irene laughed. "Flapjacks? No … I'm afraid I don't have a clue how to make those. Gotta settle for a coconut-almond protein bar."

Alex moved to a seated position, then reached for the cup. "This'll work." He took a sip, then groaned. "So, what do you want to do today?"

She smiled. "Not sure. Didn't know that your trip offered guided excursions."

"Sure! Let's see … We have several tours available. A seal- and whale-watch outing. An adventure back in time, following the same steps the early settlers took when they panned for gold. A walking tour of old shipwrecks. And the highlight of Middleton Island, the bird-watching expedition."

"You know … If we were staying at a resort or on a cruise liner, they'd charge a fortune for those trips. When do we start?"

Alex grinned, seemingly happy to make her smile. "Well, we do need to make a trip, the longest one first. At the end of the island, there's an unmanned weather station. I'd like to see if we can get inside, hoping there might be a radio. But, worse case, there's a weather cam. If we can write a sign and date it, who knows? Someone might be watching."

CHAPTER 10

~ Irene ~

I rene stuffed another protein bar into her jacket pocket and then filled up a bottle she'd found with the remaining water from the kettle.

She turned away to give Alex some privacy while he dressed. Not that he wanted it, but since he'd turned her down this morning, she hadn't wanted to put herself out there again.

"Ready," he called.

"About time!" She turned to see him dressed in jeans again and a different sweatshirt. This one had a hand-stitched logo in the upper-left corner. She walked toward him to view it better. "Oh ... it's the Midnight Sons logo. I like it. All your rescue teams are represented."

"More like, types of rescues ..." He pointed to each image. "Air, water, land, and rock." One was of a helicopter, the next a wave, the third a silhouette of a person with hiking sticks, and the last was a rock face with another silhouette holding on. "But we specialize in different areas. For example, for water, we do several things. My youngest brother, Daire, is the kayak king. Even though he's only twenty-one, if we have a rescue involving white water, Daire usually heads up the mission. But if we need to send out the jet rafts, Sam's still in charge, and then … for open water, Vince takes the lead. Even though Vince and Erik can both man a chopper, I usually take the lead on anything in the air. Erik's our mountaineer man. If you saw him at the wedding, he's the wiry one. That man can literally crawl over rock faces. Sam's our tracker. With his dogs, he can track down anyone, anywhere. He's also the boss. No matter the rescue, even if one of us takes lead, he ultimately calls the shots."

"Does that bother you?"

Alex dropped his head, shaking it, but he came up smiling. "What are you, a shrink? No, Sam calling the shots and being my boss doesn't bother me."

"No, I'm not a *shrink*; I'm a journalist. People interest me."

"Hmm …"

She planted her hands on her hips. "What does *hmm* mean?"

He shrugged. "It's just … you're always digging. I say something simple, and you assume there's more there," he said matter-of-fact like. Not as if he were upset, but more like he didn't understand why she would bother.

"Hmm …" she said in response.

"What does *hmm* mean?"

"You tell me. You said there was nothing there, so I believe you. It's just … I know how families are. Sam's older, takes the lead. That has to play on you."

"It doesn't." Alex gathered up his personal items mindlessly, then pulled a sweater over his sweatshirt. "Sam *is* older, and he's more mature. He deserves everything he gets."

"And you don't, Alex?"

He flashed his gaze upward from the table where

he was choosing one of the protein bars she'd set out. "On the contrary, Irene, I deserve everything that's come my way." He stuffed the bar in his jacket pocket, snatched up the piece of paper he'd written the SOS on, and then headed toward the door. "Let's go."

Again, Alex didn't seem angry, but rather, resigned … as if even being stuck on the island was something he'd had coming.

She pulled on her knit cap and a shawl she found and scurried out the door behind him. "Alex …" She waited while he secured the door, checking the latch to make sure it held tight. Something had been bothering her about how he'd ended up on the island. Yes, he'd saved her, but she didn't understand everything he'd said the previous day. She'd wait to ask, though, since he'd already accused her of digging. She'd wait until it came up in conversation again.

He stopped and stared at her. "Yes?"

"Never mind." She waved her hands as if it was nothing. "Let's go. I'm looking forward to our excursion."

Instead of arguing with her, demanding she finish her thought, he strolled off. His long legs had him yards away within seconds.

She rushed to catch up, then looped her hands around his arm. "So, tell me more about Middleton Island …"

The walk to the tip of the island took about forty-five minutes, but at least it was easier than crossing the dunes. While the air was crisp — about fifty degrees and humid, which meant the cold seeped right through to your bones — it was clear and sunny. She never minded the cold when it was sunny.

From the other side of the dune that lined the

airstrip, waves crashed, seals barked, and seagulls squawked ... all in a rhythm that reminded her of the ambient sounds app she listened to back home. It seemed the moment the surf died down, the seals would cry out. And then the moment the seals settled, the kittiwakes belted out their song. At least from the distance where they walked, she only caught an occasional whiff of bird poop. Mostly, the air just hinted of brine and fish, as if she were walking along Old Fisherman's Wharf in Monterey.

If she didn't think about their situation, she could imagine walking arm-and-arm with Alex, showing him Cannery Row and dining at one of the oceanside restaurants she loved. There, they'd sip something potent and fruity, and then they'd return to the B&B she always rented in Carmel.

While she daydreamed, Alex spoke of the gold rush, foxes, rabbits, and the multitude of ships that had beached. "Oddly enough," he broke into his story about the German man who'd lived on Middleton for about a year, panning for gold, "I just remembered ... the family who raised the blue foxes on the island was named Crusoe." She looked at him with one raised eyebrow, and he lifted his hand. "I swear I'm not making that up."

"Who'd think this deserted island would have such history when we didn't have all the battery and fuel-operated items we have today, but now ... it's just us."

"I know." He shrugged and went back to talking about the air force base that had closed in the early sixties.

After a while, he stopped acting as a tour guide and just walked.

"Alex?"

He peered down at her. "Yes."

"You said the best thing that happened to you in the last year was Nora ... So I was just wondering ... Did you mean ... your brother and her marrying, or her coming into your life? How long have she and Sam known each other?"

"Dig, dig, dig ..." he said through a laugh.

"I guess so ... Like I said, people and their situations interest me."

"We met Nora last May ... She came to Alaska to hike Denali, and let's just say ... her situation was interesting, to say the least." He stopped talking and walking and turned to her. "I think ... as bad as what she had going on, it actually pulled the family closer together. And hey, she and Sam found each other."

"What do you mean? What happened?"

"I think ... maybe ... you being a journalist and all, you should ask her. Hers is a story worth hearing, and I'd just butcher it. But ... I'm curious, don't you recognize her?"

Irene leaned back and looked up at his eyes, which were sparkling gold in the sunlight. "What do you mean? Why would I know her?"

"Nora is Nora Molina. UFC Champion K.O. Molina. She's played in several action thrillers, too, so I just figured with you being from California ..."

"Oh, my God! The bad-ass blonde! Of course, I know her! Hell, when I was —" She shook her head, realizing she'd almost said, *When I was lying in bed, puking my guts out* ... "I wanted to be her. What woman doesn't?"

"That's Nora," Alex said. "And I don't blame you. If I were a woman ... Hell, I think most men wish they were as bad-ass as Nora is."

It dawned on Irene. She *had* heard something. She'd been so sick, she hadn't been paying much attention, but there was something big on the news ... something about her manager. Alex was right. She would love to interview Nora. From what she could remember, no one got an exclusive; the news channels just had to go with whatever they could dig up.

"You're right, Alex, I would like to hear the story from Nora," Irene said. "So ... they've only known each other about seven or eight months, and they tied the knot, huh? And that makes you happy. That's nice."

Irene was prepared to throw some more non-threatening questions at Alex, but a building came into view. A very nice building, at that. Not a wooden shack. Why hadn't they been sleeping in it instead of the drafty cabin?

Alex trotted up to the door. "I doubt it's open, but ... you never know." He twisted the handle. Nothing. He pulled and jiggled and pushed, then shoved with his shoulder. Nothing. "It's solid."

Irene stepped up behind him. "Looks like a steel door."

He rubbed his shoulder. "Feels like it, too."

She burst out, realizing he'd hidden the fact that he'd hurt himself. Macho-itis. "I'm surprised you didn't try to kick it in like one of those cop shows."

"Nah." He laughed. "I need my foot, thanks."

Alex stepped around the side and Irene followed. Solid. Solid. Solid. No windows. No other doors. No way to get in. Definitely a government station, not a cabin erected for birdwatchers. Since it was sitting at the uppermost tip of the island, she imagined it had to be, though. The cabin they slept in was protected by massive sand dunes on either side; the radar station stood high on a cliff, where it would receive blunt force winds.

While Alex pulled out the sign he'd made, Irene walked to the edge of the island. The cliff face was steep, carved by wind and waves. At the far tip, the wind whipped her face, reminding her of a scene from *Titanic*. The island was even shaped like a massive ship sailing in the open ocean. Below her, waves crashed the exposed rocky beach. If she took one step —

Alex grabbed her from behind. "What are you doing?"

"Just playing."

"That's no place to play," he barked. "One rogue gust of wind, and it'd be bye-bye Irene."

She folded his arms around her midriff, hoping the action would soothe his tone. "I wasn't that close, but thank you for your concern. It's beautiful here, Alex."

He nuzzled her neck, his warm breath heating her in more ways than one. "It is ... And with you in my view, it's even more amazing."

She turned in his arms. "Maybe no one will come. We'll have to make do as castaways. Could we do it?"

He smoothed back one of her loose curls from her face, tucking it under the edge of her cap. "You'd want to be stuck on a deserted island with me, Irene?"

"Who else would I want to be stuck with? You're like having my own personal Survivor Man, only cuter."

He laughed. "Yeah, we could survive. If nothing else, we always have eggs. We'd probably never eat another egg in our lifetime once we made it back to civilization, but the fat and protein in eggs would be enough to sustain us."

She moved her hands to his chest. "See what I mean … You're like a walking and talking survival guide. It's like you've already figured this out."

He moved his mouth to hers, making her forget about questions and survival and drug runners. Yes, she definitely wouldn't mind being a castaway if Alex was with her.

After a few seconds, Alex's lips stilled.

She'd shut her eyes the moment their mouths had met, too caught up in the kiss to think about anything. The loss of his warmth made her open her eyes. He was just staring at her.

"What?" she asked, her fingertips touching her wet lips.

"You're beautiful."

"I am?"

He laughed. "Yes."

"Not too skinny? Too short of hair?"

He shrugged and smiled. "Well, you could stand to gain a few pounds. I feel like I'm going to crush you every time I pull you near me."

She wrapped her arms around his waist. "I'm not that fragile, Alex."

His hands moved up her arms, stalling on her shoulders. His calloused palm cupped her face and she moved into it. "Are you sure about that, Irene? I'm not the gentlest when it comes to women, as I'm sure you can already attest."

Obviously, he was speaking about more than just physical strength, and he had been a bit curt with her the previous day. But she'd never liked a pansy man. "I'm sure, Alex. I'm not delicate inside or out, I assure you."

He wrapped his hand around her back and neck and pulled her tighter against him. His mouth captured hers again, and she was instantly lost in the heat. His mouth was hot, and the sensation of his tongue exploring her mouth made that heat travel down the center of her body, heating her insides up as if it were eighty outside, not fifty.

Just as quickly as he'd taken her, he pulled away again.

She stumbled forward, grateful when he steadied her.

He chuckled as he pulled her to his side. "See, that's why we don't play on cliffs. Come on, time for shipwreck scavenging and whale watching. From the east side, there's a great spot for viewing, the highest spot on the island."

She blinked, trying to clear her head. Why had she lost balance over a simple kiss? *Probably just the lack of food*, she told herself. No man had ever made her dizzy from a kiss.

Dammit, Irene! she chastised herself. *You can't fall for Alex. You can't fall for any man. You don't have a future, remember?*

~ Alex ~

Alex blew out a long breath, attempting to stop the tingling sensation. If it was just his future, he could handle it; he was good at denying a future. He would take what he wanted and be gone before a woman had a chance to fall for him.

It was clear, though, that as much as he wanted Irene, she seemed to want him just as much. And not just physically. Physical wants diminished. The thrill of being with a new woman only lasted a few days, then he was fine with saying goodbye.

But not Irene, he'd wanted her the moment he woke up in his hotel room alone. Wanted her yesterday, all day. Not just sex. He wanted to hold her, to tell her everything. Even as he deflected her questions, he found himself wanting to answer her. He wanted to confess all and have her want him anyway.

He needed to clear his head of these thoughts. Get back to the day.

"Oh, my!" Irene said, her hand over her mouth. "Is that …?"

"Where the plane crashed? Yes."

"Alex, there's no beach!"

He touched her shoulder as she stared over the nearly hundred-foot cliff. "I know."

"I would have … drowned … if it weren't for you … I wouldn't have made it."

"Irene —"

"No, Alex. I wouldn't have made it around the island without your plane."

"I know … That's why I was so adamant that we get to the other side." He tucked her against him again and started walking along the edge, far enough away that if she stumbled, they wouldn't go over the cliff.

A few hundred yards into their stroll, Irene stopped and pointed. "There!"

Alex waited. Sure enough, a couple seconds later, he saw the black fringed flukes.

"Oh my! Is that a gray whale?"

He squeezed her hand. "No … you won't see very many gray whales or humpbacks until the water warms up. That's an orca."

Irene turned to him, her eyes wide. "A killer whale? Right here?"

"It's an orca."

"We were *in* that water."

Alex shook his head. "Did you know that other than in captivity, orcas have never killed a human being? Never. Not one. There have been four deaths while in human captivity, though, three of which were from the same whale. I've had orcas come right up to my kayak. They'll look me over, and then be on their way. They're very smart."

She lifted an eyebrow. "So … if you saw him in the water yesterday, you would have been fine?"

Alex laughed. "I probably would have grabbed a fin and asked for a ride."

"*Hmm …*" Irene mused. "Speaking of rides … I have a question. You had said that there might be fuel here. Other than a few tins of propane, I didn't see anything resembling airplane fuel."

Alex nodded, wondering where she was going with this line of questioning. From the short time he'd known her, Irene didn't seem to ask a question without a reason. "I was hoping. But since I don't have a plane, it doesn't matter, does it?"

"I was wondering about that." She stopped staring out at the water and turned her scrutiny back on him. "You said you didn't have enough fuel to take off, and obviously you didn't because Kevin had to bring down the plane, too."

Oh, boy …

"You also mentioned that no experienced pilot would take off without checking his gauges, so …"

Think, Alex! Think! Why would you come this far with-out fuel?

"And isn't there typically a reserve tank?"

"Yes ..."

"Then why, Alex?" She shook her head as she spoke, as if she couldn't even understand the question before she asked it. "Why did you fly nearly two hundred miles out into the Gulf of Alaska without fuel?"

His heart raced. He didn't want to admit what he'd planned. Not to Irene. "I hadn't planned to come this far. I saw the glint of the plane, knew it was a fresh wreck."

Irene chewed on her lip, weighing this information. "We were in the air for more than an hour before we crashed, Alex. Kevin wasn't in your plane for more than five minutes when he started to bring it down." She shook her head again, the pieces seemingly starting to make sense ... *or* not making sense. "Five minutes, Alex. You didn't use that much fuel to land and move around the island. Not an hour's worth."

"Irene ... what do you want me to say?"

"How 'bout the truth?" she spat. "Were you meeting Kevin here?"

"What?" Oh, no ... she wasn't putting the pieces together. She was thinking something totally opposite. "God, no! You thought ... You think I'd be running drugs?"

She heaved out a sigh. "I don't know what to think. I was trying to figure out everything yesterday, and then again this morning. Kevin said we were flying at 150 mph, and I know we flew for more than an hour. I just ... why are you here ... with no fuel to get back? Unless you assumed someone would be waiting for you."

Alex closed his eyes and gulped down the bile in his throat. Would it be better if she thought he was a drug runner? No, she'd asked him if he was a superhero yesterday. She thought he was one of the good guys. So, what would be worse? Him being a drug dealer ... or an idiot who planned to crash his plane in the ocean for an insurance settlement? Either was illegal ... and immoral.

"Well?" she pressed. She'd pulled her hand from his at the first question; now she'd shoved her hands in her jacket pockets. "I'm not stupid, Alex. I may be slow when my life is in danger, but I'm not ignorant of common knowledge. I know that no pilot would head this far unless they knew for a fact that there would be fuel when they arrived. I've chartered enough planes in my career to know that simple truth."

He gulped. "Irene ... can we sit down?"

She flicked her gaze from left to right, as if someone might have snuck up on them. "Fine." She stomped off toward a large boulder that overlooked the water and sat, arms folded.

Alex inhaled deeply then walked to her, sitting down in the dried grass so he was facing her. "I'm sorry that you're confused, but I promise you, I'm not a drug dealer, and I've never seen Kevin before yesterday. Never even heard his name, which *is* odd, since I know most of the pilots who fly these waters."

Her nostrils flared, but she sat quietly.

He dropped his head. "God, I don't want to do this."

"Do what?" There was a frightened edge in her voice. He'd heard fear enough times to know what it sounded like, but she didn't move from her perch. Irene had obviously lived through fear more than just these two days with him. She'd learned to mask her concerns, it seemed.

"I don't want to admit why I was in the perfect place at the perfect time."

She huffed, but she couldn't deny that his timing *had* been perfect, whether his reasons for being in the middle of the gulf were flawed or not. She'd said it only minutes ago. If he'd hesitated for even a couple minutes, he wouldn't have been able to save her. But he hadn't thought twice. Even though he'd had a plan to end his life, he hadn't wavered on doing what was right instead.

"Alex?" His name was a question on her lips, but she'd seemed to calm down a bit. She wasn't demanding, just *digging*, as she'd done a few times.

He nodded, then massaged his temples. "Ten years ago, my father died. I told you that, and I told you I didn't want to talk about it, but I didn't tell you why." He looked up again, and her eyes were expectant.

"It was a late call for the day ... I'd already signed off, and truth told, I'd thrown back a couple shots in anticipation of going out. It was a beautiful day in May. The season hadn't started, so I wasn't expecting any calls. Sam had just taken a call. Nothing big, but that had left me alone with nothing but my thoughts. I was twenty-three and pissed. I didn't want to be stuck in a Podunk town forever, rescuing people who did stupid things. But that had been the deal. Sam would work while I finished my undergrad, and then I'd work a few years while Sam took his dogs on search & rescue missions around the world. A few years was all he'd requested. Just a few years, and he'd take over the business permanently with Dad."

Alex looked up to see that Irene was listening attentively, all frustration cleared from her face. It made him want to confess, even when he knew he should make up a lie. He couldn't, though. He was certain she'd see through a lie.

"And then you'd be able to ..." she said, encouraging him to fill in the blank.

"In a few years, Erik and Vince would be old enough to help, too, and I'd be able to join the military. My grades were great. My father had already taught me to fly. But if I entered the Army or Air Force, they'd teach me to fly jets, then my career would be made. I would have been able to get a job as a pilot and travel around the world."

"But you didn't want to wait?" she surmised.

Alex sighed. "No, I didn't. I didn't want to waste three years of my life so that Sam could wander around the world. I was ticked. So, I filled my time with whiskey and women ... even before I was off duty. But then ... a call came in. As I said, it was warmer than usual. Seems like a great idea to go hiking and climbing earlier than season, but if it's too warm, sometimes avalanches are more prevalent ...

"I'd already changed clothes, ready to go out on a Friday night. My father rushed into my room, explaining there had been a snow slide that trapped a group of hikers. He took one look at me and walked back out the door. He'd seen my eyes, knew that I'd been drinking."

Alex swiped his hand across his forehead. As cool as it was, he was sweating. "I ran after him, told him I'd thought I was done for the day, and that I'd only had one drink. He said he'd wait for Sam, and I got mad. Insisted that I was fine. And I was ... I felt fine. Honestly, if I had thought I was too drunk, I wouldn't have gone. A couple drinks isn't anything for a man my size."

"What happened, Alex?" Irene's words were soft, all her earlier anger gone. He hated knowing that her fury would come back full swing when the conversation circled back around to how he ended up in the middle of the Gulf of Alaska.

"When we landed and started our hike toward the stranded hikers, I realized I'd forgotten my ice ax. I'd cursed aloud, and my father had asked. Hell, even if I hadn't said a word, he would have noticed. My father noticed everything and was always prepared for anything. He was the original Boy Scout. I tried to reject his offer, but he insisted on giving me his ax ..."

Alex closed his eyes as the scene played out in his mind. The ground was too warm. The last snowfall unstable ... He'd heard the roar above them, clambered to get a grip as the trees cracked and snapped. He'd latched onto his father's hand the same time he'd swung the ax into the ground. But it was no use. His father's grip slipped, and although Alex had let go of the ax and tried to save his father, it was too late. The avalanche had swept his father off the mountain.

CHAPTER 11

~ Irene ~

I rene watched as Alex tried to compose himself behind shuttered eyelids. Even closed, tears slipped from the corners as he obviously relived the horrific day he'd lost his father.

But it wasn't really his fault … was it? Anyone could forget a piece of equipment.

She moved from the boulder and squatted in front of him. "Alex, it wasn't your fault."

His eyes snapped open. "Yes, it was. I shouldn't have been there. I shouldn't have accepted his ax. I shouldn't have done a lot of things, but … it was my fault. My father never would have made that mistake. And he didn't. I did. I did because I didn't double check the list. We have a damn list, Irene. I was too lazy to check it. Too much in a rush to get out of there and get back so I could go out with my friends."

She felt tears in her own eyes. She knew about *should haves* and *could haves*. She'd tortured herself for years with them. "Alex, you were twenty-three, barely an adult. That's why your father handed you his ax. He understood that anyone could forget —"

Alex huffed and shook his head. "No! You're wrong!" He stopped and stared at her, his eyes roaming over her.

"You're a journalist, right?"

"Yes ..." she said hesitantly.

"You interview people, right?"

"Of course."

"What do you take? A notebook? A recorder?"

She shook her head, realizing where he was going with his line of questioning. "A recorder and a note pad. I jot down notes as I listen and record. I like the recorder in the event someone tries to retract their statement."

"Have you ever forgotten to bring either?"

"No, but —"

"An ice ax is my life in a climbing rescue. Rather, my father's life. A rescuer doesn't forget his ax any more than he would forget a rope. It's a given. Hell, it's how I got into the plane to rescue you yesterday."

"It was a mistake, Alex. You can't torture yourself for the rest of your life —" Her face flushed hot. *The rest of his life.* No fuel. Alex wasn't a drug dealer. Not even close. He'd been angry. He'd accused her of knowing what Kevin was doing. "Oh, my God, Alex!" Tears burst free. "Alex, tell me it isn't true. Were you ... you were going to kill yourself?"

She stood, stumbled backward, the tears blurring her vision.

"Irene, it was the only way."

She heard his voice, but she couldn't see him. Didn't want to see him. Her life was probably going to be cut short, and he was going to throw his away. Her sister ... Her sister had thrown away a baby, and Irene had to give up hers. Her ex had abandoned her when she'd had to make one of the most important decisions of her life.

Irene blinked, trying to clear her head. "It's not fair

… Life isn't fair."

"You don't understand," Alex continued. "Since my father died, we've lost money every year. The company that he started … that has saved so many lives … We lost so many donations in the last five years we almost went under. We've had to take out loans that we couldn't pay back. And my mother mortgaged the house. The donations are coming in again finally. With Sam's maturity, that will continue. He just needs enough to make it a few years, to pay back the debt, and then —"

She reeled. "Money? You were going to throw your life away over a few bucks?"

Alex sniffed. "One point eight million actually, enough to ensure that the Midnight Sons will continue saving —"

"Give me a break! You're weak, Alex! Throwing your life away over money. I can almost understand guilt, but money?"

He clenched his jaw. "You don't know anything. You and your posh Pacific Heights lifestyle. Hell, your mortgage is probably more than our yearly operating budget. What do you know about troubles?"

She spun away, attempting to keep her eyes dry. How dare he accuse her of being ignorant about life! He didn't know her. Didn't know what she'd been through. She ran along the edge of the cliff, looking for a place to make her way back down to the road.

A white dot on the horizon caught her attention. Then she heard the roar of the engines. A rescue boat! "Hey! Hey! Over here!" She waved her arms and jumped up and down.

SMACK!

The air left her lungs at the same time she fell. The heavy weight was on top of her, pinning her. Her face felt raw against the icy yellow straw. "Get off me!"

His hand moved to her mouth. "Shh … Stay down, Irene."

The engine grew louder, then faded.

Alex moved from on top of her, then offered her his hand. "Come on. We have to get there before they do."

Ignoring his hand, she moved to her knees then brushed straw and dirt off her pants. "Get where before whom?"

"The boat … It's the pick-up boat."

"It could just be a boat, Alex, a chance for us to get off this godforsaken island." And to think she'd been fantasizing about being shipwrecked here for months.

His eyes narrowed. "I don't have time to argue with you, Irene. Are you coming, or not? If not, stay out of sight."

She huffed. "I can't trust someone to rescue me who doesn't value life. How do I know that your family is coming? Maybe you want to just die of starvation!"

Alex threw his hands up and stormed past her. Without hesitation, he hustled down the embankment as if he were walking on flat land.

Not wanting to follow him, but not wanting to be alone either, she attempted to follow his trek. Halfway down the embankment, she lost her footing. Just as she thought she'd fall, he was there. Holding her up, stopping her fall.

He steadied her. "You okay?"

"Yes." She wanted to say, *Take your hands off me*, but she couldn't force herself, especially since she knew the reason she was so angry with him was because she was jealous. Jealous because he had a future and she didn't. Because he had the luxury of deciding to throw his life away, while she would have to fight for every breath.

He pressed his forehead against hers. "I really want to explain this to you, Irene, if you'll give me a chance, but we don't have time right now."

She pulled back and offered him a slow blink, since she didn't feel like arguing.

"Here," he crooked his arm, "hang on to me until we get to flat ground. We'll beat them to the cabin. I'm sure of it. The only safe entry is the bay we motored into, which means they have to cross over the dunes. We have mostly flat ground."

Alex moved forward, and she was amazed by his sure footing. He may have forgotten his ax the one time, but she'd lay dollars to doughnuts he'd never forgotten a piece of equipment since. Alex had said that he lived for his job, that search & rescue was the most fun he had in his life, so obviously he'd thrown himself into his career to make amends. He'd probably saved more people than he could ever count, and yet he'd intended to throw his life away over the one person he couldn't save.

Irene absorbed this as she tried not to hold his planned suicide against him, but she'd be damned if she'd miss a ride off the island because Alex was scared to leave. She had to get a look at these boaters.

~ Alex ~

Alex layered his hand over Irene's as she latched onto his arm. At least she trusted him to get her down the embankment, even if she didn't trust him to get her off the island.

He'd show her.

On flat land, he relaxed his grip, and she dropped her hands.

"Thank you," she said coolly.

"You're welcome," he tried to say with a bit more warmth. Yes, she'd made him angry, and he'd instinctively spouted out something he hadn't meant. But, if he were being honest, he knew she'd be upset. Anyone would be. No one could understand the grief he'd carried. And she was right ... it wasn't just about money. Part of him just wanted the nightmares to stop.

He turned to her. "I'm going to run up ahead so I can clear out the cabin of any indication that anyone has been there recently. Stay out of sight, please. Go behind the barracks, and I'll meet you there as soon as I finish. Okay? I doubt they'll stray from the airstrip. They're only looking for their drop, I'm sure of it."

Irene nodded. "Okay, Alex. But please find a way to make sure. This could be our ticket off the island."

"It's not, Irene. I *am* sure. No one's out this far for a leisurely boat ride in January." Instead of waiting for her to debate the issue, as he knew she would, he took off in a jog. As he rounded the curve, he looked back. She wasn't jogging, but she'd stepped up her pace. He hoped she wouldn't do anything stupid.

He waved at her and took off as he realized how ironic that thought was.

Irene hadn't done anything stupid. He was the one who had planned to do something stupid. More than stupid, really. Terminally foolish. Although ... like Kevin, the moment he ran out of gas, his preservation skills probably would have kicked in, and he would have brought down the plane and been stranded at sea.

You weren't willing to drown, he reminded himself. But that had been different … he'd been worried that Irene wouldn't make it home without him.

Shoving his pointless thoughts to the back of his mind, he edged his way toward the cabin, making sure no one had made it there before him.

Inside, he loaded all their personal belongings into Irene's suitcases. He stuffed his carry-on under the bed, but hers would have to come with him. He spied the sink.

Damn!

He knew he should have cleaned up his dish from the previous night. He stuffed the mugs and bowl under the counter upside down, then went to the wood stove.

If he poured water on the smoldering embers, he'd send up a plume of smoke.

Think, Alex! Think!

He spun, taking in the room. He grabbed up the pot Irene had used for beans and darted outside. He scooped up a large amount of sand, then rushed back inside. He dumped the sand in a heap, then smothered all the exposed embers. It would have to do. If the new-comers noticed someone had recently been here, hope-fully they'd think Kevin had stayed the night after his drop.

Alex took one more look, then hefted the purple suitcases and ran for the bird coop. Doubtful that any-one would do more than peer inside. He carried the fifty-pound bags to the far edge of the barracks, then hustled back out, his hand over his mouth.

He rounded the building and was happy to see Irene waiting, as he'd requested.

"Anything?" she whispered.

"Not yet."

Irene grabbed his arm. "The fire? Won't they see it?"

He smiled. He really liked this woman. She thought like he did. "I smothered it with sand."

"Oh, good thinking."

He pointed to the ground. "Settle in. We might be here for a while."

Her eyes widened as she lowered her body to the sand. "Where are you going?"

"I won't go far. I'm just going to make my way to higher ground. As you said, I want to make sure I'm right. I can't imagine anyone saw our SOS already, but just in case, I want to hear what they have to say."

Blinking rapidly against the bright sun, she lifted her hand to his. "Alex, please be careful."

"Of course." He stared down at her, then lowered himself until they were face to face. "My problems are far from over, Irene, but … I don't want to die; I know that now more than ever. Please believe me."

She touched his cheek. "I don't want you to die either, Alex."

"And I'm sorry for what I said about you and where you live. You obviously understand a lot about human nature. I was wrong to lash out at you. I swear I didn't mean it." He pressed his lips to hers for a quick kiss before she could respond, then stood. She didn't need to respond. He was the one who'd been a jerk. "We'll talk later. Stay here, okay? No matter what. Even if something happens to me, know that my family *will* be here soon. I promise."

Again, her eyes widened, then she blinked back tears. "Alex …"

"I'll be fine, honey. I'm just thinking ahead. Everything will be all right."

She nodded and settled back down, her arms wrapped around her knees. She looked like a little girl trying to play hide 'n' seek by just burying her head in her hands.

He forced a smile that he hoped would comfort her, then walked toward the edge of the barracks, farthest away from the cabin. The birds squawked as he passed, but seagulls always squawked. For no reason at all, the entire group would get into an uproar, and then settle down. No one who lived anywhere near the coast would think anything of them belting out a round of protest.

Alex crawled up the embankment, making his way behind a track of seagrass bordering the road. This team was coming by water, which meant they'd be coming up the road, which doubled as the runway, on foot. He moved to his belly, working his way through the sharp blades. He had the higher ground, and more than likely, the team wouldn't be looking for a couple eyes peering through the grass; they'd be looking on the ground for the duffle bags. If he were lucky, he'd have the advantage.

Minutes ticked by. What would Irene be thinking by now? That he was crazy? That she shouldn't trust a man who admitted to wanting to commit suicide? Had she believed him when he told her he wasn't the least bit suicidal? The last thing he wanted was to die; he'd proven that to himself yesterday. A part of him still wanted to fix the situation, though. Still wanted the nightmares to stop.

There has to be another way …

"Over here!" A man's voice called from the other side of the dune leading from the beach.

This is it. Alex clenched and unclenched his fists, digging his fingers into the icy wet sand. Adrenaline filled his veins as if he were rappelling down a cliff face, one of his least favorite rescues. He could only imagine what Irene was doing. Would she stay put as he'd requested?

A shaved head came into view, quickly followed by the man's body, dressed in black. All black. From his T-shirt that poked out through his open black coat, to the faded black jeans and black combat boots. Even the knife strapped to his thigh and the gun and holster clipped to a tactical belt were black. The man looked like retired military ... or a wannabe soldier.

Another man, this one with a head of blond dreads pulled back in a low ponytail at the nape of his neck, tromped over the dune. Like his older counterpart, he was dressed all in black. "Damn, dude! What's that stench? And damn ... those birds make it hard to think!"

The older man smacked the younger one upside the head. "As if you think. If you *thunked* before you jumped, we wouldn't be standing in frozen bird crap. And ain't you never seen kittiwakes before?"

"A kitty-what?"

"It's a type of seagull, numbnuts." The combat-ready man waved a black-gloved hand at the hundreds of circling scavengers above them. "Stupid hick!"

"Damn straight! And proud of it! All's we got that smells like that is chickens. But at least we can eat them bitches."

The older man waved the younger man forward this time. "Run up the road a piece. The drop is usually between the shack and the next hill."

Oh crap. As he'd thought, Kevin hadn't been trying to land. He'd just been flying low enough to find the drop point. *If they don't find the duffle bags, they'll assume Kevin might have dropped them behind the barracks.*

He inched backward, keeping his belly against the sand. As soon as he was sure he was out of range, he ran toward the bird coop.

Irene hadn't moved. She was still huddled against the siding, head tucked and arms draped around her knees.

As quietly as was possible in his alarmed state, he inched his way to her.

Her head popped up and a squeak emitted before she realized it was him.

He lifted his fingers to his mouth, and he knew his eyes must be wider than they felt, since she was staring at him as if he were a ghost. He waved for her to come up the embankment, but she stayed where she was, shell-shocked. She'd obviously heard the new arrivals and had deduced, as he had, that they weren't here to rescue, but to collect.

As much as he didn't want to waste the time, he knew, just like one of his rescuees who were afraid to move, he needed to make her move. He moved sideways down the knoll, creating deep indentations. He'd have to cover the holes once they were back at the top. He doubted either of the men would be able to climb the unstable mound.

Beside her now, he gently nudged her up and to his side.

Irene shook her head, her eyes wide. Clearly, knowing they were drug dealers made her nervous. Then again, it hadn't even been twenty-four hours and she'd lived through an airplane crash, almost drowned, and then had been taken hostage at gunpoint. She had to break eventually. He just couldn't afford for her to lose it right now.

"It's okay, honey," he whispered. "We're just going to go over the dune."

Her clammy hands latched around his arm, tighter than earlier, and he helped her up the sandbank. She slipped several times, but he managed to get a good grip on a root system. With one final push beneath her, he vaulted her up to the top of the ridge.

Alex gripped the edge, but there was nothing but sand. He dug and dug, but only came up with sand. His feet couldn't find purchase either, as he'd stripped away most of the plants with his previous two trips. His left hand burned where he clenched the root. He couldn't hold on much longer.

He threw his right arm up again, determined to grab onto anything, and Irene clamped her hand over his arm, her fingers encircling his wrist.

"Lie down, Irene," he whispered loud enough for her to hear, but hopefully not enough to rise above the squawking birds.

With her gripping his wrist, it was just enough pressure for him to dig his hand into the sand and pull himself up. He sure didn't like rock climbing, but all his practice with Erik was paying off.

"Oh, thank God!" Irene said on a quivering breath.

"Come on." Alex moved to a squat and pulled her with him, staying low as they made their way down the other side of the dune. The west side of the island wasn't as steep as the east side, where wind and waves had carved steep cliffs.

Together, they inched themselves through the sea grass.

"Try not to grab the grass, Irene. The blades are sharper than they look."

"I know," she mumbled. "You told me that yesterday."

Alex bit his lip and smiled as he moved down the embankment, Irene by his side. One thing was for sure, as sensitive and helpless as Irene could seem, she recovered quickly. Maybe he'd been wrong when he thought she was a fragile city girl. Maybe Irene could keep up with his chaotic lifestyle.

If they made it home alive, that is.

CHAPTER 12

~ Alex ~

On the other side of the dune, Alex directed Irene toward the shipwreck.

"We'll be able to spy on them from there," he said, pointing to the beached cargo ship. "We'll be above them anyway. That way we'll know when they return to their boat."

"I thought you said the ship was unsafe."

"To set up camp, it is. The top is exposed to the elements, and what's left of the hull is rusted out. Not to mention that the numerous birds that make their homes in it, won't appreciate the intrusion. We'll stay near the exterior."

Alex really wanted to linger near the cabin and listen to the men's chatter, but doing so would be unwise. As much as he doubted that the black-clad dealers would try to climb the dune, he couldn't take a chance. He assumed they'd scour the island the best they could, though. That amount of drugs had to be worth a small fortune. Hell, it was probably worth a large fortune.

The duffle bags had been stuffed to the seams, and they weighed about the normal checked-bag weight of fifty pounds each. He'd heard meth's street value in Alaska was about forty dollars a gram — his area anyway;

supposedly it went for much more in Anchorage — and there are roughly 450 grams in a pound. That's 450 times forty ...

He gave up trying to multiply the numbers in his head. "Irene, is that your phone in your jeans pocket?"

She turned to him, ducking her head as she reached for her back pocket. "Habit. Although, it does have an amazing camera, so I figured I could capture some pics."

Alex waved off her obvious embarrassment. "I understand. Can I borrow it? Or ... would you just calculate something for me. I'm pretty good at math, but the number I'm coming up with seems too high."

She stepped toward him. "Shoot."

He shot his gaze around them, making sure they weren't in eye or ear range. "Multiply 450 times 40 and then multiply that by 100."

"One million, eight hundred thousand."

He swiped his hands across his chin, but couldn't keep his heart from racing and his face from burning hot.

"One point eight million," she said softly. "That's what you said yesterday ... the amount of your life insurance."

"Thirty times my annual salary. That's the most the insurance company would let me take out."

Irene huffed and shook her head. "I don't understand. What are you doing? I thought you said —"

Alex waved his hand to stop her. Bile rose in his throat and he felt like he might puke. He inhaled and exhaled, trying to calm his heart. Irene was right. Life isn't fair.

"Alex? What's going on? I thought you decided —"

"Those men," he cut off her words, "they're looking

for the duffle bags. Two fifty-pound duffle bags with a street value of meth worth one point eight million dollars. My life is worth two duffle bags of meth, Irene."

"Oh, Alex ..." She stumbled forward, latching onto his arm as she tripped over a rock. "Your life is worth way more than that. How could you think that?"

He shrugged. "That's all I'm worth, honey. That's all the insurance company would give me because that's all that I'm worth. Sixty thousand a year times thirty years. If I can work search and rescue until I'm sixty-three, that is." He lifted his head to the heavens, hoping his stupid eyes would dry. "Two duffle bags of poison."

"Alex ..." She rested her hands on his arm again.

"I'm okay." He trudged forward. "You just never add that up, you know. How much you're worth." Irene huffed beside him, so he stared down at her. "What? Have you?"

She shrugged. "I have life insurance ... but ... what difference does it make? I haven't spoken with the people who would benefit from my death in more than seventeen years."

Alex patted her hand. "We're a pair, aren't we?"

She peered up at him and actually smiled. "Yeah, I guess we are."

Alex continued to scan their surroundings as they approached the rusted-out ship. The bird chatter increased as they grew near. He also saw the men's anchored boat, but as he'd hoped, no one was waiting on the beach.

"Pretty cool." Irene moved her gaze to the heights of the S.S. Colebrook, the sides of which were at least forty-some feet over her head. She pulled out her iPhone again and snapped a few pictures. "If we do make it home, this is going to be one hell of a story."

Only a journalist would think about a story and not the dangerous men half a mile away. He couldn't argue with her comment though, but he could argue with *if*. "*When* we make it home, you mean."

She flashed a grin over her shoulder. "*When* we make it back, Alex."

He smiled and stepped up beside her. For some reason he couldn't understand, Irene thought he was worth more than he was. Her faith in him, he realized, was important. He wanted her to know she could count on him. His family would show up by tomorrow or the next day, he was certain, so all he had to do was keep her safe until they arrived.

"Can we go inside?" she asked, her voice chipper. Amazing how she seemingly forgot about the two drug runners with weapons strapped to their sides.

With her inquisitive nature, keeping Irene safe until a search and rescue team arrived might be harder than he'd hoped. "I don't think going inside is a good idea, but we can walk to the opening in the hull and look in. We need to keep our heads down, though. No telling when those men will head back to the beach."

And they'll be mad. And they have weapons. Neither of which he wanted to suggest to Irene.

~ Irene ~

Irene stared up at the ship as they walked along its sandy berth. She'd never stood outside a ship on land, only when it was docked. But this ship had found itself beached high above the ocean. Like Alex had said, once upon a time it had been moored in water, and now she could imagine wildflowers sprouting up along its rusty hull in the spring.

Above them, the familiar sounds of their constant companions shrilled unhappily at the intrusion. Behind them, the constant rhythm of the waves crashing against the rocks and sand drowned out any background noise, so she kept her eyes scanning her surroundings, watching for any unwanted arrivals.

Similar to when she'd worked on the San Francisco streets, her adrenaline bubbled at the surface, ready to kick into gear if she needed to run or defend herself. She gripped the stun gun in her jacket pocket, always making sure that she had it in the right position. She practiced repeatedly at home, tested the on-button, knew how to slide it into the ready position. Then she'd pull it out, push the button, watch as the mini lightning bolts lit up her bathroom. She hadn't been ready when Kevin attacked her, but she'd be ready if those thugs found them.

"They can't stay long," Alex said, as if he'd heard her unspoken words.

"Excuse me?" she asked, hoping he'd clarify his statement. She sure hoped that she wasn't already getting cabin fever and speaking her thoughts aloud without knowing.

"Those men ... They anchored their boat right offshore. The shelf is wide due to the uplift from the earthquake I mentioned, but when the tide comes in, they won't be able to wade to the boat."

Irene scanned the beach. "When will that be?"

Alex looked up as if in thought, then scanned the horizon. "The tide was going out about 9:30, so my guess is that it will start coming back in around 4:30, which means the waves will be too powerful to clear."

"Four thirty is right about sunset," she added, "so those men probably won't even wait that long. Doubtful they'll want to make that hike in the dark."

Alex nodded. "Exactly."

Her hand in his as he led her to the bow, she scanned the length of the boat. "This beast's as long as a football field."

"At least." Alex looked to the front and back. "Probably a fraction more."

He removed his backpack and dug inside, pulling out a beach-size towel from the cabin. He spread it over a sun-dried patch of grass. The highest mount at the southwestern side of the island, their current spot was devoid of snow. Probably because it received the most sunlight.

Irene fished out one of the protein bars from her pack and sat cross-legged on the towel. "Whale watching, drug runners, and a picnic lunch of protein bars … I'm telling you, Alex, you could charge a fortune for this excursion."

Alex lifted a protein bar from the side pocket on his pack and settled beside her. "Hmm … maybe so. Sam has considered leading hikes. He figures he and Nora could make money on the front end, instead of hoping for donations from rescuing people who paid a fortune to visit Alaska."

Irene stared at Alex as a thought occurred to her. "You know, I'm curious … Isn't Nora willing to help the company out? From my research on blockbuster movies, she probably made several million just on her first one."

Alex sighed. "Her agent controlled everything. And

with the investigation into his practices, the money could be tied up in probate for years."

"Couldn't she get a new role ... or a fight?"

This time Alex's face was wistful, but in a good way, as if he were thinking about Sam and Nora. "She's pregnant."

"Oh ..." Irene laughed. "A UFC fight or even fighting bad guys in a movie is definitely out of the question."

Alex nodded his agreement, but she could see that he still had that far-off look. Obviously, he'd thought the same thing ... That meeting Nora could have saved his father's business and save him from throwing away his life.

Without warning, the anger simmered inside her again.

Alex lifted his hand to her cheek. "What is it?"

How could he know that she'd just gotten angry? She stared up at him. "What is what?"

He moved his thumb up the bridge of her nose, tracing the skin between her eyebrows. "These two almost-imperceptible lines. Most people don't control them well, but since you're a journalist, you've probably had practice maintaining a relaxed face. Your eyebrows dip just a fraction when you're upset."

She pushed his hand away. "What? You think you know me now?"

He looped his hand around her wrist and gently pulled her hand to his chest. "My family ... we were taught to read body language. Whether it's a team member or someone I'm rescuing, I need to know what they're going to do before they do it. People in peril do crazy things. And people who are upset, show it all over their face so, besides our obvious predicament, what did you think of just now that upset you?"

Irene stood and Alex followed, not allowing her to break the connection between them.

"See," he said. "I knew you were going to stand before you did it. You shook your head ever so slightly because you didn't want to hear what I was going to say, then pushed your right shoulder toward me, trying to create a barrier between us."

"What are you doing, Alex?" She stared at him as the wind lapped her damp hair against her face. Sitting on the ground, she'd been warmer. Now she was cold. She hadn't realized the wind had picked up and the clouds had started to roll in.

He lowered his head and stared at her from beneath his long lashes. "What do you mean, *What am I doing*?"

"I mean ... why do you care what upsets me? I know your goal is to get me home safely, but what happens after that ... when you decide you still want to kill yourself?"

He sighed long and deep, rested his head against hers. "Irene ... I don't want to kill myself. I promise you, I'm not suicidal."

She stepped away from his too-warm embrace. "But you said it ... your problems will still be there when you return home, and if you thought that killing yourself was the way out, then what's to keep you from thinking that way again?" *Besides*, she reminded herself, *you can't be there for Alex. You can't be there for anyone.* Just what he needs: a woman who has a fifty percent chance of dying in the next five years.

Alex's brow lowered, but he didn't reach for her again. "I'm not suicidal, Irene. I just wanted what was best for my family, and I thought I was brave enough to pull it off, but I'm not. Is that what you want me to admit? That I'm weak? You're right. I am weak. I *want* to live. I didn't realize it yesterday. I thought I was a hero, but I *do* want to live. As unfulfilling as my life is, I like my life."

Irene thought of a hundred things she wanted to say, but she held her tongue. It was better this way. She'd always hated soap-opera drama. While she'd been in the hospital, her hospital roommate had watched one soap opera after another, and Irene had found that the stupid shows were sucking her in, too. But mostly she'd just wanted to scream at the characters, *Tell him you're pregnant! Tell him you love him!*

Now she understood the vital importance of shielding her secret from Alex. She couldn't tell Alex that there was a fifty percent chance that she'd die in the next five years, because then he'd want to save her. She didn't want his warm embrace if it came with a side of pity. And she didn't want Alex to care about her only to lose her. She knew the grief of loss, and she wouldn't wish it on anyone.

CHAPTER 13

~ Irene ~

Irene stared up at Alex. "You said that you're not suicidal, and yet you set it all up, so what am I supposed to think?"

Alex blew out a breath and headed back to the beach towel. "I don't know. The same thing everyone thinks about me, I suppose. That I'm a screw up. My own brother doesn't even trust me to run the business. When he leaves, he puts Vince in charge." He looked back at her, then plopped down on the ground. "I told you I get everything I deserve. I make my own bed, so I have to sleep in it."

Irene crossed her arms and stared at him. "I don't understand. Sam doesn't know, right?"

Alex shrugged. "He suspects. But mostly, he just holds it over my head that I ran off after my father's accident. I couldn't deal with it, so I just left for the coast, stayed out of sight for a few months. I bartended at night, slept and drank all day."

She closed her eyes and shook her head. "And yesterday, you were going to run away for real ... forever, because you're upset that Sam holds your running away over your head?"

"That's about right." He patted the towel beside

him. "Would you sit down, please? Your beautiful bronze hair is like a beacon in the wind. No way would those men miss it if they come back now."

She lowered herself next to him, pulling the shawl she'd found in the cabin tighter around her shoulders. "If you suspect he knows anyway, why don't you sit down and talk to him?"

Alex tilted his head and peeked up at her. "This coming from the woman who hasn't been home in seventeen years?"

"That was different, Alex. I wasn't the one who lied. I wasn't the one who took a non-family member's word that I'd gotten pregnant and had an abortion. My parents didn't even ask me if it was true; they just blasted me. So yeah, I left. I was leaving anyway. I just left sooner than I'd planned and never looked back."

He dropped his head against his hands and rested his elbows on his knees. "Sam will never forgive me. My mother will hate me. My baby brother grew up without knowing our father because of me. He'd never look at me the same."

Irene traced the lines of the sweater he wore. "Would you forgive Sam? Would you hate your mother? Would you look at your brother differently?"

"I don't know."

"Alex ..." She grazed the new stubble on his face. "You said yesterday that my sister would appreciate my forgiveness. I think that's because you know it's what you want ... what you need. You can never be forgiven if you don't tell them the truth. I know you blame yourself, but ... couldn't the accident have happened even if he'd had an ax? Didn't you try to save him?"

He nodded slightly. "Yes, but I'll never know the

truth."

"We never know the truth ... Not really. Every action has a different reaction. We can torture ourselves with *what-ifs,* but it doesn't matter. What will be will be, right?"

He turned to her, a small smile playing on his lips. "Sounds like a song."

"It does —"

Curses came from the other side of the dune, followed by, "You better run! If that boat goes out any farther and we're stuck here, I'm gonna eat your ass like one of those rugby players who crashed in South America."

Alex pulled her down so they were both horizontal. He inched on his belly toward the edge of the cliff face.

"That's sick, man," a second man replied. "You'd really eat me?"

"Nah. Probably not. You've poisoned your body so bad with that crap you smoke. But I'd use you as bait and catch me a fish."

"Damn, man. You're as cold as ice. What the hell'd they teach you in the Marines?"

The other man harrumphed. "To stay alive when punk asses like you screw up."

"Whatever, man. I didn't pick that pilot; you did."

"Maybe so, but if your mother hadn't mortgaged her property to bail you out of jail, I wouldn't be running drugs to save her and your sorry ass."

"Nobody asked —"

"Just get the damn boat!"

Irene watched as a head finally came into view as one of the men jogged onto the beach and into the surf. The man was right. The boat looked a lot farther out than it had been when she and Alex first spotted it. The young man, mid-twenties, she guessed, dove into the surf and came up with long strokes, making short work of the distance.

At the boat, he latched an arm onto a ladder. Only then could Irene see how high the waves were. Every few seconds, the man's body disappeared as the boat rocked up and down.

The other man came into view. Older, early to mid-fifties, she assumed. From their conversation, he was the younger man's stepfather, though he obviously didn't claim that title. He was just involved with the young man's mother, it seemed.

She'd always thought of drug dealers as users themselves, who supported their habit by selling, or someone who just wanted to make money off the weaknesses of others. She never thought about someone selling drugs because they were desperate to save a loved one. Not that it mattered; it was still wrong. The repercussions of selling drugs went way beyond selling to degenerates; it left a path of destruction miles long, often with innocent children in its wake. She'd definitely seen the ugly side on the streets.

The older man waded into the water, checked his surroundings. He obviously wasn't as confident diving into the surf as the younger man. He backed up into the wave, ducking his head as the wave crashed around him. Past the break, he swam on his back until he reached the large speedboat. The man in the boat offered him a hand, but he swatted it away.

Seconds after entering the boat, the engine roared to life and the boat sped away. The young man stood behind the wheel while the older man spoke into a hand-held speaker. She couldn't hear, but his hands told a story all their own as he waved his hand at the beach, the boat below his feet, and even the air.

"Whew!" Alex rolled to his back. "That was close."

"They didn't even look our way. They were so preoccupied with yelling at each other that they didn't check their surroundings."

Alex nodded, allowing that. "Yeah... but I kept waiting for one of them to suggest that Kevin had dropped the bags into the wreck, thinking it'd be safe there."

Irene scurried to her knees. "Then why did you have us wait here?"

"Because it was the best place to watch. I knew we could get away before they saw us if they circled back." He rolled to a seated position, his legs stretched out. "Now we know we're alone again, so we can relax. At least until the next wave of drug runners arrives. I just hope my family gets here before they do."

"Do you think there will be more?"

Alex laughed, and not his normal goodhearted laugh; this one was condescending. "Did you not hear that calculation earlier? One point eight million, and that's based on the value in my little town. Cities like Seattle and San Fran probably pay twice as much."

"What do we do?"

"Same thing we just did. Stay out of sight and hope my family gets here before they send in the muscle."

"We can't stay here forever, Alex. As you said, 1.8 million is a lot of money. They obviously won't wait until the weather clears up to comb the island, and there aren't too many places for us to hide."

~ Alex ~

Alex hopped up, pulling Irene with him. He wrapped his arms around her waist. "What happened to surviving on a deserted island with me for a few months?"

She stared up at him. "That was when I thought you had a strong will to survive."

He shook his head and dropped his arms, but scooped up her hand to lead her down the dune. Her words had stabbed him deep. His heart ached, his stomach felt like an empty pit, even more hollow than when he'd taken off on his fateful flight the previous day.

At least she didn't fight him on helping her down the mound, but maybe that's just because she didn't want to topple head over heels through razorblade seagrass.

Head over heels ... He'd never thought he could fall head over heels for a woman, but he was pretty sure this was what it felt like — Her foot lost traction and she started to fall, so he thrust his hands beneath her arms and pulled her back up.

"Sorry."

For breaking my heart before I even knew it was yours to break? he wanted to ask, but instead he just said, "It's okay. I'm used to walking on uneven ground. I've done it almost as long as I've known how to walk." And it was true ... He'd always been accustomed to treading lightly, physically and mentally. He'd been tiptoeing around the family as long as he could walk, too. Even before he screwed up, his father had always looked to Sam. True, Sam was five years older than he was, but he'd been twenty-three when his father died. Yeah, he would party at night, but he'd never not shown up for work. He'd never made a mistake that had cost a life.

Not until the day he'd lost his father ...

They'd made it to the road and Irene allowed his hand to fall away. But maybe not because she didn't want to hold his hand. He'd realized he'd broken into a sweat as he'd thought about his father and Sam ... even his mother. No one had ever trusted him like they did Sam; they'd always just looked on in concern. Why? He wasn't the baby; Daire was. Why had his mother and father always treated him like he was the baby? Even yesterday, his mother had voiced her concerns about him taking out the plane. She never would have done that to Sam. He'd always just brushed it off, but now he wondered.

Maybe he'd been wrong when he told Irene that Sam being the oldest and always in charge didn't bother him.

"I was thinking ..." Irene's soft-spoken words broke him from his thoughts. "For dinner, maybe I'll make us some canned beans and black coffee."

Alex stopped walking and looked down, saw the corners of Irene's lips turn up. He laughed and shook his head. "That sounds good. Can't wait. Maybe when we get back to the mainland, I'll take you out on the town, show you some of the places you didn't get a chance to see in Anchorage —" Her expression cut off his words.

The look had only lasted a second, but he recognized it: sadness ... regret ... Her lips had turned down quickly, the fine lines framing her mouth deepening. But then she'd hidden it. As he'd suspected, she knew how to mask her feelings. But some feelings were impossible to hide, and sadness or remorse was the hardest. He'd seen the look a hundred times. He'd seen it when they'd been called too late to a rescue and someone had already died. And he'd seen it on his brother's face more times than he cared to count.

She raised her hand to his arm. "Alex —"

"It's okay, Irene," he cut off whatever excuse she was going to give him. He was the king of excuses for why a relationship wouldn't work; he didn't need any new suggestions. "I understand. We've been thrown together these last couple days. That doesn't mean we have to prolong it once we get to safety." He shrugged off her touch and walked toward the cabin.

She jogged to catch up to him. "It's not that ... I just ..."

He stopped again, stared down at her. She was too good at masking her feelings. If he was going to have to endure an excuse, he wanted to make sure he heard the *real* excuse, not the one she made up. "You just ..." he offered as she stared up at him.

Irene inhaled deeply, then spoke quickly, "I have a lot to handle with my family." She blinked repeatedly before continuing, "I can't ... I'm not ... ready —"

"For a relationship?" He forced a smile. "That's my line, honey! What makes you think I'm looking for a relationship? I was just trying to be nice. No worries. I get it. I'll still get you home safely. You don't owe me anything."

He walked off again, this time faster than before. She didn't try to keep up, just tromped behind him as if she were angry. What reason did she have to be angry? She was the one who insisted she'd only wanted a one-night stand, and then practically seduced him with her little question game the previous evening. She'd gotten him to open up to her today, and then had dumped on him.

And when he tried to take their ... whatever they were doing ... to the next level, she'd rejected him.

Maybe he hadn't been mistreating women all these years. Maybe it's what they wanted. They sure seemed to flock to him, even though he'd never hidden what he was. They'd call him a scamp, but then show up on the tailgate of his truck. He'd never had to beg.

He sighed. Irene didn't seem like the type, though. Yeah, she'd slept with him, but he could tell it wasn't the norm for her. She smiled and danced seductively that first night, but he could see the pain in her eyes. Someone had definitely hurt her. Is that what she was trying to do ... hurt back? Make him suffer the way someone had made her suffer?

That was hard to believe too. Maybe she just didn't like him. That was easier to believe. She studied people for a living, so as much as he perceived about her, she probably saw through him too. *What does she see?* he wondered. A man who easily snapped when he got frustrated? A man who was willing to throw his life away because he was weak?

He wasn't weak. He was tired. Tired of the fighting and the nightmares. But for the first time in forever, he'd been imagining a life. That's why he'd asked if he could show her the town. He wanted to, he realized. He wanted a future. How could he convince her of that?

At the last bend before the cabin, he stopped and waited. Not that there was anything dangerous on the island, but he didn't want to take the chance and let her out of his sight.

After all, the owner of those drug-laden duffle bags knew they were missing now, and he'd be ticked. Obviously, the older man had been telling someone on the radio that the cargo was missing. Based on the men's conversation, they couldn't afford the gas to run that powerboat, let alone buy it. Even used, a Fountain 47 Lightning probably sold for half a mil. He understood why a drug runner would want it. It could outrun most Coast Guard boats and power through waves like a tank through a card house.

Irene looked up from the road and caught his eye. "You don't have to wait for me, Alex. I know you feel responsible for me and will get me home safely."

He resisted rolling his eyes. *You started it*, he wanted to say, but that would be even more childish than rolling his eyes. Even though it was true. He'd not come on to her the first night ... or really the second night. He turned and walked toward the shack. She was close enough, and she certainly didn't have a light foot. He'd hear her coming from a mile away, he was certain.

In the event another one of the drug runners had managed to creep onto the island unseen, he carefully opened the cabin door. He doubted it, though. They had to come by air or boat, so he'd hear them either way. Still, he peeked in, making sure it was safe, then pushed the door wide, leaving it open for Irene.

Before she asked, he snatched up the bucket and went in search of more snow. In just the day they'd been on the island, a lot of it had already melted. He walked over a dune that received less sun. He scraped away a top layer, then scooped up handfuls, picking out tiny pieces of twigs.

When he returned, Irene had retrieved the cups and bowls he'd stashed under the sink and was walking them outside. "I just need to clean these up."

He took them from her. "I'll get them."

"Thanks." She stepped back inside.

So much for paradise ... Alex walked to the outhouse and carried what was left of the bucket of water he'd filled for her the previous evening. He washed out the cups and bowls, and then headed over the dune again. He didn't have to be as careful with bath water.

"Aaaah!" The high-pitched wail coming from inside the cabin sent Alex careening back over the dune. He dropped the bucket at the door and ran inside the cabin without a thought.

Irene was up on a chair.

Alex scanned the room, looking for the threat. "What happened?"

She pointed below the sink. "It's down there."

"*It's?*"

"An animal of some sort."

Alex stooped down, examining the shelf below the sink. Nothing jumped out at him. He moved the few cleaning products around. Nothing. But there was a tiny hole leading outside. He wadded up a dishrag and stuffed it in the hole, and then pushed the heaviest bottles against it.

"I think you'll be safe now. There was a mouse hole, but you probably scared him worse than he scared you."

"I doubt that."

"Regardless, I clogged up the hole, and I'll do a search when I get back." He stood and went outside again, retrieved the dishes he'd washed and took them inside, setting them on the table, and then headed back to fill the bucket with snow so he could clean up later.

As he headed back up the knoll, he realized his heart was racing. Not from the exercise. He could hike for days if need be. His concern for Irene is what had his heart nearly pounding out of his chest.

Adrenaline was his favorite drug, more than alcohol and even women. He'd pushed himself to extremes for years to experience greater highs. Irene walks into his life and, suddenly, she's got his heart racing as if he were in a free-fall.

And yet, in as little as a day or so, she'd be out of his life.

CHAPTER 14

~ Irene ~

I rene hopped down from the chair, then plopped in the seat, head lowered. "What an idiot!" she grumbled beneath her breath. "Screaming at a damn mouse. What's wrong with you?"

It wasn't as if she'd never seen a mouse. Hell, she'd had to deal with plenty of them on the streets. And if she had screamed, she would have been dead.

It was Alex's fault. All his concerns about those men bringing back an army had her on edge. The stupid mouse had just startled her. Because she hadn't been paying attention.

She'd been thinking about Alex and his request to *show her around*. She knew what he'd meant. He hadn't just wanted to be top dog in the welcoming committee. That had been Alex's way of asking her out ... asking to see her again once they made it home.

And she hadn't wanted to turn him down. Yeah, she was mad at him ... furious that he'd wanted to throw his life away. And yeah, she wasn't a hundred percent sure that she could trust him to do the right thing, since he obviously didn't value life as she did.

But worse, what if he did? What if he did care for her? She knew without a doubt she cared for him, so how could she ever hurt him? And letting Alex get closer, knowing there was a good chance she wouldn't even make it to her fortieth birthday was cruel. Especially cruel to do that to a man who'd already contemplated suicide over the loss of a loved one.

Footsteps sounded outside and Irene sprang to the window, her hand curling around her stun gun. She peered through the crack between the drawn curtains and exhaled.

"It's just me, Irene," Alex said as he opened the door.

"Oh, I know. I just thought we should get some light in here before the sun goes down."

Alex offered her a quick raise of his head. "Good idea."

His tone indicated that he didn't believe her. Probably thought she'd been sitting in the cabin wringing her hands, waiting for her knight in shining armor to rescue her. Well, she kind of had been, but not because of the men. She knew they'd hear them if they showed back up. Alex obviously had the instincts of a watchdog, always popping his head up with every creak and crack, and now he had her doing the same thing. Heck, she'd been the first to spot the boat.

Alex dropped her suitcases on the mattress, dug his own bag out from beneath the bed, then walked toward the door again. "I'm going to go get cleaned up."

In other words, *I want to be alone for a while.*

She couldn't blame him. She'd been hot and cold, she knew, but it was for the best. Without comment, she followed him to the door, watched as he rounded the cabin, then stepped back inside and locked the door.

Maybe she couldn't blame him, but he was still behaving grouchier than he should for someone who wasn't *looking for a relationship* and was just *trying to be nice.* "Ugh! Men! He was hot and cold too."

Trying to ignore the way his cold shoulder affected her when she was the one who stepped on the brakes, she ventured back beneath the sink for the kettle in the pot. Before reaching for either, she nudged the items, hoping the critter really was long gone. She set up the kettle and pot and then left them on the counter. No way was she going to start a fire without his okay. He'd definitely bite her head off.

Instead, she rummaged through her luggage. She did a quick clean up with her face wipes and then reapplied deodorant and her vanilla body mist. It was light, nothing that screamed, *Take me now, flyboy!*

Next, she sifted through the contents for something decent to wear. Oh, to hell with decent! Do what you want! She screamed internally. Isn't that what this trip — the new you — is all about?

She snatched up the white sweater she'd purchased before she left San Fran. The low V-neck front and back and sheer, practically see-through thread, made the top essentially worthless as a sweater, but it was sexy as hell. She swapped her jeans for black yoga pants that showed every curve of her hard-earned glutes.

She wasn't being a tease, she assured herself. It wasn't as if she didn't want to spend another night with Alex; she just knew they couldn't go further. He was tough ... he'd find another woman and forget about her the second they touched down in Anchorage. She, on the other hand, would suffer for her actions for the rest of her short life.

But ... if tonight's the last night we'll be together, I don't want to spend the long cold evening without him.

~ Alex ~

Dammit! Alex groaned into his hands.

"Damn. Damn. Damn." Yesterday, he'd been free, knew exactly what he wanted and what he needed to do. "Dammit, Irene!"

Couldn't she have just hated him from the beginning? He never should have danced with her. He knew it. The first time he saw her he knew it.

"Stupid. Stupid. Stupid." Now you want her, and she doesn't want you. *Because she doesn't trust you.*

No ... He shook his head. It's more than that. She'd done everything he'd suggested would keep them safe. Yesterday, even when she thought he was dragging her off to rape her, she'd settled down and listened. Then earlier, even after she knew what he'd planned, she'd followed him to the wreck to wait for the men to leave. She'd allowed him to help her.

Something else was standing in the way of him finally moving on with his life. And it wasn't their predicament. Vince would find them tomorrow, he was sure of it. Vince would know that if the plane was going down, he would have headed toward Middleton. Hell, he'd taught Vince that. To always be ready for the unexpected ... to always have an out.

So what was it? Irene obviously liked him, so why didn't she want to see him again?

Frustrated but determined, Alex washed up extra well, slipped into his last clean shirt and jeans, and even shaved. Not a fun thing to do without hot water, but ... he made it work with just the shaving cream.

Outside, he scanned the road and air, noticed the

birds were already settling down. The sun had dipped behind one of the larger dunes.

Another long night. What kind of games would Irene want to play? Or maybe he should lead with the questions ... or games.

He tapped on the door. "Irene?"

"It's unlocked," she called from the other side of the closed door.

He didn't want to get distracted by going inside. Plus, she liked a mystery. "Come on out. I want to show you something. Bring my bag."

She cracked the door and peeked out. "What's up? Everything okay?"

He nodded. "Hurry up. We only have a few minutes."

She sighed. "Okay. I have to put on my shoes and coat."

"Hurry."

Alex waited, listening as she tromped across the wood floor. She sounded like Vince clopping in his boots. Hell, even Vince, at six-four and two-ten, was quieter than she was.

The door opened and she stepped out, handing him his pack. "What's up?"

"Come on." He slipped on the pack and took her hand, hustling up the road to the northwest part of the island.

At the end of the road, instead of heading west, he led her up the east side, to the high cutaway cliffs.

"Where're we going, Alex?"

"Don't worry, it's only one climb in this direction. Not like the dunes heading to the beach."

She trudged beside him, holding on as he climbed the mound. It wasn't as soft as the other side, so working their way up wasn't nearly as difficult.

At the top, he led her to the far eastern side, so they could stare down at the seventy-five-foot cliff face.

Wind whipped at her hair again, so he pulled up her hoodie, fastening it around her. He turned her to face north. "Do you see them?"

Irene craned her neck forward. "What am I looking for?"

"The platform on the next cliff. It's not easy to get to, but here ..." He rummaged through his pack for the binoculars. He adjusted the sight then handed them to her.

Irene looked through them, and he maneuvered her so she was looking in the correct direction. "Oh ... How cool! Eagles. Up close!"

Alex laughed. "They prefer trees, obviously, but since the entire island is a bird sanctuary, the platform was built for them. Although, I've heard some have hustled in on the wreck's mast and some even try to sneak in at the kittiwake lodge."

She lowered the binoculars and laughed.

"And now ..." He turned her to face west.

"Isn't it amazing, Alex?"

"It is. You know, I say I love the summers in Alaska, but the winters are also amazing. I love the way that even when it's dark, the snow literally illuminates, sending off a blue hue."

The sun melted behind the horizon, leaving behind layers of dark red and violet.

"Shouldn't we be getting back, Alex?" She shivered, wrapping her arms around her midriff.

Alex moved behind her and wrapped his arms around her. "Is that better?"

"Hmm …"

"It's a clear night. Let's watch a few minutes, see if we're rewarded. I promise you I won't get lost."

"I have no doubt about that, Alex."

He heard her unmentioned doubts. She didn't have doubts about his survival skills, but she doubted him. Still, they had tonight. He'd do his best to continue with the excursions, as she called them.

The last strands of red and violet dissipated, leaving an indigo sky splattered with millions of sparkling diamonds. And like a genie escaping the confines of its bottle, swirls of lime green and fuchsia moved toward the heavens in a mystical dance.

"Oh, Alex. I forgot how magical the aurora borealis is."

He pulled her tighter, hoping that his passion about the beauty surrounding them would convince her that he wasn't suicidal. That he wanted to live. That she could trust him.

She covered his arms with hers. "Thank you."

"I figured if it's the last night on the island, we should appreciate the lack of people and light pollution."

She released an almost inaudible sigh. "True. We should appreciate what we have while we still have it."

He started to defend himself, but then realized, she wasn't just referring to his choices. If she had, she wouldn't have said *We*. So was she referring to the two of them, or something else she might lose? As he'd thought before, Irene had secrets. What had she lost … or what was she about to lose? The boyfriend from high school? That didn't seem likely.

He stepped beside her, but kept one arm latched around her. "Hang onto me."

She huffed out a light laugh. "You're not getting away from me until we're on flat land, mister."

Then you'll let me go? he wanted to say, but again held his tongue. No sense in recapping the earlier conversation. The only thing he could do was show her.

Neither of them spoke as they worked their way back down the ridge and to the cabin.

Once again, he investigated the cabin before stepping inside, making sure she was out of range if anyone were waiting.

Irene scooted past him. "Can you start a fire? I have our grand two-course meal ready to go."

"Sure." He swept away the sand and set up the logs and kindling. He rummaged through his pack for another firestarter, and then struck a wood match. He held the flame to the starter log only for a couple seconds and the flames burst to life, licking at the logs.

"Man, you're good at that."

He turned to see Irene watching him, her hands on her hips. "I've never been able to get a fire going like that. Well, except for those wax logs. That's all I use in my apartment anymore."

"I cheated," he admitted. "Since I'm positive we won't be here long, I used my firestarter logs."

Irene set the kettle on top, then stood in front of the fire, wiggling her fingers. "So you're not the last Boy Scout?"

"Hardly."

She raised her eyes to him. "Could have fooled me. I bet you walk old ladies across the road."

Since she was being playful — and obviously chilled — he moved behind her again, wrapping his arms around her. "Only if they have beautiful daughters."

"I don't believe that." She pressed her cheek against his arm; it was cold. He shouldn't have kept her out after sunset, but he'd wanted her to remember how beautiful Alaska was, even in the winter months. He wanted her to know how much he appreciated beauty.

He shrugged. "It's not often that little old ladies walk across roads in Alaska, not where I live anyway."

She turned in his arms. "You don't live in Anchorage?"

"No, I live in the sticks — Falcon Run — halfway between Anchorage and Denali. Most of our search and rescue calls are in Denali, so it's better to be close."

"Oh ..." Her one word came out as if she were disappointed.

Alex moved his hands to her face, and the kettle sounded its long cry, breaking the moment.

Irene stepped back. "I, for one, could use a large cup of coffee. I'm chilled to the bone."

As she stepped away with the kettle, Alex added another log. Might as well get it hot early.

Irene returned with the pot of beans in one hand and a cup of coffee in the other. "Here."

Alex accepted it and moved for one of the chairs instead of the love seat, where they'd gotten too intimate too quickly the previous evening.

Irene returned with her cup, settling down with a sigh. She stared into the fire, and he couldn't help but stare at her. He loved the way her bronze strands shimmered just like the fire. The firelight flickered in her hazel eyes, making them look as magical as the northern lights.

Pop. Pop. Pop. The beans bubbled and spurted upward, so Irene stood and retrieved the pot with an oven mitt, then filled up two bowls.

She kicked off her untied boots and settled back on the love seat, pulling her legs up beneath her.

"Kudos to the cook," he said. He hopped up and took both of their bowls to the sink.

"Yes, it was such a difficult meal. I've never claimed to be a great cook, but I can certainly do more than open a can of beans."

Alex sighed internally. It wasn't as if she were going to cook for him, so why tease him? He needed to get the truth. One second she acted as if she was interested, and barely in the next breath, she'd be saying, *Not gonna happen.*

He sat across from her on the sofa again. "So, Irene, tell me, other than your parents and sister, is there someone else waiting for you on Saint Paul?"

She guffawed, nearly spitting out her coffee. "Umm … no way. Who'd be there?"

"I don't know … That boyfriend you mentioned."

"That was seventeen years ago, Alex." She shook her head. "Nope, I'm going to show up, forgive my sister, hope that she apologizes back, see if my parents still think I'm Satan's spawn, and then go from there. If things go well, I'll spend a bit of time. If not …" She sighed. "There's a hostel on the island. If they don't want me, I guess I'll be holing up there. Maybe wait until March when I can charter a respectable pilot."

"I could come get you …"

Her slow blink indicated he'd struck out again. "Alex, let's just call this what it is —"

"That's right, a one-night stand — two-night actually. Man, I feel so cheap."

She laughed. "I'm sure."

"So, what's in San Fran? Pretty nice that your job has given you so much time off. Don't you have someone back there —"

She lowered her eyes and looked at the table before he could even finish his question. She shifted her gaze to her lap, where she was cradling her hands, her fingers massaging the back of one hand.

Alex reached out and touched her arm. "Irene ... if you only knew how loud your soul is crying out. I thought I was messed up."

Her eyes lifted, nostrils flared. "You don't know anything about me, Alex."

He dropped his hand. If he hadn't been so moved by her sorrowful — or was it shameful? — actions only seconds ago, he'd laugh at her onset of anger. "Maybe not, but I can read you like a book."

She shook her head. "If you know so much about what people are thinking, maybe you should be a detective instead of a pilot."

"Nah ... I don't think they'd accept me anyway." He scooted closer, but kept his hands to himself. "Irene, I told you all my dark secrets, won't you share just one with me? I'm a good listener too."

"I told you my dark secret."

"That's when you were a kid. You've had seventeen years on your own. I'm sure you've screwed up somewhere."

She reached for her cup and lifted it to her lips. Hiding. "Actually, I haven't." She exhaled loudly. "My life has been a straight and narrow path. I knew what I wanted, and I went for it. I didn't take time to screw up. I worked my ass off from college, to interning, to the bottom of the ladder, to the top of the ladder ..."

"Go on..."

"I don't want to talk about my career."

Alex moved a fraction closer. "Okay, what's the best thing that's happened to you this year?"

It worked. She smiled. So whatever road she'd gone down that caused the hurt and pain in her eyes, he'd try to steer away from that line. Did it have something to do with her scar? Had she been attacked while interviewing someone on the street?

"Would you believe me if I said getting in a plane wreck?"

"No!" He lifted his head, cracking his neck back and forth. "You don't even want to see me again, so how could wrecking be the best thing that's happened to you?"

"I didn't say that I didn't want to see you, Alex. I said, *I wasn't ready* ... You're the one who filled in all the blanks. But, it's true; wrecking was the best thing that has happened to me all year. If my plane hadn't wrecked, you wouldn't have seen it, and you may have —"

"Irene, I told you—"

"Let me finish, Alex. You *are* brave. I watched you go back in that plane yesterday without hesitation. If you thought that giving your life would save others, you would sacrifice yours. But you saved me, Alex ... because you have good instincts. And I'm betting that over the years you've saved countless lives, and you'll go on to save countless others. These few days with you have been crazy, but they've been the best days I've had all year. So yes, my plane wrecking was definitely the best thing that's happened to me all year."

Alex couldn't take it. If right now was all he had,

he'd take it. Yes, he could read Irene like a book, and no matter what her words said ... she wanted him. Tomorrow, they could be rescued or killed. All they had was tonight.

He reached forward and pulled her into his arms. She didn't resist. She opened up to him as she had the previous two times. He stood up with her in his arms and carried her to the bed.

"We don't have to do anything—"

"Alex ..."

He lowered her to the bed. "Yes ..."

"Make love to me."

CHAPTER 15

~ Alex ~

A lex fell back. He was exhausted ... euphoric ... enamored. Maybe he *was* in heaven ... because that was the best experience he'd ever had in his life. No, it was because he was in love.

It wasn't just the amazing sex ... It was because that great sex had been with Irene. The way she'd asked him to hold her. The way she felt in his arms. The way he wanted to protect her — forever. Yes, he'd said that word in his head several times. It had taken every bit of willpower he'd possessed not to tell her while they were making love. He couldn't do that. It was too cliché, like something out of a country song ... *I'll even tell you that I love you*, kind of thing.

That wasn't him. Never had been. He'd always been upfront. And now, he felt he needed to be upfront again. He had to tell her how he felt. He had to say those three little words he swore he'd never utter to a woman. He had to make her believe ... in him.

"Irene ..." He moved to his side and ran his fingers along her creamy skin.

Her eyes opened, and there were tears in them.

"Oh my God. Did I hurt you?" She was so delicate. He'd thought that he'd been so careful. Even when she'd asked for more, he'd held back.

She lifted a hand to his cheek. "No, Alex. You were wonderful. Like I said earlier, I just have a lot to think about."

"But … you will think about it … whatever it is, right? And us? Irene, I'm pretty sure I'm falling in love with you." He shook his head. "No, that's the coward's way. To not give completely. And you're right. I'm not a coward. I'd walk into a burning building for a stranger, so how much more do you think I would give you? I love you, Irene. And I know we barely know each other, but I'd like to —"

"Alex … I …" She sighed. "We'll talk when I return from Saint Paul, okay? But that's all I can promise."

"That's all I'm asking. A chance. I'm not going anywhere, Irene. And I'm definitely not dying."

She closed her eyes and gulped. "No, you're definitely not dying. Please don't die, Alex. The world needs you."

He pulled her into his arms and settled back on the pillow. She hadn't said she needed him, but she said they'd talk. It was a start. Two days ago, he had zero future, so, he'd be happy for what he had. Not just because of Irene, but because he wanted to live. And right now, he'd enjoy this time in paradise.

He stroked her hair, watching as her eyes closed again. She looked so tired. She needed to rest. She didn't need to worry about him.

As soon as she was deep asleep, he gently removed his arm from beneath her. He wasn't sleepy. Not in the least. Exhausted from their lovemaking, but that was a different kind of exhaustion. Unlike some men, he didn't roll over and pass out after sex. Actually, he felt a glorious high ... and hunger.

He pulled on his sweatpants and shirt and rummaged through his pack. Only two bars left, but Irene had some too. If he didn't eat now, he'd have a hard time sleeping.

He opened the bar, took a few bites, then decided he'd better take care of nature before it got too cold out.

As always, he checked his surroundings, making sure nothing had crept into the bathhouse. He washed up again, then stared into the mirror. He almost didn't recognize himself.

He laughed. "Who is that stranger in the mirror? Is that hope I see in your eyes? I think it might just be."

He massaged his shoulders and neck, then pulled his clothes back on. Maybe if she wasn't too tired, she'd be ready again. He knew he was.

Alex strolled back to the cabin, but then looked back at the bird coop. Several of the birds were in a tiff. One must have tried to move in on another's nest.

At the door, he kicked the sand off his boots and stepped out of them into the cabin. He dropped them by the door, then looked in the direction of the bed, where it sounded like Irene was having a nightmare. The cast iron stove was in his line of sight, but she was clearly upset.

He didn't want to wake her, but he knew what it was like to be trapped in a nightmare. "I'm right here, honey."

"Mm-mm!" Muffled sounds, louder than before, filtered from the bed.

A long shadow quivered from the roof to the opposite wall. Alex turned to the right just in time to see

Kevin's long arms coming down, a brown object aimed right at his head.

Alex deflected and dropped to a squat at the same time. The log split open on his forearm, sending shards and splintered wood pieces across the floor. The pain soared up his arm immediately, but not as bad if he'd taken the swing full-on to his head.

Without waiting for Kevin to come up from the swing, Alex plowed into him, crashing against the dinette. Glass and metal, toppled to the floor, crashing and clanging.

Behind him, Irene's muffled screams filled the room. It sounded as if she were fighting too.

On his back, arms flailing like an upside-down turtle, Kevin groaned. "You son of a bitch!"

Alex picked up a chair and swung, but Kevin rolled over in time to avoid a full hit.

Without waiting for him to get to his feet, Alex swung again, but Kevin staggered backward out of his reach. Alex lunged forward, holding the chair as if he were a lion tamer.

Kevin braced himself against the counter, then raised his hands, realizing there was no escape.

Alex held his stance, his breaths coming quickly. He wasn't accustomed to fighting. The adrenaline was taking away his breath.

Kevin, also bent over, was panting loudly. And then he twitched, ready to barrel straight toward Irene.

Alex moved toward him, but this time Kevin deflected the chair, sending Alex toppling backward. Alex righted himself, ready to pummel Kevin into unconsciousness.

Free from the restraints, Irene lunged for the jacket

she'd tossed on the floor the moment Alex had carried her to the bed. Kevin pushed through the chairs and loveseat to get to her. Without a doubt, Kevin knew if he got to Irene before Alex did, he'd have a hostage, the best weapon of all.

Alex leapt the fallen chair Kevin had knocked over, just as Kevin lunged for Irene and knocked her down.

Irene screamed at the same time a metallic clicking sound and flashes of miniature lightning bolts filled the room. She didn't release; she held the hot pink stun gun against Kevin's neck while his body convulsed, arms floundering.

Alex pulled the man's jerking body off her, then reached for the extension cord the monster had used to bind her wrists, tying Kevin's hands behind his back. "Get me some rope, Irene!"

She ran toward a cabinet at the back of the room, as if she knew exactly where there was some real rope.

Kevin started to buck, so Alex brought his fists down hard against his kidneys.

The man let out an *Ooof*, but still tried to move from Alex's grip.

"What the hell, man?" Alex shouted. "You smoking that meth too?"

Irene tossed Alex the rope as she neared them, and then squatted down and gave Kevin another long shock. "You gonna behave?"

The effect of the shocks didn't last long, but evidently Kevin had had enough. He didn't move, allowing Alex to tie his feet too.

"Bring me a chair, Irene."

Irene ran to the shattered dinette and brought back one of the chairs.

"Get up!" Alex demanded.

Kevin struggled, but got to his feet.

"Sit," Alex said, then looked at Irene. "Is there any more rope?"

She shook her head.

"Dammit!" Alex stared down at Kevin. His hair was matted, face scratched. He looked like death warmed over.

Kevin spit to his side. Blood.

Alex thumped the man's head. "There's a lady present, and that's just disgusting. Do that again, and you'll be sleeping in the bird coop. I should probably put you out there anyway. What happened? Did you lose your gun in your swim?"

The man looked up, pure hatred in his eyes.

Alex grabbed the pillow from the bed, removed the case. He walked back to the man, watching as his eyes widened. Fear this time. "Don't worry. I'm not a killer like you. I just don't want to see your face." He dropped the case over the man's head and turned to Irene.

She sighed. "Serves me right! I should have known that no reputable pilot would fly to Saint Paul this time of the year. What are we going to do with him?"

Alex sighed too. "I don't know. I guess we're going to have to take turns watching him until my team arrives." He walked to the bed and retrieved the sheet. He wrapped it around Kevin, strapping his arms down, and then tied the two ends together behind the chair. It'd have to do.

Well, it looks like I'm not sleeping tonight. Then he realized something really, really awful, something he didn't even want to think about, but he had to. If Kevin was back ... "Oh, no."

"What?" Irene's eyes were wide. She paced back and forth, as if looking for something to do.

"Kevin, where are the drugs?"

The man said nothing.

"You want me to zap you again?" Irene asked. "Tell him whatever he wants to know."

The man groaned. "They'll kill you, man."

"Let me worry about that," Alex said. No way would those men give up. They had to know the plane crashed here. Alex needed an advantage. "Where are they?"

"Just above the beach, so the surf wouldn't wash them out to sea like you tried with me."

Alex harrumphed. "Hey, man, I tried to warn you. Where's my plane?"

"On shore. I didn't think I'd ever make it back."

"Lucky us," Alex growled, then he caught Irene's eye and mouthed, *I have to go.*

She nodded and held up her stun gun.

No man would want to take that more than once. *I'll hurry. Be careful.* He mouthed each word separately. He hated leaving her for even a second, but there was no way Kevin would try anything. And how could he anyway. If Irene hadn't been asleep, Alex doubted Kevin would have been able to sneak up on her. The woman unquestionably had street smarts — and actions.

He snatched up one of the shovels, handed her the other, just in case, then left the cabin as quietly as possible. He rushed toward the beach. Had to be the same beach.

Outside, he looked up at the stars, thankful for the bit of light. So much for his glorious evening. *One thing's for sure ... This sure isn't paradise. Maybe I ended up in hell after all.*

~ Irene ~

Don't talk, Irene disciplined herself internally. *Not a word. Not even a grunt. Anything you say, can and will be held against you. No matter what this jerk says, ignore him.*

Kevin whipped his head back and forth, jerked against the extension cord tied around his hands and the chair. "What's going on?"

Irene slid the stun gun to the on position and pressed the lightning bolt on the side. The loud crackling broke the silent air. She didn't touch Kevin. Didn't have to. He froze instantly.

"Irene, I never would have hurt you. I just had a job to do." He shook his head. "These men ... You don't know what you're dealing with. They'll kill you without as much as blinking."

Obviously, Kevin knew instinctively that Alex had left to retrieve the drugs. *Still*, she reprimanded herself. She knew the first person to talk in these situations lost. Kevin was obviously desperate. She wasn't. She had a weapon, and Alex would return soon.

Alex had said he loved her, and that he'd walk into a burning building for a stranger, so how much more would he do for her ... He'd not even blinked when Kevin attacked him. Alex had charged him without one concern for himself.

Irene paced behind Kevin. As much as she wanted to be angry with him, she'd told Alex the truth. She'd forever be grateful that Kevin's stupid actions had inadvertently saved Alex. Her parents always said that everything happened for a reason, but she'd never bought that. Yeah, she believed in God, but she was of the belief that he'd created the earth and then had allowed humans to walk away from him.

Her mind spun, though ... If her sister hadn't done what she'd done. If her parents hadn't done what they'd done. If she'd never gotten cancer. If her fiancé had stuck by her... Understood the choices she'd been forced to make ... Every little thing that had happened in her life had brought her to this deserted island.

"Hey!" Kevin yelled. "I need to —"

She touched the stun gun to his exposed skin, but didn't activate it. Just enough to let him know she was still here and that she wasn't falling for the, *I have to use the bathroom* routine.

"Irene," he said in a low seductive voice. "Please untie me ... I'll make sure you're safe. I'll take you to Saint Paul. There's fuel in the radar station. We can—"

She tapped the metal against his wrist again, cutting off his pleas. *Fuel in the radar station?* Alex had suspected, but they hadn't been able to break in. Then again, they hadn't taken tools. When Alex returned, she would see what he wanted to do. She wasn't going anywhere without Alex.

"Can I at least have some water? I'm dying of thirst."

Irene held back a sigh. He probably was, but ... another hour wouldn't kill him, would it?

"Please, Irene. Just a sip of water."

Damn ... He might die. He probably hadn't drunk anything for nearly two days, then he'd fought with Alex. She lifted the kettle, making sure she kept her eyes trained on him. She filled a cup with the still-warm water.

As she walked back to him, she realized she'd have to remove the pillowcase. Was she being stupid? His hands were still tied, though, right?

She stepped behind him again, checked the knot. She lifted the pillowcase, and he swung his head left and right, then tried to look over his shoulder. She backed to one side, then the other, as he whipped his head back and forth.

"Do you want this or not?" she growled. "Or you want another zap?"

He stopped moving, so she moved to the side, holding the cup to his lips.

Instead of drinking, he slammed his head against the glass, snapping his teeth at her hand. She yanked back, but he somehow managed to lift his entire body and the chair off the floor, toppling against her. The weight of his body knocked her back, along with her only defense.

He was still tied, but he inched his way on top of her. "Untie me, you bitch!"

She scrambled her fingers across the wood planks, desperately seeking the stun gun.

"You couldn't be reasonable, could you?" He pulled his head back and then thrust it toward her. She moved to the side, but his chin still caught her shoulder.

Her fingers looped the cord. She searched for the grip, hoping she was clicking it in the right direction, and then pressed the button.

ZAP!

She held the metal against the back of his neck at the same time his teeth pierced her flesh. She cried out as warm blood trickled over her shoulder, but held on until he released his grip.

She pushed him off her, then scooted out from beneath him. On her feet, she scrambled for the shovel.

"I swear ... if you even move to get up, I'll bring this shovel down on your head until you don't have a head."

Kevin peered up at her, but remained where he was, cheek smashed against the floor.

She snatched the blanket off the bed and threw it on top of him. "Not another word from you! I swear to God I'll kill you."

She pulled her sweater back, tried to see how bad the bite was. Blood stained her fingers ... her new white sweater, but she couldn't see how deep the bite was.

"Freaking animal!" she growled under her breath. She snatched up her toiletry bag, pulled out the face wipes. She wadded one up and pressed it into the bite.

"Everything for a reason? Ugh! Thanks for nothing!"

A knock on the door pulled a yelp from her.

"It's me, Irene."

She pulled on her jacket. What would Alex do if he saw what Kevin had done to her? Should she let him kill the man?

She inhaled deeply to calm herself, then unlatched the door.

Even though the temperature had fallen into the thirties, Alex was sweating. Not a good thing in the cold.

"Get in here and warm up," she barked. He shouldn't have left her. He shouldn't have gone for the drugs. She looked down at his empty hands. "You didn't find them?"

His eyes were wild. "No. The plane wasn't there either." Alex looked at her face, then the lump of blanket on the floor. "What happened?"

Irene shrugged, then cringed. "He fell."

Alex stared at her. "Did he hurt you? Why did you

flinch?" He pulled back the lapels on her jacket and hissed. "What the fu —" He charged across the room, heading for the lump that was Kevin.

"Alex!" Irene followed him, grabbing the back of his jacket. "Stop!"

Alex turned on her. "Why? He caused you to be in a wreck, nearly killing you. Took you hostage, and now he ... what? How did he hurt you?"

"I was stupid. I was trying to give him some water."

"How?"

"He bit me."

Alex kicked the lump, and Kevin shrieked. "You like to hurt women?" He kicked several more times as Irene tried to grab him.

"Alex! Stop! I mean it!" she screamed, since her attempts to pull him away did nothing.

"Give me one reason why I shouldn't kill this asshole."

"Because I'm begging you not to." She stared at him, pleading with her eyes. "We're not like him."

His eyebrows shot up.

She shook her head. "Please. You said so yourself, Alex. You're not like him. You're a rescuer, a hero, not a murderer."

Alex grabbed the shovel from her, setting it on the back of the chair. "Move a muscle, asshole, and I will kill you. I may be a rescuer, but I'm not above killing the son of a bitch who hurts someone I love. Try me."

Alex took her hand and led her to the sink. He pulled a chair next to the cabinet. "Sit." He grabbed the kettle and then his backpack. He rustled through it, pulling out a white box with a red cross on the front. He pulled off her coat, then gently removed the wipe. He lifted the sweater over her head and one shoulder, and then carefully held the opening wide as he slipped it down her hurt shoulder and arm.

As much as she wanted to feel embarrassed, his face was passive, focused. "Watch him, Irene, not me," he ordered.

She cringed when he poured the water over the site, dabbing it with gauze. Then he poured a dark solution into it, and she bit down on her hand to keep from screaming.

Alex loosely applied more gauze, tape, then he stared down at her. His eyes were glassy. "I'm so sorry, Irene," he whispered. "I'm not doing a very good job of taking care of you, am I?"

She blinked back her own tears. "You're doing a great job. If it weren't for you, I would already have been dead." It wasn't Alex's job to take care of her — or her problems.

"I've screwed up right from the beginning. I should have offered to take you to Saint Paul the first night. I shouldn't have trusted your life in anyone else's hands." He rested his head against hers. "I ran all the way back from the beach. I just ... I knew something bad was going to happen. Something bad always happens."

"Oh ... Alex."

What was she going to do? Every time she wanted to tell him the truth, he said something that made her realize she couldn't. She had no doubt Alex would accept her, short lifespan and all, but she couldn't do that to him. As soon as they made it to the mainland ... if they made it to the mainland, she'd have to make a clean break. She couldn't hurt him more than she already had.

CHAPTER 16

~ Alex ~

Alex sat watch while Irene slept. She'd offered to take a turn, but it wasn't the first time he'd stayed up all night.

When he was on-duty, he was working. He'd worked rescues where they'd searched for days, taking only two-hour naps before continuing. Besides, if he were correct, and he sure hoped to God he was, Vince would have a search party out today. The grid wasn't that large. Vince knew he left from Lake Hood. He had to know that he would have headed out into the gulf. After Cordova, Middleton was the logical place to start a search.

He needed coffee. He stood, stretched, cracked his neck, then reached for the kettle. Empty.

"Want me to go find some snow?" Irene whispered.

Alex walked over to her. "You're supposed to be sleeping."

She yawned. "I was, but I'm awake now."

He handed her the zapper and moved his mouth to her ear. "I'd rather go. Don't let him move an inch. I'll be back in a few minutes."

She nodded, so he quietly slipped into his boots and unlatched the door. "I'll put another log on the fire so it gets hot in here before the sun comes up." He spoke loudly, even though Kevin would be able to hear him even if he whispered. He wanted Kevin to think that Irene had left, not him.

Outside, Alex ran to where he knew the only mound of snow remained. He filled the kettle and darted back toward the cabin.

Hopefully the embers were still hot enough to melt the snow because it was too late to get the fire going again. The eastern sky was already a bright orange. He stood for just a second as he watched the golden ball quivering at the horizon, rising slowly like a giant Mylar balloon that had slipped through the fingers of a child.

Would Irene slip through his fingers today? As much as he wanted a search party to arrive as soon as possible, especially since Kevin had made a reappearance, he knew that the longer he was on the island, the more time he had with Irene.

With that thought, he rushed back to the cabin. He doubted the man would try anything again, knowing he was only seconds away, not on the beach, but he still didn't like her alone with him.

At the door, he kicked the sand free, then hustled inside, not concerned with being quiet now that he was back.

He made a quick summation of the cabin and breathed a sigh of relief when he saw her on the opposite side of the room, curled up, the stun gun held at the ready. Kevin's lump hadn't moved, so she was obviously just being cautious.

Alex peeked into the kettle, making sure no foreign objects were inside, and then set it on the stove. He poked the fire just enough to cause a spark. It was still early. Most rescue missions would wait until the morning fog burned off, as it would be impossible to see any plane wreckage anyway.

Irene walked to the sink but didn't say a word as she readied the two cups of coffee.

Alex approached the counter where her back was turned. He bent his head over her good shoulder. "You okay?" he whispered. Not that he cared what Kevin heard, but she was obviously uncomfortable.

She nodded and turned, tears in her eyes. "It freaking hurts," she said softly. "That's what I get for being nice."

"I know, honey. Here …" He pulled the chair beneath the window so he could get a good look. He pushed the curtain to the side as she sat. Carefully, he removed the gauze.

Seeing the deep indentations where Kevin's teeth had lacerated her skin, he wanted to kick the man again. Hell, he wanted to bash the man's teeth in with the shovel so he could never do this to anyone again.

"Is it that bad?" she asked.

"There's no pus, but it's swollen and red, so we need to watch for infection." He reached for the first-aid kit and repeated the process he'd done yesterday. He added a clean gauze square and tape, then kissed her forehead. "I really am sorry, Irene."

"It's not your fault." She stood and made her way back to her luggage, pulling out a clean sweatshirt. She lifted a protein bar. "I'm down to my last protein bar. Do you have something to eat?"

"I have a couple left. We'll make it."

Irene walked back over to him, then motioned to go outside.

Alex looked in Kevin's area of the floor, then followed her lead. "What's up?"

"Kevin said there's fuel in the radar station. With tools, maybe we could break in."

He shook his head. "The plane's not there, Irene. What good is fuel going to do if we don't have a plane?"

"But how did he get back?"

"If I had to guess, the life raft."

Her brow furrowed. "And the drugs?"

"Gone," he lied, but he had his reasons for not telling her. He couldn't let her know that they were here. Her actions spoke louder than words. No way would she be able to lie if it came down to it. And those drugs were the only leverage they had if the owner showed up before a search team.

"I don't understand. Why would he lie? How would that benefit him?"

Alex clenched his fists. "So he could do exactly what he did: get me out of the cabin." She shivered, so he directed her back inside. "Let's get some coffee in us."

"I'm down to my last four packets."

"After this, it's nothing but hot water and eggs. Sure hope Vince is as good as I think he is. The man's got a sixth sense. He's almost as good as Sam at tracking people."

"Which one is Vince again?" Irene filled up her mug and sat at the dinette. Her eyes traveled to where Kevin had spent the night. "You sure he's okay? You might have given him a concussion."

Alex resisted rolling his eyes. "He's fine. He was sawing logs earlier, and I can see him breathing. Not that I'd fall for that whole *I'm unconscious* routine again anyway." He grabbed his mug and sat beside her, making sure his back was to the wall. He inhaled the aroma, took a sip, and then set down his cup. "Vikentiy Kolya, or Vince as I've always known him, was a neighborhood kid who followed my adopted brother Erik home from grade school twenty years ago."

"So you're not really brothers."

"We're as close as any blood brothers could ever be. Hell, we're the Midnight Sons. When you have to trust someone with your life, you tend to get close. Plus, as I said, I've basically lived with him since I was thirteen."

Irene took a sip of her coffee. "I don't understand."

"His father wasn't a good man. Even as young as eight, he'd whipped Vince with a belt until he sliced open his skin. But thankfully, the ogre hadn't minded when his eight-year-old son decided he liked another family more than his. One less mouth to feed, I guess."

"What about his mother? Why didn't she stop him? Didn't she care?"

Alex shook his head. "Of course she cared, but he was a big man, and she had a three-year-old to protect. As soon as Vince came to us, she took off. When Vince turned eighteen, he tracked her and his brother down, and—"

"What happened?"

"Vince has had a hard life, that's all." Alex closed his eyes as he realized what his death would have done to Vince. Sam and his mother were strong. Although Vince was always the rowdiest in the room, seemingly indifferent to what life had tossed at him, he was more sensitive than any man he'd ever known. He also had a heart of gold. Vince had already lost one brother; it would have devastated him to lose another. Alex could literally kick himself for even considering throwing his life away.

Irene nodded, but didn't press him for details. Then she looked up.

Alex peered through the window.

CHK-CHK-CHK-CHK. CHK-CHK-CHK-CHK.

CHK-CHK-CHK-CHK. CHK-CHK-CHK-CHK.

The *CHK-CHK-CHK-CHK* sound rose and fell, a mind-numbing rhythm that he sometimes played on his iPhone to help him decompress. A chopper. A rescue copter, to be exact.

Kevin finally joined them, squirming and griping, "Untie me. You're gonna need me."

Alex scoffed. "That's a rescue copter. You'll be behind bars in a few hours."

Alex pushed the stun gun toward Irene, then opened the door, peeking out. Sand whipped up in a twist of dust. He picked up the shovel and stepped outside. Whether the crew was there to rescue them or not, they'd check the cabin, so he might as well meet them head-on, do what he could to protect Irene. But he was sure it was a rescue chopper.

Alex stepped a few feet from the door and stared up at the red and silver Temsco chopper. He blew out a breath of relief when he recognized the registration numbers. Not that Cal Landrum was his favorite person in the world — they'd had more than one difference of opinion over the years — but unlike the man's brother, Abe, Cal ran a first-rate charter business. When needed, Cal would pitch in with search and rescue efforts. Obviously, Vince had already been on the horn, calling in favors from all the charter companies.

Alex shielded his eyes with one arm and waved with the other. The glare on the windshield made it difficult to see, but it looked like Cal was in the co-pilot's seat. As always, Cal flashed a million-dollar smile. His pearly whites stood out more than others because, even in January, his skin was always golden brown. Cal was one of the only men Alex knew that sported a year-round tan. Probably had a tanning bed in his million-dollar home. Not to mention a personal barber that kept his hair highlighted as if he didn't live in *Seward's Icebox*. If Cal lived in Cali, he'd probably look like an everyday Joe, but here in Alaska, he looked like an out-of-place Ken doll. Obviously, Cal had done well in the charter business … better than Alex's family had done in the search & rescue business. But SAR Team Alaska wasn't about money — not a lot of money, anyway. Alex — and his brothers — just wanted to make a living without closing the doors.

The skids touched down and Cal hopped out, a rifle slung over his shoulder. Not uncommon for Alaska, but unwarranted on Middleton. Cal knew polar bears don't live this far south, and grizzlies certainly hadn't swum to the island.

"Morning, Alex!" Cal crooned as he slipped the gun forward in his grip.

"Uh … morning, Cal. Um … you can put down the gun. We have everything under control."

Cal lifted a brow. "Not what I heard."

In his peripherals, Alex saw Irene pocket something, then move to the back of the cabin. He prayed she'd stay put — rather, hide. He hadn't thought to tell her to hide, since he'd been sure that the helicopter was here to rescue them. It didn't compute, though. Why would Cal level a gun on him?

Alex laughed. "What did you hear, Cal? I was just out

on a routine service check, and I heard an SOS. I hadn't planned to fly so far, so I hadn't fueled up. Isn't that what Vince relayed?"

Cal sucked his teeth and laughed. "You always were a good liar, Alex. Even in school." He motioned Alex to the side with the gun. "Where's my man?"

"*Man?*" Alex feigned ignorance. Kevin had been right; he was in over his head. Alex had always known that Cal's brother was a tweaker, but he hadn't known that Cal had been the one keeping Abe high.

Cal motioned over his shoulder at the pilot, and the big man hopped out. Alex recognized him now. The man from the previous day, the big bald man dressed all in black combat wear. The pilot leveled an AR-15 at Alex's head while Cal kicked in the cabin door.

A few seconds later, Cal dragged Kevin out by the scruff of his collar as if he were an animal that had gotten into a scuffle. Cal's cold dark eyes moved from Kevin to Alex. "Where's the woman?"

Alex remained silent, hoping a back door had mysteriously materialized at the rear of the cabin and that Irene had escaped. The windows were too high and narrow, but she was small.

Cal nodded to the pilot. "Go find her."

The pilot made a wide arc around Alex and Kevin and stepped into the cabin sideways. Seconds later, Alex heard a THUMP, and the sound of the zapper, but then a second crash told him the big man had knocked the stun gun out of her hands.

"Let go of me!" Irene screeched.

The big man pushed her through the door, and she landed in a heap on the sand. "Bitch tazed me." He rolled his shoulders then stepped next to Cal.

"Put her in the chopper," Cal ordered.

As much as Alex wanted to scream, *No!* what good would it do? The men had two guns trained on him. Well, one now, but if Alex made a move, the other guy would be back in a second.

Cal motioned the gun at Alex again. "Sit down!"

Again, now wasn't the time to play hero. All he could do was wait for the moment when Cal didn't find his drugs.

Cal approached Kevin, eying the restraints. "Where are my bags, Kevin?"

Kevin stared up at him but didn't speak. He'd warned that they would need his help. So he'd known that Cal also worked search & rescue. Here Alex had thought that Cal's charter business had been doing so well, and it was just a cover for dealing drugs. He had to give it to the man; it was a great cover. Perfect way to not only deliver the drugs, but also to launder the money. After all, who knew how many passengers the planes were carrying? Kevin's plane could have held ten tourists, and yet, he'd only had Irene onboard. One passenger was a lot easier to convince that the pilot needed to travel a different route than ten.

"I said ... where're my bags, Kevin? Don't make me ask you again."

"On the southwest beach," Kevin spat.

Cal turned his gaze back to Alex as if asking him for the same information. Alex just shrugged.

"He moved them," Kevin growled. "He went to the beach last night and then came back and said the bags weren't there."

Cal released a long breath through his nose, then glanced back at the pilot. "She cuffed?"

"Y'sir!" The man hopped out again.

"Go check the beach," Cal ordered. "And be quick about it." He walked back to Kevin. "You worthless piece of garbage. I give you a chance to pay back your loan, and you screw up on the first run."

"I —"

"I don't want to hear it." Cal pressed the barrel to Kevin's head and pulled.

Alex jolted and Irene screamed.

"And I liked him," Cal laughed. "Imagine what I'm going to do to you and the pretty woman."

"Cal, this isn't you, man," Alex pleaded. "Hell, we've known each other since high school."

"I figure if I kill you, our family's square. Since your family's responsible for my brother's death."

"Your brother was a meth head, Cal. You said so yourself. It wasn't our fault —"

Cal shoved the gun in Alex's direction. "He was my baby brother. I was helping him. He was getting better."

Alex gulped, but didn't say a word. There was nothing to say. And if he told Cal where the drugs were, he and Irene would both be dead. Maybe if he didn't find them, at least he'd only kill him. After all, he'd cuffed Irene inside the helicopter. All he could hope was that Vince would catch up with Cal.

The radio on Cal's side clicked. "Yeah?"

"Not here, boss."

Cal lifted his head and sighed, then turned back to Alex. "Where are my drugs, Alex?"

Alex shrugged. "I don't know what you're talking about."

Cal's radio clicked at the same moment that he'd raised the gun, ready to strike Alex in the head. "Did you find them?"

"No, sir, but we gotta go. Fire up the bird. That man's family is on the way."

Cal shook his head, then stepped back. "I'm taking your girlfriend here. If you want to see her alive, you better contact me and tell me where my drugs are. Do you hear me? I don't have time to scour the island, but I know they're here." Cal reached into his pocket and pulled out a phone, handing it to Alex. "I'll call you in a few hours, which will give your brother enough time to rescue you. You'd better have my drugs and be ready to make a swap, or I swear, I'll pull her apart limb by limb and drop the pieces on your lawn. And it goes without saying ... but any cops come sniffing around my business or me, I'll be out of the country faster than they can identify her body. You know I have the means, Alex, so don't screw around with me."

Alex clenched his fists, but didn't move or speak. Cal held all the cards here. A trade was his only chance at keeping Irene and himself alive.

The big man huffed his way around the bend, then stared down at the pool of red staining the sand. "We leaving him?"

Cal rolled his eyes. "No, we're not leaving him. Put him in the back with the girl. We'll dump him off the coast."

"What about this guy?" The big man shot his thumb over his shoulder.

"That one's gonna deliver my bags to me, or you and I are gonna have a field day with the lady."

~ Irene ~

Irene strained against the cuffs but didn't make a sound. Even as the helicopter lifted, she realized that begging was futile, and the last thing she wanted was to force the man's hand against her — or Alex.

Even though Alex obviously knew where the drugs were, he'd been right not to tell this Cal guy. If he had, they'd both be dead right now, she was certain.

She stared down at Kevin and tears broke free. Yeah, he'd been in the wrong line of business, which had caused her to be in a plane crash. Yeah, he'd taken her hostage and then had returned and bit her ... But he was still a living and breathing creation at one time. She had no idea why he was running an illegal operation, but maybe he had a reason. As much as it would make it easier, she couldn't bring herself to think that he deserved death. So often when there was a heinous news story about how a person killed an innocent, the question was always: why? She'd learned that there wasn't always a why. Just like this Cal guy ... She knew why this other thug was dealing with drugs ... because his woman had gone into debt trying to bail out her son. But Alex had known Cal and obviously hadn't suspected him.

Irene stared down at Kevin's still pale form, thankful that she couldn't see his face. Crusted blood matted his dark hair, making the ends curl up as if he'd just hopped out of a shower and towel dried his hair without combing it. Small bluish patches dotted his hands and wrists, assuring her there was no chance he was alive.

It wasn't the first dead body she'd seen, but it still upset her. She never understood why one human would want to take another human's life — or their own, for that matter. Even as she'd threatened to kill Kevin, she knew she never would. Well, maybe she could have. If she was truly convinced that it would be her life or his, she was pretty sure she could pull a trigger. But not like Cal did. He hadn't even cared about an explanation.

Wind ... When it came down to it, a rogue burst of wind had caused Kevin's death. Or ... if she really wanted to know, she guessed she'd have to go back to the beginning ... to the first choice Kevin had made that led him to work for Cal. If Cal was willing to kill one of his workers without a second thought, what chance did she have? And what chance would Alex have if he met Cal with his drugs?

No way would Cal let her go, which raised another concern ... Would it help her case or hurt her if he found out who she was? She'd told Alex that she was a journalist, which was true, but she hadn't told him everything. Hadn't told him whom she worked for.

Thankfully, she hadn't told anyone about her little trip back home. As far as her ex knew, she was still on medical leave. He probably assumed she was lounging around her condo eating bon-bons, waiting for her hair to grow back. Thankfully, she'd only been on chemo for a while, so she hadn't lost all her hair. The doctors had decided that operating was the way to go, and then had stuck with radiation treatments after the surgery.

Irene focused her gaze out the window, at the tiny dot of land circled with water. Whatever she did, she tried not to look at Kevin or the two men holding her hostage. No, she only wanted to focus on Alex. He would find her, and he'd be smart about it, she had to believe that.

Although she'd given Alex a hard time about his suicide solution, she'd noticed that everything else he did, he did with precision and forethought. He had a plan for every step of their situation.

A CLICK snapped her to attention. The bodyguard, or whatever he was, climbed through the center of the helicopter and reached for the door.

She did her best not to scream or cry or spit ... none of those ridiculous things she'd seen in movies. She'd sworn that if she ever found herself in a hostage situation, she'd be smart about it. Instead of ticking off your captors, she'd read that you're supposed to remind them that you're a human.

The man pushed open the door opposite her. "Out you go, Kevin!" He pulled a rag from beneath the seat and wiped up the few drops of blood staining the floor, then tossed the rag out after Kevin.

As cold as it was, Irene broke into cold sweats, the kind she got right before she threw up. *Don't throw up. Don't throw up. Don't throw up.* She closed her eyes and focused on her breathing.

"You okay, Miss?"

Eyes still squeezed together, she nodded.

"You don't look so good." The vinyl seat crinkled. "Boss, she looks green. I think she might barf."

"Well, give her something to throw up in!" Cal barked. "I don't need her DNA all over my rig."

"But her hands are zip-tied," the man tried.

"Jeff, do you want to be with Kevin? As I told both of you, if I have to do your work for you, then I don't need you. Kevin made me fly out to Middleton. You want me to take care of the woman?"

"No, sir," Jeff said.

The current conversation was enough to bring her

around, but at the chance of being untied, she decided playing it up might not be a bad idea. "Ohhhh …" she moaned. "I didn't know I'd be flying today." She dropped her head, letting her hair shield her face, since she was sure she'd gotten a lot of her color back. "I would have taken my motion sickness pills," she groaned.

"There's Dramamine in the first-aid kit!" Cal ordered. "Give her some."

"Noooo …" she drew out the word in a whine. "Too late … for … that. I'd just throw it up." She added a few more groans and even a small burp.

"She's right," Jeff said. "You have to take it like a half an hour or more —"

"If she pukes in my chopper," Cal cut him off, "I'm throwing you both out!"

Irene peeked beneath her curtain of hair to see Jeff climbing out of his seat and into the back seat. She heard the *Fffft* of a switchblade, then felt the cool metal against her wrists. A second later, her hands were free.

"Here." Jeff handed her a 64-oz-size Styrofoam cup. "Use this if you get sick." He pleaded at her with his surprisingly beautiful baby-blue eyes. She understood what he was saying. Don't throw up in the plane and get us both killed.

She accepted the cup and nodded, still doing her best to look sickly, which wasn't that hard. She was en route to heaven-knows-where with a maniac that might do god-knows-what to her, but Jeff didn't strike her as a killer. And he obviously had some sense of humanity, since he loved a woman so much he was willing to work for a homicidal maniac to get her out of debt. That was something she could work with.

She could reach for the pocketknife she'd stuffed in her jacket, but no sense in bringing down the helicopter. One aircraft wreck in a lifetime was more than enough. She'd wait until the precise moment. Again, something she'd screamed at her TV a hundred times in the last year. Never failed ... a woman in a movie would have a knife or gun, but they'd reveal it too early, or try to wield it when the bad guy was looking. She had called foul on the action every time.

Not her; she had tons of patience. She'd been patient for everything she ever wanted in life. And she'd be even more patient with the life she'd fought so hard to keep.

No matter what, she wasn't going down without a fight.

CHAPTER 17

~ Alex ~

A s soon as the helicopter disappeared from his sight, Alex strapped on his backpack, grabbed the shovel, and sped toward the shipwreck.

"Dear God!" Alex appealed aloud, hoping someone up there was listening. "I know I haven't made many good choices, but please let me have made the right decision this time."

Hiding the drugs had to have been the right decision ... If he'd handed over the bags on this deserted island, Cal wouldn't have had any reason to keep him and Irene alive. No, instead of just Kevin, the three of them would be sharing a watery grave. As much as he hated that Cal had shot Kevin in cold blood, he couldn't dwell on that fact. Kevin chose his destiny when he'd chosen to run drugs. Irene hadn't chosen this fate, so he would be damned if he'd allow her to pay for Kevin's sins.

Alex navigated the dunes once more, vowing he'd never set foot on this island again once he escaped. The cold air stung his lungs, and he was seriously lacking energy. A couple of protein bars a day weren't enough sustenance to replace the calories he'd been burning. Not only was his body burning calories by trying to stay warm, but also multiple fights, survival tactics, and even sex had drained his energy stores. He'd probably lost ten pounds in the last two days.

Still, he pushed his legs until he thought he might drop. The faster he found the drugs and got rescued, the quicker he could make a trade for Irene. The longer it took, the more time Cal had to come up with a plan.

As Alex jogged, he contemplated the scenario. He needed to come up with a surefire way to exchange the duffle bags for Irene. Somewhere public. But someplace they wouldn't stand out and attract authorities. More importantly, a place where Cal wouldn't be able to take the drugs and then leave Irene and him for dead.

Although Cal had taken Irene as a hostage, Alex was sure that he — not Cal — was holding the cards. No way would Cal want to lose nearly two million dollars in merchandise, especially since Alex doubted this was a one-man operation. As with most ventures — even illegal ones — there was usually someone higher up. In the world of drugs, that often meant the Cartel, and from what Alex had seen on the news, the Cartel didn't mess around — and they didn't offer second chances. Cal didn't know Irene, but he knew Alex. He knew Alex was a man of his word, so Alex would have to bank on their past. Hell, they'd gone to school together, and Cal's younger brother had gone to school with Erik and Vince.

Alex climbed the last dune, tromping his way to the wreck. He scanned the skies, making sure Cal hadn't stayed within range. But he doubted he would. Cal would have had a tracker on Kevin's plane, so he knew exactly where it was: 26,000-plus feet into the Aleutian Trench. Cal was also on the rescue circuit, so he would have heard a call go out on Alex's plane. Cal wasn't stupid; he would have put two and two together and assumed that the plane had sunk. So now, Cal would wait for Alex to deliver.

Alex drove the shovel into the frozen ground. It was easier than it had been the previous evening, but still hard because the ground was frozen more beneath the wreck than where the sun shone daily.

Shovelful by shovelful, Alex removed the top layer of dirt, careful not to drive the metal through the canvas and into the plastic-wrapped bags. Above him, the shipwreck's residents weren't pleased. Once again, he was invading their space. The Audubon Society would have plenty to say, but at least he could assure them that no birds were harmed in his task.

CHK-CHK-CHK-CHK. CHK-CHK-CHK-CHK.

Once again, the sound of a rescue copter caused him to breathe a sigh of relief. The chance that he'd encounter more than one drug-running charter/rescue service was hopefully slim to none. He dug through the pack and pulled out the binoculars. Unlike earlier, when he'd assumed the chopper was Vince, he peeked out from behind the ship's rusted hull, spying through the lens to make sure that the colors and numbers belonged to his team.

When he saw the blue and white chopper, he threw back his head and huffed out an exhausted breath. "I knew you wouldn't let me down, Vince!"

Alex dug inside the pack again for the flare gun. He stepped outside the ship and shot the flare, then fell to his knees. "Dear God," he prayed again, "please don't let anything happen to Irene. Give me an opportunity to atone for my past sins."

For the first time in his life, Alex now knew what it

felt like when the rescue team arrived. He now understood why, especially in the water, rescuees would almost die at the last second. He'd never quite grasped why before, but the sheer relief that your life was now in someone else's hands was enough to make you want to relax and finally stop fighting.

He couldn't do that, though.

Alex picked up the shovel and went back to work as the rescue copter hovered overhead, finding a place to land.

Alex discarded the shovel and tore at the sand with his hands, not concerned with the cold that burned his numb fingers as if they were on fire. He'd be warm soon enough.

As he bared the bags from their resting place, the blades wound down and voices filtered from beyond the outer walls of the wreck. "Alex?" Erik called. "You in there, brother?"

"Yes!" he huffed out, exhausted. "I need some help, though."

"Told you he'd be okay," Daire said through a chuckle. "What're you doing, bro? Diggin' for buried treasure?"

Alex dropped his head. He didn't have the energy to joke around. Of course, there was no way his brothers could know what he'd been through. For all they knew, Old Betsy had just gone kaput.

Erik stepped through the rusted-out hull first. "Why you burying your luggage, dude?"

"It's not mine, and I'm digging it back up, not burying it. A hand, please."

Erik fell to his knees, and Daire followed suit.

Alex stepped back and let his younger — and, right

now, stronger — brothers finish the task of digging up the duffel bags.

First Daire, then Erik, pulled out the fifty-pound bags. "What the hell?" Daire laughed. "You really are digging up treasure."

Alex took the bag from Daire and dropped it. He unzipped the length of the canvas bag and pulled out one of the wrapped packages. Both his brothers stepped back. He might as well have pulled out Medusa's head.

"You freakin' kiddin' me?" Daire whipped his head from side to side. At twenty-one, he was probably more familiar with drugs than any of his brothers. "I know everything ain't so good with finances, but —"

"They're not mine," Alex scoffed. "These bags belong to Cal Landrum, and he wants them back. He took someone very important to me as a hostage."

Erik narrowed his eyes. "You've only been gone for two days. What the hell has been going on?"

Alex zipped up the bag. "Load these up, and we'll talk on the way. Where's Vince?"

"He's in the boat," Erik said. "I'll radio him and tell him to turn around."

Alex stood and handed the bag to Daire. "Load it up please and get me some food and water ASAP." He turned to Erik. "Tell Vince to meet us at Lake Hood. We have to figure out how to exchange these for Irene."

Both his brothers stopped and looked at him, but he waved them off. "Yep. Not only did I manage to get mixed up with a pack of drug dealers in two days, I also fell in love somehow."

Imagine what tomorrow might bring, he thought.

~ Irene ~

Irene maintained her sickly disposition, hoping they wouldn't see the need to restrain her again. Whenever possible, though, she monitored her surroundings, doing her best to figure out where they were taking her.

She recognized the Kenai Peninsula, so it looked like they were heading back the way they'd come. It'd been cloudy when she'd left the mainland, but today was clear to the heavens.

Irene kept her head down, allowing her gaze to shift to the window every minute or so as they got closer to land. If she was going to have to make an escape, she needed to know what was surrounding her ... wherever she ended up.

No conversation emanated from the cockpit. Since Cal was piloting the helicopter, he obviously saw no need to include Jeff in his plans.

Irene's heart quickened as the seaplane base came into view. The hotel where she'd stayed wasn't far. If she ran as soon as the aircraft touched down, she'd be able to get close enough for someone to hear her. She had a loud scream; she'd used it more than once in her life. It not only attracted attention, it seemed to work as a momentary distraction for her abductor.

She shifted her focus to the door, hoping helicopters didn't have child-proof locks like cars. The exit was clearly marked, but it looked like she needed to pull the emergency release before the silver handle. She imagined the moves it would take, preparing to jump out before the helicopter even landed.

As she concentrated on the door, she watched Lake

Hood, the hotel, and then Anchorage fade in the distance. Cal flew a straight path north, following one lone highway. The farther they traveled, the more densely forested the earth below her appeared. To her left, nothing but the Alaska Range, to the right, trees and trees and more trees, and then more mountains to the east.

Less than fifteen minutes past Anchorage, the helicopter started to drop.

Irene stared down at a cleared plot of land. One side of the property had a concrete square with a large black X. Next to the concrete pad sat a hangar larger than the one at Lake Hood. She could only imagine how many planes this man owned. He'd reminded Alex that he had the means to leave the country, and he hadn't been lying. He could be in Russian or Canadian airspace in less than an hour.

Next to a swath of birch trees on one side and a frozen lake on the other, sat an impressive three-story home. Although covered with snow, the deck jutted out around the second story, offering an extraordinary view of Denali.

Maybe if Cal isn't married, I can convince him I'm interested. I'm certainly interested in his home.

The helicopter dropped, and Irene thought she might really get sick. "Ohh ..." she groaned. She could have held the moan in, but most men, she'd learned, didn't like puke unless it was in a scary movie. Whenever she'd gone undercover and a man was her cameraman, she'd catch them gagging faster than when she worked with women.

Jeff looked back at her, eyes wide. "You okay? We'll have you on the ground in a few seconds. Keep that cup close."

Irene scooped up the cup she'd set in the seat beside her. She held it close to her face but swept her eyes back over the property. The dirt road leading to the estate was miles off the main road. No way would she be able to escape on foot. She could run into the woods ... But no, she'd rather take her chance with Cal or Jeff than face a grizzly.

Alex would come through, she was certain. She'd behave and hope to hear of a plan to swap her for the drugs. Alex had to know that he couldn't just drop off the drugs somewhere in hopes that Cal would let her go. Cal had everything to lose even if he recovered his drugs. He wouldn't be able to take a chance that Alex or she would turn him in.

No, there was no way that Cal was just going to hand her over. Alex would have to take control, regulate the time and place.

The helicopter rocked forward and back as it finally touched down. Cal was out of the aircraft and at her door faster than she could even have thought about opening it. Then Jeff was beside him.

So much for that plan.

As soon as she saw the acreage, she knew she wouldn't have been able to run. Cal had to own darn near a hundred acres.

So, flirting it is.

Irene covered her mouth and hunched over a bit to maintain that she was sick but allowed herself to breathe in the fresh air. "Wow! This place is beautiful. So much nicer than San Fran ... or that Godforsaken island with all those birds and seals. I think I have some type of bird flu." She stretched her arms and neck, then peered up at the house. "Is there someplace I can clean up? I haven't had a hot shower in days."

A hint of a smile played on Jeff's lips, but Cal huffed through his nose. "You're not a guest; you're a hostage."

Irene waved her hand. "Anything's better than that island with that surly pilot. But seriously, I think I might be sick ... or dehydrated ... or both. If you want me as a hostage, you need to make sure I don't die."

"Lock her in the basement!" Cal barked, then turned for the hangar.

Jeff nudged her arm. "Come along, miss."

So ... Cal isn't interested, but maybe Jeff is. He didn't seem to still be upset that she'd shocked him.

Jeff was older, and supposedly in a relationship with the man from yesterday's mother. If her womanly wiles couldn't get her anywhere, she'd appeal to his humanity. If neither worked, she'd keep the pocketknife ready.

She didn't want to kill anyone, but she wasn't above maiming any monster who tried to hurt her first.

CHAPTER 18

~ Alex ~

Alex downed one bottle of water after another. He'd not been eating or drinking his share, allowing Irene first rations. His body was accustomed to going long stints without food and water. Even though he was always prepared, often there just wasn't enough time to stop a search to eat or drink.

Erik kept the bird steady, hovering the tarmac while Alex scanned the base. No sign of Cal's aircrafts — or Cal. He could have gone to his property in Falcon Run, but that seemed risky. Then again, maybe Cal assumed that Alex wouldn't come to look for him there.

Cal was right. Cal lived on nearly a hundred acres. He'd see Alex or the police long before either of them would have a chance to touch down.

So, Anchorage it is. He needed to figure out where to make the switch. But first, real food and a chance to gather his thoughts. He and the team needed to come up with a plan.

"Go ahead and land, Erik," Alex said. "Obviously, Cal thought we might try something on his turf, and that's not going to happen. Not today. I'm not endangering all our lives."

Daire turned. "What about Mom? What if Cal decides this Irene woman doesn't mean enough to you?"

Alex gnawed his lip. "Good thinking. Call Mom. Tell her to go to Joanne's. Cal would never show up at Sheriff Wheelans' house. He'd be as good as dead. Erik, let me borrow your phone, please."

While Daire called their mother, Alex called Vince.

The throaty roar of the Mercury engine filled the line before Vince said, "Yeah?"

"You on land?"

"Docking now. Where you wanna meet?"

"The hotel is as good a place as any. Less locals. Less chance anyone will overhear or understand what's going on."

"See you in twenty." The line clicked. While Vince was the man to lead a room in conversation, when it came to business, he used clipped words and direct speech. The man was raucous and fun until things went south. Then he would seamlessly transform into the leader Sam always relied on.

Alex didn't have time to be jealous of that fact. Not now. He intended to capitalize on his family's individual strengths and wisdom, the secret weapon that made them the Midnight Sons. Each of them specialized in different areas and even thought differently. If two heads were better than one, their five heads were unstoppable.

If his family couldn't bring Irene home safely, no one could.

Before the skids hit the tarmac, Alex started crawling out.

Daire followed while Erik shut down the chopper. "Mom's on her way to the Wheelans' house now. She had a couple questions but said she'd wait patiently for you to call her."

Alex wrapped his arms around Daire. "It's good to see you, brother. Thanks for finding me."

Daire shrugged. "It wasn't me. The three of us had been fussing back and forth — as usual. Vince left the room then came back with a map of the gulf. He spread it across the kitchen table and pointed. He said, 'If I were in trouble, I'd head to Middleton.' And he was right. Y'all think a lot alike."

"And here I thought you and Vince were besties."

Daire smirked. "You know you'll always be my favorite brother, Alex."

Alex stared up at Daire, then back at the asphalt. He didn't try to play favorites, of course, but when there were five of you, some just got along better than others. Daire and he had always gotten along. While Sam was the oldest and Daire was the youngest, and Alex had done much more with Sam, he and Daire were almost always on the same page when it came to rescues and just life in general.

Once again, Alex felt like a heel. How could he have thought for even a second to end his life? No matter what happened with the business, they would always be the Midnight Sons. They didn't need a company to help rescue others. They could volunteer just like most of their volunteers.

No matter what happened, the news would always be ready to announce that someone was saved by Alaska's own Midnight Sons.

Alex stopped. "That's it!"

Daire stopped too, eyes wide. "What's it?"

Erik caught up with them. "What did I miss? What's it?"

"The news ... No police. But we need to call the news. But first ... I need to think about where to call them to."

Erik's truck chirped as he clicked the key fob. "Vince drove yours to the marina."

Alex just nodded as he hopped into the passenger side. Really, he just wanted to walk to the restaurant so he could brainstorm, but he was cold and hungry. And he had a hard time thinking when he was hungry.

Where can we make the swap safely? He thought of every stupid thriller movie he'd watched in his lifetime. Hostage situations just didn't work. Neither side ever had an advantage. Whether you dropped the hostage off or the goods, the other side could welsh on their word.

It took only seconds to return to the hotel where he'd met Irene. *If only I'd — STOP!* he ordered himself internally.

He was tired of all the *what-ifs* in his life. From now on, he wouldn't allow *what-if* to dictate his life; he'd just do.

Erik parked, and Alex and Daire strolled past the check-in desk, making their way to the hotel restaurant.

The waitress he'd given a huge tip hustled to the host stand. "Hi, guys. Will there be a large group again?"

Alex wasn't feeling friendly, but that wasn't her fault. He forced a smile as he read her nametag. "Just four of us today, Beth. You got a booth in the back, away from everyone? We're having a business meeting today."

"Sure thing, hon." She counted off four menus from the stand and then weaved her curvy figure between tables, heading to the rear of the restaurant. "This work?"

Alex smiled again. "Yep! Would you do me a favor, please? Bring us four glasses of water and an extra pitcher right away. No ice."

"Will do!" Beth trotted off, her hips swaying a bit more than necessary. Odd that while he noticed, he wasn't the least bit interested. Irene had definitely done a number on his heart.

Daire scooted into the side with his back to the wall but craned his head, eyebrows rising. He stared up at Alex for confirmation that the woman was hot, but Alex waved him off.

"Wow ..." Daire crooned. "You really are in love."

"Move over," Alex grunted. "That woman's too old for you anyway."

Daire shrugged. "I'm legal, and she definitely qualifies as a MIL —"

Alex turned to Daire, cutting off the acronym that he'd clearly used too many times around his baby brother. He hoped it wasn't too late for Daire. He truly wanted Daire to find someone that could complete him before he became too old and got set in his ways.

Erik rolled his eyes as he approached the table. "I'd complain that you two took the side of the booth with your backs to the wall, but I know you have my *six*. Vince won't like it, though. Twenty years with us, and he's still waiting for his father to make an appearance."

Alex shook his head. The five of them were something indeed. Too many demons hiding in the shadows, always looking to take one of them out. And way too much testosterone between them.

Vince appeared in the doorway and shot a cursory glance around the dining room; then his long legs carried him to the table in seconds.

He stepped right up to Alex's side of the booth, narrowed his eyes, then pulled him up from the bench. "Don't you ever scare me like that again!" Vince wrapped his long arms completely around Alex, smacked his massive hands on his back, then released him and plopped down in the booth next to Erik. "What the hell happened to your radio? Where's Old Betsy? Daire said she went down? I just thought you needed to land somewhere —"

Alex cut off Vince with a half-laugh, half-sigh. "I'm fine, thanks." The last thing he wanted was to admit why he didn't have a radio, and he didn't have time to go into the details. They had to figure out how to get Irene back. "We'll talk about my ordeal later." He lowered his head across the table. "Right now we need to figure out how to exchange Cal Landrum's drugs for an innocent woman who doesn't deserve the situation she's found herself in."

~ Irene ~

As Jeff directed Irene through the house, Irene made note of any possible exits, weapons, electronics ... anything that she could use to escape or alert someone of her whereabouts.

Jeff brought her through a side door, not a main entrance. When they entered, they walked below the deck, into a dark, seventies-throwback-looking living room. The carpet was dark, green or black, she wasn't sure which, and the sofa and chairs were upholstered with some brown and tan hunting theme. The only window was narrow and high, much like the windows in the cabin on Middleton. Jeff had used a key to open and lock the door, and no phone or computer was visible, so definitely not a room she'd run to if she managed to get away from Jeff.

Next, Jeff led her down a hallway with two rooms on the side. As she peeked in, she saw that they were small rooms, nothing in them but a bed and dresser. The windows, again, were high and narrow. She suspected that being on the bottom floor, it was better to have high windows because of the snow drifts.

Jeff passed a circular staircase that led to the second floor, but the opening was so narrow, she doubted he could use this set of stairs. The house was a labyrinth. Apparently this was the original house, and the part with the wide-open windows and surrounding deck must have been an add-on.

At the end of the long hallway, Jeff used his key to unlock a dark walnut door. The door was solid. Not one of those hollow-core doors so popular in new construction. So much for finding a tool and digging her way out. On the other side of the door, a long stairway led straight down into black nothingness.

Irene stared wide-eyed at Jeff. "I don't do so well in confined places." Which was true. When Cal had said *basement*, Irene had been thinking of a modern basement with whitewashed walls, large projection screen, and movie-theater seating like her ex-fiancé had set up in his beloved Painted Lady.

Jeff hit a switch, and the bottom floor lit up. She relaxed a bit. While the basement didn't have the clean beige walls with cream trim she was accustomed to, at least the area didn't resemble Buffalo Bill's hole in the *Silence of the Lambs*. Instead, a long five-shelf wine rack took up much of one wall, and opposite, a kitchen set up monopolized the other wall. A long rectangular table sat in the middle of the room, and another rustic sofa and grouping of chairs lined the back wall. It looked like the kind of room where a low-life Mafioso might meet with his rebels to discuss renouncing their allegiance to the Godfather.

Clearly, I've watched too many movies in the last year. It's just a basement, Irene. Chill! It's not like there are shackles and chains hanging from the walls.

"Better?" Jeff asked as he nudged her down the stairwell.

She laughed to lighten her words. "If I say no, do I get another option?"

Jeff returned her laugh. "Doubt it."

At the foot of the stairs, she looked up at the open door, and then lowered her head as she whispered, "What's he going to do with me?"

Jeff shrugged. "I guess that depends on your friend. Cal just wants his bags back — all hundred pounds of them."

"Was Kevin his friend?"

"Listen, lady, I just work here." He huffed through his nose. "My suggestion is you do whatever Cal tells you to. This ain't no *Romper Room*. The man means business. He's got some mean people waiting for his product. If he doesn't show up with the merchandise, it's his ass on the line."

Irene nodded. That information was something she could use anyway. Cal had a boss — or business acquaintance. If said associate doesn't get his merchandise, he'd be ticked, and Cal would be the one who'd end up as fish food. Yes, she could definitely use that information. If only she could sit in while Cal and Alex discuss her swap. Maybe she'd get lucky and Alex would pull one of the I-need-to-talk-with-Irene-first demands. If so, she could let Alex know that Cal wasn't the kingpin, that they had an ace in the hole.

At least it appeared Jeff didn't intend to tie her up or search her, so ... she'd wait patiently. If anything went sideways during the switch, she'd fight her way out.

But what if she was wrong? What if Cal was wrong? What if Alex really didn't know where the drugs were? Would he even try to barter for her life if he didn't? After all, she'd turned him down, said she wasn't interested in Alex showing her Anchorage.

Was it possible that she'd survived everything she had only to be killed by a low-life drug dealer?

CHAPTER 19

~ Alex ~

Alex downed two more glasses of water before he finally felt sated. Then, he downed the plain burger he'd ordered in four bites. He sat back, his stomach feeling the full weight of all the water and food he'd consumed in such a short time. Still, he wanted more. He hoped that Cal was being a good host and making sure that Irene had plenty of food and water.

Vince eyed him. "Full?"

"Not even close, but we have to come up with a plan."

Erik glanced over his shoulder, taking in the restaurant, then turned back to the booth. "Shouldn't we just call the cops?"

"This is Cal," Alex said. "He has more money than all the families in Falcon Run put together. And how many aircraft? Eight, ten … that we know of. He'd be out of the country in minutes. And by the time the police get a warrant, Irene could be dead." Alex shook his head. "We'll worry about his illegal ventures after we get Irene back."

Vince nodded. "I agree. Cal's a loose cannon, worse than his brother. So, what are you thinking, Alex?"

Alex picked up another sweet-potato french fry, then pushed the plate away so he had space to think ... to plan. "Cal instructed me not to call the cops, but we all know how excited the news gets when there's a rescue. I'm thinking I could call in a tip. Only problem, I'm not sure where to make the exchange and how to keep the news away until we need them."

Vince stared at the ceiling. Erik swept up a few crumbs scattered around the table. Daire tapped his glass.

Alex stared from face to face, then focused on Daire. "Come on, Daire. You watch more movies and play more video games than all of us put together." Alex realized he was talking too loud, so he lowered his voice before he asked his question, "Haven't you ever seen a hostage situation that works?"

Daire shrugged. "Nah, man. The bad guys either play nice, or they don't and someone gets killed."

Alex thumped his head. "Never say that again—"

"Wait!" Vince cut him off. "Where are the ... you know?"

Alex jutted his chin in the direction of the parking lot. "In Erik's truck."

Vince waved his hands. "I mean ... what are they in?"

"Two duffle bags. Why?"

One side of Vince's wide mouth turned up. "I know exactly where we can do the swap."

***

Alex paid the tab as his brothers headed to the parking lot.

When Alex left the hotel, he spotted Erik and Daire moving the bags from Erik's truck to Alex's truck.

He smiled. *Vince is right. It looks perfectly normal.*

If Alex were waiting outside the *Arrivals* lane with two duffle bags, no one would look twice about some-one picking him up. Except, he wouldn't get into the van. He'd allow Cal and his thug to load the van as Irene hopped out to hug him. Perfectly normal. The only difference ... after the bags were inside the van, Alex and Irene would head back to the terminal, and Cal would speed off.

Cal wouldn't dare try something at an international airport. And Alex was pretty sure that, even if there were drug-sniffing dogs, they'd be inside, monitoring the TSA checkpoint, not the area where people have al-ready finished their flights.

The only question was ... would Cal view the airport as the best place to make the swap?

***

"You're out of your mind, Belgarde!" Cal's voice boomed through the phone. "You think I'm gonna dan-gle a hundred pounds of meth in front of the cops?"

"No," Alex said. "You're not. I am. I'm the one who's going to carry them. You'll just be picking me up. I'll be on the far end of *Arrivals*, which means I'll have to walk past all those exits. But ... you know I'm right. It's the one place that neither of us can pull something. You'd see if there were any police, and if there are, just drive off. You've done nothing wrong that they know of. I'm the one taking all the chances. I don't care about your ventures; I just want Irene back."

"You got *cojones*, Alex. Maybe you should come work for me. One run and you'd be out of the red, my friend."

Alex wanted to growl *I'm not your friend*, but that wouldn't get him anywhere. And running drugs. He'd definitely kill himself before he ever ran illegal drugs. Drugs killed people. He'd dedicated his life to saving people, so the last thing he would do was play a part in something that endangered the lives of both the users and the dealers. He'd only been involved two days, and he'd already watched a man murdered in cold blood.

Still, Alex had to keep the peace. If Cal thought that Alex was interested, he might not want to kill him. "Hmm ... never thought about that, Cal. After Irene is back home in San Fran, we can discuss terms."

The line was quiet. Cal seemed interested. Guess the man didn't harbor as much animosity over his brother's death as he'd claimed.

Cal huffed out a laugh. "Damn, Alex. Here I thought you Midnight Sons were all straight and narrow. Sure ... we'll talk. Right now, let's get this business squared away. Just so you know ... if you get busted, even if the DEA comes sniffing around my place, they won't find anything. I'm clean. My business is clean. You'll be going to jail a long time if you get caught at an airport with a hundred pounds of meth. You could just do a fly-over at my house, you know."

"That's okay. I'd rather take my chances and be assured that I'll get Irene back."

"She really worth it? Thought you were the forever bachelor."

Alex shook his head. Seemed that Cal had kept tabs on Alex's life. Then again, he lived in a small town. The problem with a small town is that everyone knew everyone's social business, even though no one knew what went on behind closed doors. Like Cal's doors.

"I don't know what you mean. I promised to get her home. That's my job."

"Hmm ... I don't believe you, Alex. I think you're in love with her, and when people love someone, I can use them —"

Alex exhaled and tried to control his temper. "Make no mistake, Cal, you harm a hair on her head, and I don't care where you seek sanctuary ... I'll find you."

"Ah, shucks, Alex, no need to make threats —"

"It's not a threat, it's a vow."

Cal laughed. "I think we might work well together, Alex. What time am I picking you up from Ted Stevens?"

Alex relaxed his grip on the phone. Cal was a businessman. He understood what was at stake, and since he'd murdered Kevin, maybe he did need another pilot. "One hour. one o'clock sharp."

It'd take Cal less than thirty minutes to fly back to Anchorage from Falcon Run, which meant that he wouldn't have time to set up any traps. One o'clock in the afternoon was also a slow time of the day. If there were officers or agents stationed outside, chances are they'd be swapping lunch shifts. Plus, since Alex was only minutes away, he could use the time to make his phone calls from the cell parking lot. He still wanted reporters inside the terminal in the event something went wrong.

"No can do, Alex. I can't make it before five. I sent my pilot on a run."

Alex sighed. Just when he thought everything would run smoothly. Five o'clock was after sunset, so it'd be dark. Busy. More chances that officers would be on watch.

"You're a pilot, Cal."

Cal scoffed. "If I'm flying, who's gonna watch your girlfriend?"

Alex shook his head. "She's not my girlfriend, Cal. But fine. Five o'clock sharp. I'll be in the last pick-up spot."

The line clicked.

"Damn!"

Vince turned to him. "What happened? It sounded like it was going well. As well as can be expected anyway."

Alex rubbed his temples. "It was, and then I folded. Cal made a show of dominance at the end, taking back the control I had. Now, we have to wait until five. What the hell am I going to do for four hours?"

"Call a reporter."

Alex groaned, and Vince grinned. "Hey, you said she was a reporter. Who knows who you can get to come?"

"Yeah ..." Alex gnawed on his bottom lip again. He stopped when he tasted blood. Either he'd worried his lip too much in the last forty-eight hours or the dehydration had caught up to him. He downed more water as Vince drove.

"Where to?" Vince asked.

Alex threw his head against the headrest. "Hell, I don't know. I feel so utterly helpless. What am I going to do for four hours?"

"We could drive there —"

"No!" Alex said a bit too loudly. He picked up his phone, though. He didn't want to alert Cal, but he could make sure his mother was safe. He turned the rear-view mirror so he could see behind the truck. Erik was less than a car length away, obviously making certain no other vehicles separated them.

"Yeah?" Daire answered. "Where to?"

"Vince," Alex said, "pull into that gas station." He pointed to the next block. "Daire, tell Erik to follow us in. Tell him that we're going to leave the chopper at the base, and he'll come with us for now. I want you to drive home. Take care of Mom, okay?"

"Got it!" Daire didn't fuss about wanting to stay in Anchorage, as Alex probably would have done if he were him, as he always wanted to be part of the action.

Vince parked at the far end of the parking lot, and Erik hopped out. In seconds, Erik was crawling into the back seat, and Daire was squealing off, heading toward Falcon Run.

Erik moved to the middle seat and practically knelt on the center console. "What's the plan?"

Alex turned to face Erik. "We have four hours to waste, and I can't think of anything to do other than to head to the airport and start making phone calls."

"Four hours?" Erik echoed. "Cal might call in a troop in that amount of time."

"Who's he got?"

"Hell, I don't know. Abe hung out with a bad sort, though. They were all probably working for Cal, so no telling what he has planned. I like the idea of meeting at the airport, but what guarantee do we have after that? What if he ambushes us on the way home? With only one main road home, he could pick us off and disappear."

Alex didn't plan to spend his life looking over his shoulder. It'd been bad enough that he'd lived in the past for ten years.

"Just head to the airport, Vince. I can't worry about

what might happen later; I need to concentrate on now."

Alex opened a browser in the phone and typed: report news tip. The first page that popped up offered a form. He didn't have time for that. The next page had a phone number to correct errors.

"Damn!" Alex growled. "I thought news stations wanted hot tips. Who do people call when they see us rescuing someone? How come the news always seems to be the first to arrive?"

Erik snatched the phone from him and started tapping on the keys. Seconds later he stuck his arm in between the seats. "I found a number for the editor of the local news."

Alex grabbed it from him. "Where did you find that?"

"I have more patience than you. Plus, you're more frazzled than usual, Alex. I've never seen this side of you."

Ignoring Erik, Alex clicked the number.

"Ahh ... love sweet love ..." Vince said in a singsong voice. "'Bout time Alex got bit. Why should it just be my lonely ass always strung up over a woman?"

Alex may have been a player, but Vince loved women, really loved women. He couldn't live without some honey keeping him in line. Although, he hadn't been tied down since his wife walked out on him, taking everything with her, including the money that was supposed to have been earmarked to pay for his commercial fishing boat.

"Hello?" a man answered.

"Hi ... ummm ... is this the number to call if I have a ..." Alex felt awkward. What would he say ... that he had a hot tip? The plan had sounded simpler in his head.

"Hello?" Irritation was clear in the man's tone.

"Yes, umm … I'm one of the Midnight Sons. Ever heard of us?"

The man laughed. "Yes, son. I've heard of the Midnight Sons. How can I help you?"

"Well, sir," Alex said, since the man had called him *Son* and knew about his search & rescue team, he figured he must be older. "I just … um rescued a woman from a plane crash, and I think she might be important. She was reluctant to give her name, you know … like she might be someone."

He laughed again. "Go on."

The man was placating him. Alex would take whatever he could get. "Like I said, her private plane went down, and now I'm supposed to deliver her to Ted Stevens at five o'clock sharp. But get this … she said to drop her off at arrivals, so that no one would see her. She said if anyone saw her, she'd have me drive off. But that she usually just enters through *Arrivals* and makes her way to the checkpoint —"

"Son, what are you trying to pull?"

Alex raked his teeth over his chapped lips, then cringed from the pain. "Nothing. I just … umm … I was hoping there might be some sort of finder's fee in it for me."

The man sniffed. "This woman have a name?"

Here goes nothing … Would the man care that some journalist from San Francisco had crashed her private plane off the coast? Probably not. If the plane had crashed in Anchorage and was on fire, then maybe —

"Son, I don't have all day."

"Her name is Irene Rose …"

"Irene Rose?" the man repeated as a question. A snap of fingers came through the line, then it sounded like the man had covered the phone as he mumbled to someone else. "You mean to tell me that you just rescued *the* Irene Rose?"

The food and water that Alex had just gorged on threatened to make a reappearance. He'd made a grave error. He should have looked up Irene's name first.

He clicked *End* and opened the browser again. Who was Irene Rose?

~ Irene ~

Irene paced the cellar.

As much as she wanted to break open one of Cal's prized cabernets to calm her nerves, she needed to keep her wits.

What if Alex didn't come for her? How long would she be stuck down here? How long would they keep her?

She rifled through the cabinets that served as a galley kitchen. Jeff had stuffed the knife block, along with the long butcher and filet knives into a plastic sack and then had done the same with the set of steak knives he'd pulled from the silverware drawer. But maybe Cal had stashed a weapon down here in the event something went wrong during his meetings — or whatever he did in this windowless hole.

First chance she'd had, Irene had moved Alex's pocketknife to a more secure location in her boot. Since Cal hadn't ordered Jeff to search her, she doubted they'd search her now. A pocketknife wasn't an easy weapon for a woman to use against a man, though. One, her adversary would hear the moment she used the spring-loaded assisted-opening feature. Two, both men stood nearly a foot taller than she was and outweighed her by more than a hundred pounds.

"I need a gun," she said nearly inaudibly. Drug dealers were notorious for being paranoid. She imagined hidden cameras and recording devices stuffed into the air vents, capturing everything she said and did. Still, she needed a backup plan. She needed a real weapon.

She hated guns, but ... she wasn't against defending herself. She'd gone through too much to keep the life she had to let someone steal it away from her.

Irene moved furniture pieces, fished through dust-covered boxes, tapped along the floorboards, hoping to find a hollowed-out nook. Didn't all drug dealers have hidey holes for their stash? Had all the books she'd read gotten it wrong? Cal certainly didn't fit the profile. Even Alex had seemed shocked when Cal had shot Kevin in cold blood.

Alex ... Was he okay? Had his brothers really been on the way to the island? She and Alex had eaten the last of the protein bars, so he would be starving by now.

CLICK.

Irene hopped up from the floor and darted to the nearest seat: a chair next to the rectangular plastic table in the middle of the room. She stared up at the stairwell as the door opened.

"Yeah?" The man in the doorway wasn't looking at her. He'd turned to look down the hallway before descending the steps. Although the silhouette was nothing but a black mass with light outlining him, it had to be Jeff. While Cal wasn't a small guy, Jeff looked the role of a bodyguard or bouncer. Albeit a retired one, who'd slacked a bit on training and diet, but she doubted his fighting skills had deteriorated along with his midsection. "Five o'clock, Ted Stevens. I know, I know," he called back to whoever was speaking to him. Was that where they were making the swap? Had to be. And it had to be Alex's idea. No way would Cal want to be caught with two duffle bags of meth at an airport.

Irene couldn't hear anything from the other person, not even muffled words. Then again, Cal had never raised his voice. In fact, he always spoke in that quiet and calm manner, which was somehow more disturbing. An image of one of the James Bond villains popped into her head. She couldn't remember which movie, as she'd binge-watched them in only a few days while she was sprawled out on her sofa. He'd been a spy too, she remembered. A Russian one. He came off as sophisticated and debonair. If he'd been English, M might have chosen him over Sean Connery.

The door finally closed, and the shadow started down the stairs, arms full. She sat quietly, hands clasped above the table, but she maintained her scan of the room, looking for anything that might aid her escape if Alex fell through.

Jeff was halfway down the stairs when light hit his face. She could rush him. Maybe knock him over the railing and charge the door. It hadn't sounded as if he'd locked it behind him.

Even if that worked, she'd have to deal with Cal upstairs, and he'd shot Kevin without a passing thought.

"Hungry?" Jeff asked as he hopped off the last step. "I have leftover lasagna, salad if you're vegan — or not — and water."

"I'm not vegan." She had been. She'd spent more than

ten years on a strict plant-based regimen. For years she'd led a stringent path of what she ate, what she drank, and even what she thought. It wasn't easy to lead a stress-free life with everything she'd seen and done, but she damn well tried. She'd exercised regularly, meditated, took supplements, ate only organic, and still, the cancer monster had tracked her down. After she'd gone through the couple chemo treatments before the doctor decided to operate, she'd eaten anything she could keep down.

Jeff set the items on the table, then walked toward the cabinets she'd just scavenged. He came back with two plates and two sets of utensils. Maybe she did have a chance of seducing him. At least he'd been treating her well.

Irene picked up a serving spoon and ladled salad onto her plate. Even if she wasn't eating healthy, she loved salad, and she was in desperate need of something other than the protein bars she'd basically lived on the last couple days.

She started to scoop up a spoonful for Jeff, but he stopped her. "Cal may not be hungry, so let him serve himself."

She stared down at the other place setting. "You're not eating?"

He nearly choked on a laugh. "Umm ... no. Don't think Cal would like that."

The door opened and closed, then the sound of creaks and cracks filtered from the stairwell as someone else joined them.

Cal stepped into the light and clapped his hands. "Perfect. Dish some of Jeff's lasagna out for me, would you, dear?" Cal motioned for Jeff to join him as he walked back to the steps. Cal whispered something, but Irene heard nothing but *psst, psst, psst ...*

Maybe I need to get my hearing checked.

Heavy footsteps took to the stairs again, and Irene knew immediately she'd be dining alone with Cal. Why did that bother her so much?

She was certain Cal didn't keep Jeff around for his stimulating conversation, as Jeff came off as more of a laid-back country boy. Not that she wouldn't enjoy talking with Jeff, but Cal came off as a wannabe celebrity, so she doubted he shared his plans with his hired muscle.

Cal approached again, a wide bright smile lifting his face. He rubbed his hands together, then pulled out the chair. "What a find Jeff is! He can scare the crap out of anyone we do business with, and he's also a great cook." Cal took a bite, chewed, then stood. "This calls for a bottle of ... *Hmm* ..." He turned back to look at her. "Maybe a full-bodied red? What do you suggest?"

Irene shrugged.

"Ahhh," he said as he chose a bottle. "Not too expensive for my unscheduled houseguest and yet a perfect choice." He dug in the kitchen drawers and came out with a corkscrew. She was glad that she hadn't chosen the twisty metal contraption as a second weapon. She'd thought about it. Held it in her hands for all of two seconds, but then decided it was useless as a weapon.

Cal pulled two wineglasses from the upper cabinet, then carried the items back to the table, setting one in front of each of their plates. "Donnafugata 'Mille e Una Notte' Contessa Entellina," he said in what sounded like perfect Italian as he held up the bottle for her inspection.

Her ex was the one who'd ordered wine at restaurants, who'd enjoyed the show and sampling. Even when she'd gone to Napa with him, she simply followed his lead and sipped. All she cared about was how the wine tasted and how well it swept away her cares of the world.

Cal uncorked the bottle, poured a couple ounces in her glass, then stood back.

She wanted to roll her eyes, but she remembered her earlier promise not to overreact or be stupid. Cal was obviously putting on a show. Maybe he was interested in her after all. Not that she would allow him to touch her without stabbing him in the groin, but a little harmless flirting couldn't hurt.

She lifted the glass, swirled the liquid. She knew squat about good wine, other than how it tasted, so instead of trying to figure out if it had great *legs* — as her ex had always looked for — she lifted it to her lips and tasted the dark red liquid. No surprise, the wine was delicious.

She smiled up at Cal. "It's very good."

"The 2014 vintage is *terrific*." He'd emphasized the word *terrific*, so apparently her use of the words *very good* wasn't showing the proper amount of gratitude that an unscheduled houseguest should.

She blinked a couple times, not enough to make it look like she was flirting. "I'm afraid I'm not that educated on wine."

He filled her glass, then his, and sat again. "But you know a lot of other things, don't you, Irene Rose?"

Irene did her best not to gulp or fidget. Instead, she shrugged off his question, which was really a statement. He'd obviously done some checking up on her. "Not anymore."

Cal's lips turned up for a brief second. "*Hmm* ... yeah, I read something about that. That you took a leave of absence. That was about a year ago, right?"

Her mouth dry, she simply nodded and picked up her glass.

"But those highfalutin people you work for are still your friends. I'm sure if you brought them a big enough scoop, they'd be all over it."

Irene bristled. "I'm the one who brought the news *and* delivered it. I didn't ask someone to find or report my news. I found the interesting stories, then *I* shared them with my viewers."

Cal's lips turned up for real this time. "I bet you did, Victress." He picked up his fork and dug back in. He lifted his hand in front of his mouth. "So, what happened? You were on top, the queen in your field." He leaned over the table, smiled a closed-mouth smile. "Hell, some would say you were better than the men who dominate your field."

"I *am* better." Irene followed his lead and started eating. She lifted her hand to cover the bite she'd just taken. No sense in grossing him out since he had good table manners anyway. "I got burnt out."

He nodded and chewed. "So, not looking for your big break? A chance to get back in the game?"

She set down her fork and stared at him. "You know, I'm not sure what answer would seal my fate faster, so I'm going to stick with the truth." She dabbed at her mouth. "As much as you might be big news here, Cal, in Alaska. Believe me, San Francisco — most of the United States, for that matter — won't give two hoots about a meth dealer from Falcon Run, Alaska. So, if you're thinking I need to crawl back to my editor with a hot news alert, you're wrong. Of course, I'm hoping that's what you want to hear."

Cal downed another forkful of lasagna and followed it up with a hefty swig of the dark red wine. "That *is* what I want to hear. Although, you could have let me down a bit softer, especially since I opened an eighty-dollar bottle of wine."

She stared at the glass. "Really? See, I don't know anything about wine other than it goes straight to my head." She added a soft giggle for good measure.

"Clearly ..." He shook his head instead of continuing.

She could deduce his unspoken words, though. She'd just offended a cold-hearted killer. *Smart, Irene. Really smart.*

Then again, Cal was here, eating delicious Italian food and drinking expensive wine with her, and staring at her as if she held some magical key. He could have just tossed a peanut butter sandwich down the stairwell if he only wanted her as a hostage. Clearly, he wanted something from her. Or maybe, he just wanted companionship. It couldn't be easy trusting women with what you do for a living when you deal drugs and murder your employees.

"Cal ..." she drew out his name a couple seconds. "I walked away from my job for a reason ... several reasons actually. No matter where I wanted to go in the world, I would have had to deal with ..." she trailed off. She wanted to give him a good enough excuse without telling him the truth. She also wanted to connect with him, even if her reasons for hiding weren't the same as his. "Well, let's just say I suffered some extremely personal issues I'd rather not share with you — or my entire viewing audience, for that matter."

The ruthless murderer wiggled in his chair like one of her male *BFFs* in San Fran. "Do tell. I love a good piece of gossip. You know, growing up in such a small town and all. You'd be surprised how easily people hide their dirty laundry around here."

She couldn't resist, and she assumed he was proud of hiding in plain sight, so she offered, "Like being a drug dealer?"

He threw his head back. "Touché! Woman, no wonder you climbed to the top. You're not afraid of stepping on a man's balls to move up a rung. No wonder Alex fell for you. You're probably the only woman who's never taken his crap."

Fell for me ... How did Cal know Alex had *fallen* for her? She'd called Alex a surly pilot earlier. Had Cal been thinking she was talking about Kevin?

Cal stopped laughing, his head cocking to the side. "You didn't know Alex was in love with you?" he asked in that sickeningly soft voice again. "Well, I'd love to burst Alex's bubble if you don't feel the same way, but the thing is ... I need him to care about you, Irene. I need him to be willing to die for you. Nothing like love to provide leverage. Like my man Jeff." Cal waved his hand toward the upstairs portion of the house. "Threaten to cut one insignificant little pinky finger off his woman and he's all gung-ho to pay off her debt. Hell, I'm pretty sure he'll continue on even after his debt is paid."

Irene gulped but held her posture and composure. She'd seen worse than Cal. She just never had to dine with the brutes she wrote about. While she'd gone undercover numerous times, she never infiltrated any of the rings she'd broken up; she just observed from a distance.

Cal reached across the table and stroked her hand. "Don't worry, Victress. I have much larger plans for you, so I wouldn't think of disfiguring these beauties."

CHAPTER 20

~ Alex ~

Alex closed out the web browser he'd been using and plugged in the phone.

"Damn ..." He ran his hands through his hair. If Cal found out who Irene was, how would he ever let her go?

Vince looked up from the game he was playing on his phone. He'd turned off the noise when Alex had asked him, but he'd still been noisily tapping the keys. Not that there was much else for them to do for several hours as they awaited, so Alex couldn't begrudge him filling his time.

Erik had stretched out in the back seat of the truck and was now snoring.

Vince finished whatever he'd been doing and turned his phone over. "What'd you find out?"

"Irene's more than just a reporter ..." He shook his head, feeling like a total idiot. She earned more in a year than he'd made in his entire life. No wonder she'd been so upset and confused about his stupid plan. She obviously couldn't comprehend needing two-million dollars when she was worth ten times that much. "She's flipping famous. She's worked as a columnist for New York magazines, appears regularly on Fox and CNN, and personally knows the POTUS."

Vince laughed. "You and Sam need to get out more. Both of you have your heads in the Denali cloud cover."

Alex turned to his brother and somehow resisted snapping. "Did you know who she is?"

"'Course I did. What else do I have to do on the boat all day other than read."

Erik mumbled beneath his arm. "Can't believe you never heard of Irene Rose."

"Whatever." Alex banged his head against the head-rest. "Think! If not reporters, who?"

"Why change the plan?" Vince said. "I think it'll work. Maybe even better now that it's clear the editor at the station knows who Irene is."

Alex flopped his head to the side and just stared at Vince. "You think?"

"I *do* think. You're right. Publicity is our best bet. Call him back."

Erik poked his head between the seats. "I think so too."

Alex picked up the phone and hit redial.

"Hello?" asked the man he'd been speaking to, breathless. His one word said everything. He'd been anticipating a call back, and he had questions. "Are you the man who just called ... the Midnight Son?"

Alex gulped. "Yeah."

"Okay," the man said. "What do you want in exchange for this info?"

Alex hadn't thought about what to say concerning a finder's fee. He'd mentioned the payment just to sound authentic. But he didn't want money; he wanted safety. For Irene. How could accepting a referral fee help Irene?

"Publicity!" he blurted out after a couple seconds.

Publicity would help Irene, and it would be good for his business. "I want as many cameras as you have inside the terminal so you can capture a Midnight Son bringing Irene Rose safely home. I want you to mention that we work off donations."

"That's all you want?" The man sounded surprised.

Alex sighed. "That's all I want. But ... you must remain inside the terminal. If she sees you, she won't leave the vehicle. We'll enter through the last doors in the *Arrivals* area at exactly five o'clock this evening."

Alex clicked *End* without offering anything else. If he offered additional info, the reporter might not show up, but now he'd be intrigued.

He looked up at Vince, who was shaking his head. "I know Sam busts your balls, but we all know you're a true family man. Only you would think about asking for donations."

Erik smiled. "Of course, he's a family man. He's a Midnight Son, and we stick together through hell or high water — err ... snow." He laughed at his own words as he squeezed Alex on the shoulder.

Alex shrugged. "I had to give the reporter something. Otherwise, he might not have believed me." He blew out a long breath. "Please tell me this will work."

"This will work, Alex," Vince said. "In fact, why don't the two of you drop me off now? Then, Erik can drop you off before five. I'll find an inconspicuous place to wait. If Cal tries anything, the two of us can take him down."

Alex chewed on a nail, then shook his head. "He killed a man, Vince. Right in front of me. Didn't hesitate a second, just shot him." He shook his head again. "No, I can't let either of you get involved. Just drop me off."

"Like that's gonna happen." Vince huffed and opened the driver's door. "I'll walk to the terminal."

Erik grabbed Vince at the same time Alex did.

Alex felt his face get hot. Yeah, they risked their lives for their jobs, but they were good at what they did. Asking his brothers to take down Cal, knowing the man had just shot someone in cold blood ... wasn't something he was willing to do. "I already carry the guilt of our father's death. Please don't do this to me."

Erik spoke first, "Bro, you weren't responsible for Dad's death. We have a dangerous job. But think about that ... If you feel guilty, imagine how we'd feel if we let you do this alone? After I drop you off, I'll swing back around. I'll run that bastard down before I let him run off with either of you."

Vince smiled. "See, Alex, that sounds like a good plan."

Alex didn't like the plan. Didn't like the idea of his brothers' involvement. But ... he couldn't lose Irene either. And the Midnight Sons worked better as a team; they always had.

He reached out and rested his hands on a shoulder of each of his brothers. "Okay ... You're right. We're better if we stick together."

Alex wished Sam were here. Sam was the one person who could talk sense into their brothers. Then again, Sam might not be willing to jump into icy water to rescue an animal, but Alex knew for certain that he would for him or anyone else. Maybe it was good Sam wasn't here.

If things went badly, at least their mother would have her eldest and youngest child to comfort her.

~ Irene ~

Irene wrestled with what she should do. Fight, or allow Cal to use her as bait?

As she trailed behind Cal and Jeff, exiting the house through the same door she'd entered, she scanned the surrounding wood.

Would they shoot her in the back if she ran? Probably not. Would they track her down? Probably. That could mess up whatever Cal had planned at least. If Cal arrived at the airport late, chances are Alex might not be there.

But then he'd set up another rendezvous. The next one might not be in Alex's favor, and she was positive that Alex had come up with the airport swap.

Cal tossed a look over his shoulder. "Let's go, Irene! Your lover awaits."

Once again, Irene struggled to keep her face void of any emotion. Cal had said lover, but he didn't actually know that she was in love with Alex. If Cal knew she loved Alex, then he'd have twice as much leverage. No, the best thing was to go along with whatever Alex had planned, and then pull her weight when the time was right.

Jeff held the rear door open for her, then climbed into the co-pilot's seat. Obviously, Cal was flying again.

Before Jeff buckled in, he turned to her, handing her the large cup. "Here ya go, hon. It's a short run, but —"

Irene cut him off with a smirk but accepted the cup. "I'm sure I'll be fine. But thank you."

Cal turned to take her in. "You'll see lover boy soon enough. Just settle in."

The man was obviously testing her, seeing if she'd scream or cry ... or jump.

Irene glanced down at her boot but waited for the two men to preoccupy themselves with flying. She had opened the pocketknife in the cellar, and then carefully slid it back into her boot, aiming the sharp edge against the inside lining. The blade's cold spine dug into her ankle, but it'd be worth the discomfort if wielding it bought Alex enough time to get away.

She held the cup in her left hand, preparing to yack in it if either looked back, as she slid her right hand toward the boot. She'd kept the top laces loose, hoping she wouldn't slice open her fingers. Bleeding profusely wouldn't be very covert. Gingerly, she felt along her ankle, reaching for the sides of the blade.

"Beats driving, huh, Irene?" Cal offered good-humoredly.

Irene immediately bent over the cup and moaned. "Not if you get airsick."

"Woman, you're gonna have to get used to flying; it's the backbone of my business."

"Hm," she groaned.

While Cal and Jeff laughed, Irene pulled the knife up with her fingers. She palmed it, her eyes remaining on the men, not what she was doing. She hadn't felt a slice, but the blade was sharp. It could have sliced her open without her even feeling it.

She slowly moved the knife to her pocket, then removed her hand. She stared down at her fingers and exhaled softly. No blood.

She returned her hand back to her pocket, curling her fingers around the handle. She could stab Cal in the neck right now, which would probably cause them to crash. She wouldn't be able to get to Jeff, though. The moment she attacked Cal; Jeff would react.

Or ... is it possible that Jeff would be happy if she killed Cal? Could she even kill Cal? Sure, he was a murderer. But technically, she wouldn't be killing him in self-defense. He hadn't threatened to kill her. Just the opposite. Cal had made it sound as if he planned to keep her indefinitely. As what? A slave?

She could argue with herself all she wanted. She didn't have it in her to kill in cold blood. She would build up her courage to defend Alex, though.

She stared out the windows as the plane paralleled the Alaska Range. Beautiful. Majestic. For the millionth time in her life, she wondered: *What could I have done differently? In my life ... in the past few days?* No way to know. She sighed and stared out the front window as the bay came into view. They were landing at the same port. Cal must keep a car there. He probably had vehicles everywhere.

Once again, she checked her surroundings, even though she knew it wouldn't do any good. Other than a police officer, who would come to her aid if she screamed? It wouldn't be fair for her to endanger another person's life anyway. No, the only thing she could do is follow along, waiting for her chance.

Alex wasn't stupid. He and his brothers were accustomed to getting people out of sticky situations. She'd originally wondered if Alex would have washed his hands of her, but based on Cal's comment, he obviously hadn't. Again, where did that leave them? Maybe she needed to scream at Alex to run the moment she saw him. After all, she might be a dead woman walking anyway.

She sighed, then latched her hand around the grip when the plane lurched. "What was that?"

Jeff looked back at her, offering her a soft smile. "Just a change in the wind. Nothing to worry about."

The wheels touched, and Irene released the breath she'd been holding. Yeah … she was ready to die. *Not!* She could say that she'd willingly sacrifice herself, but no matter what, she knew she'd fight until her last breath. Maybe that was what Alex was saying. He'd wanted to do what he thought was right for his family, but in the end, he'd fought to live when he was drowning. He hadn't gone down without a fight. She'd watched him fighting for every breath. And now … he was risking his life again … for her.

Jeff and Cal jumped out and were at her door in seconds.

Cal wrapped one arm around her waist. His other hand was in his pocket, pressing a hard object against her side. *A gun?* "Smile, darling. We're a happy couple. Hell, we own a plane … can go anywhere in the world. That would make any woman happy, right?"

Irene glared up at Cal, then turned to see a group standing by a plane. Most of the bystanders were paying attention to a man with a clipboard, listening intently as he went over rules and regulations. But a couple of them were watching her and Cal.

She forced a smile, then waved to the onlookers. "Have a good trip!"

Cal rushed her toward a van. "No one said you had to be friendly."

She sneered up at him. "I *am* friendly." Truly, she hoped that a few of the travelers might recognize her. At least if she disappeared, they could say they'd seen her and hopefully describe her kidnapper.

"Well, save it!" Cal growled, obviously aware of what she was doing.

Jeff tugged open a sliding door on a stretch van with blacked-out windows. Of course Cal would have a private van. He owned a charter service, so this looked completely normal.

Cal escorted her inside, sitting beside her. He patted her leg, and she resisted cringing.

Jeff opened the driver's door and climbed in. The digital clock on the dash read 4:55.

Five minutes. Her heart rate quickened. She'd stuffed the knife in her right pocket. Now Cal was on her left side. Not what she had hoped. Of course, she didn't know what she'd hoped. How could she?

She stuffed her hands into her pockets. Her left hand found nothing but lint; her right gripped the cold metal. She'd do it. To save Alex, she'd hurt Cal. Just enough for Alex to get away, though, she decided. Her fate didn't matter.

They were meeting at the airport, which had to have been Alex's idea. No way would Cal fire a gun on airport property. So, what was Cal's plan? Was he really going to let her go? No, he couldn't. She'd witnessed him commit an unprovoked, cold-blooded murder. No way would he just let her go.

Within minutes of leaving the seaplane base, Jeff was pulling into Ted Stevens. Not much time to plan an attack.

Irene sucked in a breath as she inspected the area. *Arrivals*, Cal had said. Alex said he'd meet Cal at the end of the *Arrivals*. Then what? She wished she knew the plan, then she could do her part.

Her heart raced as Jeff entered the long line of cars. She eyed each person on the sidewalk, looking for a man with two duffle bags, as if she could somehow help Alex if she spotted him before Cal or Jeff did.

"Pull over, Jeff," Cal ordered.

Jeff followed Cal's direction without question.

Irene craned her head, looking for Alex. Maybe he'd gotten smart and hadn't showed. Good — no, not good. She saw him at the end of the lane. He stood with the two bags beside him, as if he were waiting on a ride.

"Up ahead," Cal announced, leaning forward. "That's Alex standing at the end. Wait until a spot opens, then pull directly in front of him. You know what to do, Jeff … Grab the bags and take off."

"That wasn't the deal!" Irene shouted.

Cal fastened his hand over her mouth and squeezed. "Keep your trap shut, or I'll kill Alex — and you — and then disappear. Trust me, darling. I can be in the air and in international airspace before your blood stains the concrete."

Irene gripped the knife tighter, focused on the handle, imagined the moves. She could slam the knife into Cal's leg right through her coat, then remove it and shove down the door handle before he knew what happened. If she aimed for his femoral artery, he'd have to take action to save his life, giving her and Alex time to escape.

The van lurched forward. Irene shot her gaze to Alex. Jeff pulled next to the curb, and before Irene could blink, Cal lurched over her and hopped through the opening doors, knocking Alex backward with what looked like a bear hug. "Alex!" Cal crooned as if Alex were his long-lost brother. Jeff had already exited the front passenger door and was lunging for the bags.

Irene darted for the open door, but Jeff was shoving the bags against her. They'd planned what they were going to do! Jeff had activated the power door as soon as they stopped, and Cal had known to occupy Alex while Jeff retrieved the bags.

A tall blond-haired man knocked Jeff away from the door and reached for her. "Come with me, Irene!"

Irene lurched back in shock, but then realized she'd seen the fair-haired man. At the wedding. Alex's Russian brother.

Jeff bounded upright and knocked the man down before she could take his hand, but she was free of the van.

She tried to move around the two men, but Jeff slammed the man into her, pinning her against the van.

The sliding-glass doors of the airport opened and, all at once, the sidewalk came alive with shouting onlookers screaming her name, asking questions she couldn't make out.

Cal released Alex and raced toward Jeff. "Let's go!" He grabbed Jeff's arm and the two of them hopped into the van. Irene stumbled backward as the van screeched away.

A second before her head smacked the concrete, a set of hands grabbed her. She blinked, trying to clear her mind as she took in the face of the man who'd caught her. "Andrew?"

"Oh, my darling. Are you okay? I'm so sorry about what's happened to you. I never should have let you—" Her ex-fiancé shook his head as he righted her.

On solid footing, Irene stared at the hundreds of flashing cameras, and then Alex's face.

"Irene Rose!" shouted a tall man. "We're told the

Midnight Sons rescued you after your plane crashed in the Gulf of Alaska."

Irene stared up at Andrew and then at Alex again, who was backing away from the crowd.

"Sir!" The same reporter shoved a microphone in front of Andrew's face, since obviously she wasn't answering any questions. "You said you were waiting for your fiancée. What was your reaction when you heard her chartered plane had crashed?"

Andrew, always public-ready, wrapped his arms around her, turning her toward the camera. "I was devastated. Irene and I have been through so much over the last year, what with her cancer and all. The thought of losing Irene —" He wiped away a non-existent tear.

Irene closed her eyes, wishing everything would go away ... except Alex. The only person she wanted to see ... but she could no longer find him among the crowd. Dozens of reporters circled her and, before she knew what was happening, she felt her body being moved inside the terminal.

"Alex?" she croaked out. She tried to see over the heads, but everyone was taller than her. "Alex!" she cried again.

She caught a quick glance of Alex shaking his head in between a break in the bodies surrounding her. That one look told her everything she needed to know ... He was angry. Angry because she hadn't told him that she might die. Alex had obviously called the reporters here, knowing that if they showed up, Cal wouldn't try anything. But he'd also heard her ex tell the reporter she had cancer, and he'd heard the reporter call Andrew her fiancé. She'd told him that she wasn't in a relationship, and Alex had proven repeatedly that he could read her like a book, so he knew the reporters had gotten their stories crossed. But she hadn't told him that her days were numbered, that she had a fifty percent chance of dying in the next five years. How could she explain that she only had his best interest in mind?

Any trust she'd built up with Alex over the previous days was gone — shattered. She'd had her chance, and she hadn't told him the truth. And now that the press knew, the world would know that she was a woman on borrowed time.

She'd never see Alex again. But she would also have to worry for his and her safety. No way would Cal let either of them live. Not when their testimony could put him away for life.

"Alex ..." she pleaded again, hoping he'd break through the crowd and usher her away from the nightmare that would soon be her life.

CHAPTER 21

~ Alex ~

*F*iancé? Cancer? Alex backed away from the crowd — and the stranger he thought that he'd fallen in love with.

How could he have fallen in love with someone he didn't even know? How could he have fallen for a woman who not only hadn't told him the truth, but had also cheated on her fiancé? The answer was simple: he couldn't have; it was all a mind game. A mind game she had played with him. And a game he'd played with himself. He was far, far from innocent. He'd *wanted* to believe that someone could love him … even after all he'd done wrong. He'd wanted to believe that he was worthy … Of what? To go on living?

Vince wrapped an arm around his shoulders, cutting off the ridiculous thoughts bombarding his brain. "Well, it worked, Alex. Not the outcome we wanted, but at least you and Irene are both safe. We'll catch up with your woman after the vultures stop circling—"

Alex turned to his brother, cutting off his words with a frown. Irene wasn't his woman, nor would she ever be. Even if it somehow worked out for them; Irene would never be any man's woman — and that was one of the things he had loved about her. *Had* … was the opportune word. He couldn't think about Irene or what could have been. He had to track down Cal, but not with his brothers. No way would he be responsible for another fallen family member. Cal's thug could have killed Vince right there outside the terminal.

Instead of trying to explain the Irene situation to Vince, he turned the subject to something far more important. "Did you hear from Erik? Does he have Cal in his sights?" He had to make sure that Erik wasn't doing anything stupid.

"Yeah ..." Vince said with a shrug. "Erik just texted me. But, no, he lost the van. He's circling back to the airstrip now. But I doubt Cal will head back there. What should we do next? Maybe Erik's right. Maybe we need to call the authorities."

Alex shook his head. "If we call the cops here in Anchorage, they won't find anything in his plane, and I doubt they'd issue an all-out manhunt for the van based on our word alone. No, we need proof. The only thing we can do is watch and wait for Cal to screw up."

"So, you're just going to let him get away?"

Alex threw up his hands. No way would Vince back down from a fight; he had to convince him. "We rescue those in peril, Vince. We're not crimefighters. Look what happened last time we ran up against a criminal? Sam almost died."

"No, we're not," Vince said, "but ... we have to do something—"

"We're going to do something," Alex said, cutting him off. "We're going to make sure mom and Daire are okay. Then we'll play it by ear."

Vince nodded a tightened jaw in the direction of the terminal. "What about Irene?"

Alex closed his eyes and shook his head. "I don't know who Irene is. A woman lost in the wilderness will obviously say anything to get home safely. I was just the right man for her at the time, it seems. We did our job. We rescued her from peril. That's what we do. Nothing more."

"Oh, Alex … I thought a few days in the wilderness had changed you, but you're as jaded as ever. How do you know what's really going on? She looked as shocked as you did."

Alex shook his head again. "Of course she looked shocked. Her fiancé is sure to have a million questions for her. She was caught dead to rights. Irene isn't stupid. She knew what she was doing."

Alex sighed internally at his words. *So why did she give me such a hard time? Why did it matter why I was on the island if she didn't care?* The answer was obvious… *Because if I didn't live, I couldn't save her.*

He pulled Vince from the doors and walked to the end of the drive. "Tell Erik to come get us. We need to get home. Make sure Mom and Daire are okay."

Vince did as he requested while Alex just stared at the terminal doors. *As always, I got what I deserved. What did I expect? For Irene to come running for me when she has a supermodel fiancé holding her? Idiot!*

Not wanting to wait, Alex walked past Vince, tromping down the side of the road. Erik would be here in minutes. All his troubles came rushing back, as if a few days in the wilderness — as Vince had so eloquently put it — could make things go away. He still had money trouble, and now Cal was probably planning to off him, his entire family, and Irene.

He snapped his head up, as if Cal would be standing

right there, ready to offer him a job again. If he were working for Cal —

Vince caught up to him, smacked him on the back. "Sorry, Alex. Women suck. Hell, I know that more than anyone. But you can't —"

Alex huffed out a breath, cutting off his brother's words. "I don't want to talk about it."

Yeah, he knew how some women were, what Vince had gone through. First with his high school sweetheart who'd upped and left him right after prom, and then his ex-wife who'd emptied his house and bank account while Vince was out to sea for three months … But Irene had seemed different than all the women Alex had dated or that his brothers had dated. Plus, she was from Alaska. Even if he visited the lower forty-eight and found a bride, it'd be damn near impossible to convince a woman to move to Alaska. All most people thought when they heard Alaska was a barren snowy land, but it was so much more. A land he never wanted to leave really. He could whine and cry all he wanted, but the fact of the matter was … he loved his homeland.

And he didn't intend to leave it for a woman — or Cal. No, he couldn't think about Irene right now. He needed to concentrate on the real threat to his life and his family's lives. He'd been prepared to sacrifice his life before, so he would do this.

Two soft horn taps sounded behind them, then Erik pulled up alongside the curb. Alex and Vince hopped into the passenger front and rear. Erik pulled away before they shut their doors, so as not to get stuck in airport traffic.

"What happened?" Erik asked. "I saw you, made one loop, came back around, and all hell had broken loose. I saw Cal and his partner hop into a van, so I followed, but lost them at a busy intersection."

Alex rested his head against the cool leather seat. "I don't want to talk about it. Just drive home, okay?" He had to plan. He had to figure out how to track down Cal Landrum.

~ Irene ~

Irene blinked, then blinked again. She shook her head, but nothing worked.

Nothing cleared her head of the millions of stars shooting at her eyes. She'd lost her hearing too. Minutes ago, Andrew had been pressing her for answers, reporters had been shouting questions, and the overhead speakers had been blaring out orders of what passengers should and shouldn't do.

Now, her head felt heavy and fuzzy. Blood rushed inside her skull, throbbing in her ears and behind her eyes.

She tried to grip onto something, anything, but felt nothing. Her hands and feet tingled, as if her entire body were asleep.

A loud muffled voice sounded in her ear. "She's going into shock. Call 9-1-1!"

Irene blinked again. A fuzzy outline of a man stared down at her. She moved her lips, trying to form the name she wanted, but unsure whether anything came out.

Then the world went black.

Beeping. Cold. Footsteps. Chattering. A T.V. commercial. Laughter. A groan. Soft whimpering.

Irene's eyes felt soldered shut, but she heard the

mixture of sounds clear as a bell. She wasn't on the island anymore. Had she really been on an island? Or had she played out some soap opera drama from months of watching nothing but T.V.?

She strained to hear the surrounding noises. Yes, she was in a hospital.

Had it all been a bad dream? Was she still in the hospital after her surgery? Had she wanted to escape from her nightmare so badly that she'd conjured up an action-adventure romance starring a good-looking pilot and drug runners?

Something cold touched her arm, and she jumped.

"It's okay, Ms. Rose," a woman said. "I'm just checking your vitals."

Irene cleared her scorched throat. "I can't see."

The woman touched both sides of her face, lifting something. "You can see, Ma'am. Your fiancé covered your eyes, said it wasn't dark enough ... that you required a completely dark room to sleep."

Irene blinked in the darkness. The only light streamed in through a cracked doorway at the end of the room. "My fiancé is here?"

"Yes, ma'am. He went to get coffee when I came in."

Irene rolled her shoulders, attempting to work out the stiffness. "How long have I been here?"

"You came in last night."

Irene smiled up at the woman. "Umm ... what city am I in?"

The nurse tilted her head. "Your fiancé said you didn't hit your head. Do you feel okay?"

"I'm sorry ... I think I know where I am. I think I was just hoping this wasn't a dream." The dark-haired Alaska native was a major clue that she wasn't dreaming.

"I'm in Anchorage, right?"

"Yes, ma'am."

The door to the corridor creaked open, and a man, based on his shape and height, walked into the room. Bright white surrounded his silhouette, making it impossible to distinguish his face.

The nurse patted her arm. "I'll tell the doctor you're awake."

"Oh, darling," Andrew cooed as he approached the bed. "I was so worried." He leaned over the bed and kissed her forehead. "Why didn't you tell me you were coming here? I could have had my private jet bring you."

Irene stared up at the man she hadn't spoken with in more than a year. Their last conversation was a knockdown, drag-out, and now he was acting as if it'd never happened.

As hard as she tried, she couldn't force herself to be pleasant. "There are no cameras here, Andrew. No need to put on a show."

His face instantly transformed to the hard edge she knew so well. Once upon a time, she'd loved that hard edge. Hell, her own personality had nearly mirrored his. Until he'd let her down. Until he'd not supported her when she needed him the most.

"I was worried about you, Irene. I flew all the way to this godforsaken state to come to your aid."

"I needed you a year ago —"

"You know I couldn't take part in your decision," he growled. "It would have ruined me."

"Oh ... *Now* it's the woman's decision? As if you didn't take part creating the baby. I didn't hear that stance in your political campaign. What you meant to say is that you *couldn't* make the decision with me because it would have ruined your political career. A conservative democrat is hard to find, huh? Can't have him making one of the hardest decisions in life." She stared up at him with all the hatred she'd built up over the last year. Everything that she thought she'd resolved came roaring to the surface. "Tell me, Andrew ... How will you make important government decisions concerning the entire state of California, when you can't even stand beside your fiancée to make one decision? It's not like you cared one way or another, you just didn't want to *make* the decision."

Andrew bolted upright. "That's not true. I wanted our baby. I wanted you!"

"I didn't have a choice, Andrew. I sat there all by myself as the doctor made it clear I had to decide. I was barely a month along. If I'd waited eight months, it would have been too late ... the cancer would have overtaken every part of my body. And not that I expected you to make my decision ... I didn't. But you couldn't even sit in the same room with me —"

He knelt by the bed again, but she waved him away. "It's not over, Andrew. I still have only a fifty/fifty chance that I will live, so the last thing I will ever do is get pregnant. I can't go through that again, and you don't want a wife who won't be able to give you children."

Andrew blinked repeatedly, as if shocked by her statement. "Never ... Even after five years?"

"Never," she repeated. "I won't abort another child to save my life, and there's no guarantee the cancer won't come back so, no ... I will never bear children."

He nodded slowly. "And your job? Will you come

back to the station?"

She wanted to scream, *And, see you daily? Never!* But she'd thrown all the daggers she had left. She just couldn't carry the pain and resentment in her heart for the rest of her life. All it did was bring her down. Made her collapse in the middle of an airport, when she should have been chasing down Alex, begging him to understand why she hadn't told him.

"No, Andrew. Sorry. That part of my life is over too. I'm going to enjoy the rest of my years doing what I want to do, not what everyone else wants me to do."

He forced a smile. "I understand. You're welcome any time, you know. I'm sure the world would love to hear what happened to Irene Rose." Andrew offered her hand a squeeze and then turned and walked out of her life for the second time.

His last words echoed in her head long after he was gone, until a soft rap sounded on the door, followed by cries and squeals and *amens*.

Irene felt a tear slide down her face as she took in the three familiar faces. The auburn hair that matched her own topped her very pregnant sister. Next to her sister, her mother, as short and dark-haired as she remembered, with extra crinkles around her soft Aleut face, hustled toward her, dragging Irene's father in her wake. Her father, tall and lean, but with a head-full of gray hair where there used to be red, kept hold of both women's hands as they all moved toward the hospital bed.

Together, the three of them approached her. Together, the three of them embraced her. Together, they all whispered *I love you* and *Thank God you're okay* and *We missed you so much.*

Together, the four of them cooed and cried kind words and encouragements for untold minutes.

Her ex-fiancé was out of her life. She might not ever see Alex again. A madman probably wanted her dead. But this ... her family holding her without any questions of where she'd been or how she ended up in the hospital, was what she needed right now.

Tomorrow, she would decide her next steps ... and figure out what to do about Cal Landrum.

CHAPTER 22

~ Alex ~

For the third day in a row, Alex switched from channel to channel and repeated the identical message. "Interested party, got a 10-20 on Kevin's Kodiak near Middleton. Copy?"

The message was vague enough that it wouldn't rouse attention from the wrong listeners. But Cal would understand. Just by Alex mentioning Cal's dead pilot and the plane he flew, it'd be enough. But adding Middleton sealed the deal. If Cal heard the transmission, he'd know that Alex wanted to talk to him. He just had to find the correct channel ... at the correct time.

He'd driven by Cal's hangar and house repeatedly, at all times of the day and night, but there was never any sign of life. Had Cal really fled the country? It seemed unlikely, especially since there hadn't been word one about his illegal affairs. Apparently, Irene had also decided it was best to let him get caught on his own. Irene had called numerous times, but Alex told Vince that he wasn't taking any calls, which included Irene. He couldn't talk to her right now. Maybe in the future ... if he had a future. But not right now.

After sending out the message countless times, someone finally clicked a response. It could have been anyone, someone who was getting tired of hearing the same message. But when the click wasn't followed by a transmission, he knew he'd reached his mark.

Alex sucked in a breath as the line remained quiet. He leaned forward, hovering over the radio, waiting. It had to be Cal ... or perhaps the bald military-looking man.

He held down the mic. "Are you the party looking for a pilot?" That question would definitely interest Cal. After all, Cal had mentioned that maybe they could work together, and the man was down a pilot.

Nothing but dead air followed his direct question.

Realizing his head was pounding from not breathing, Alex sucked in a breath and released it slowly. He leaned back and massaged his temples. What else could he ask? Nothing. If the person at the end of the frequency was, in fact, his interested party, Alex had said all he should. He had to let Cal make the next move.

A crackle on the channel had Alex darting forward again. "Yeah," a gruff voice offered. Cal's military thug, he assumed. "We're interested. We've been wanting another Kodiak. You got one for sale?"

Alex released a long breath as he looked over his shoulder, making sure none of his brothers or mother had returned home. If they knew what he was doing, they'd kill him. Not that they'd need to. One wrong move with Cal, and Alex would end up at the bottom of the Aleutian Trench.

Alex licked his lips and clicked the mic. "Yeah. When would you like to see it?" He released the mic and closed his eyes. *What am I doing?*

Minutes passed slowly, to the point that Alex was certain he'd been too forward. Hell, he had no idea how to handle situations such as these. Cal needed someone, though. It wasn't as if he could advertise for a drug runner. No, he imagined those situations happened just as this one. A pilot owed him ... or needed money and knew about his illegal enterprise.

CLICK! "Seven o'clock. Falcon Run strip."

Alex's heart sped up. Seven o'clock. All the staff would be gone. It'd be pitch dark. *I must be nuts, but I'm really doing this. It's the only way.*

Alex clicked the mic again. "I'll be there."

Alex stood outside his plane at the non-towered airport, his gaze roaming between the entry and the moonless sky. He had no idea how Cal and his goon would arrive ... if they'd even arrive.

He tugged his coat higher up his neck, attempting to tilt his head down to block the wind, while keeping his eyes focused on his surroundings.

Hours earlier, he'd left the house, so he'd be long gone before his mother or brothers returned home. Without the excuse of a rescue call, the family would have had endless questions about where he was going. After all, they knew he wasn't seeing anyone. As much as his mother had pried, he absolutely refused to talk about Irene Rose.

He'd spent the last few hours driving ... thinking. He'd driven by Cal's again but still hadn't seen any indication that he was home, so he decided to keep with their scheduled meeting.

Two bright beams lit up the vacant lot.

Alex's heart pounded fiercely. *I don't know if I have what it takes ...* But it didn't matter. He had to do this.

The vehicle sped toward him, not slowing.

"Well, Alex, it won't be painless, but it will solve all

your problems. You'll be dead, and Cal will go away for murder."

The vehicle skidded sideways, spraying Alex with a mixture of snow, mud, and gravel, then turned straight and squealed to a stop. The bright headlights made it impossible to see through the windshield. Cal hopped out of the driver's side, his thug from the passenger side.

Cal lifted his arms, the gesture playful and friendly. "Alex! It's been forever! So glad to see you again." He nodded to the bald man. "Jeff, say hello to my old friend."

Jeff crossed the distance of about ten feet with barely three steps. Then he was on him. He whipped Alex around, lifting each hand and placing it on the plane's exterior. Systematically, Jeff patted down each of his arms, his legs, back, and chest. The big oaf dug into his pockets next, pulling out his cell phone and tossing it to Cal.

Cal popped open the back like a pro, then nodded at Jeff again.

Jeff pulled out a gold walkie-talkie-looking thing no larger than a business card and ran it up and down Alex's body and then moved to the plane.

Alex shook off the feeling of being man-handled and jutted his chin to Cal. "What do you think? I'm an idiot?"

Cal forced his lips up. "Alex, my old friend. Just making sure we're still friends."

We were never friends, Alex wanted to growl, but he figured that wouldn't help his situation. "Do you normally spray your friends with slush?"

Cal had always been a nerd, even in high school. He'd

made stupid jokes and pulled ridiculous pranks. No wonder his brother had turned to drugs. He'd probably gotten the worst of Cal's bullying.

Made Alex appreciate Sam even more. Yeah, his big brother gave him a hard time sometimes, but it was usually when Alex was doing something dangerous. Mostly, Sam had always encouraged him. It was Alex's own guilt that had turned Sam's gentle instruction into taunts.

Cal smiled widely this time. "You know me. Always looking for a good time."

Jeff finished his sweep of the plane, and Cal gave him another signal that the man obviously understood because he walked back to the SUV, to the rear liftgate. Cal pulled out a fob and clicked, and the door opened on its own. Jeff reached inside the cargo area, then returned to where Alex and Cal stood with two familiar black duffle bags.

Alex sighed. *I'm really doing this.*

"Where's Irene?" Cal asked flippantly. "I was really looking forward to seeing her again."

Alex clenched his jaw, so he didn't explode. Instead, he shrugged off Cal's question, as if it didn't even make sense. "How would I know? I haven't seen her since the airport. I got her there safely. That was all I promised."

Cal's eyebrows lowered. "I was under the impression that you two were a hot item."

Alex forced a smile. "You assumed. You know what happens when you assume, don't you?"

Cal laughed, then tossed the two pieces of Alex's phone next to his feet. "You mean what *almost* happened to me. I was one step ahead of you, Alex. Just like I've always been."

No sense in commenting on that absurd statement. Cal had never been a step ahead of Alex. Then again, Alex had never kept track. Of what? The girls they dated in high school? The wrestling team or track wins? Was it possible that Cal had gotten involved in the drug trade because he'd felt second-best?

"You're right, Cal. The income from your tour company far exceeds our little search and rescue non-profit." Alex had decided to give the man something, even though he now knew it wasn't true. He used to think that Cal had done well for himself with his adventure tours. He'd even been jealous a few times.

"Hm! Well, we're going to see how well you do." Cal dipped his head to the bags, and Jeff picked them up and carried them to the plane. He tossed them inside without saying a word. "You know where to drop them. I'll have a boat pick them up tomorrow."

Alex stared from the plane to Cal. "And my payment?"

Cal winked then turned for his vehicle. "You owe me one, Alex." As he reached for the handle, he looked back. "You know ... Irene and I got along pretty well. If you're not seeing her, maybe I'll drop in on her."

Alex bit his tongue as both men piled into the SUV. Then Cal sped off as quickly as he'd arrived.

His breath came out ragged as he watched Cal's hundred-thousand-dollar SUV disappear behind a track of trees, then in his peripheral, he caught a tiny flicker of light inside the small terminal.

He snatched up his phone, then hopped into his plane. Middleton. *Humph!* He had vowed never to go back there.

~ Irene ~

Irene clicked end and shoved the phone in her jeans pocket. "Grrr ... Men!"

As the last few times she called, Vince had been more than pleasant, and she'd thanked him profusely for his help in rescuing her from Cal, but he'd repeated the same words, *I'm sorry, Irene, but Alex still isn't taking calls — from anyone. It's nothing personal, I'm sure. He's a good man, I promise you that, so please don't give up on him.*

Give up? What is there to give up? We don't have anything to give up. And they never would have anything. But she wanted to explain that she hadn't been lying to Alex about her feelings for him. How could she explain if Alex wouldn't give her the time of day? She'd thought about tracking him down, but she'd waited too long to see her family and had come too far. She intended to spend at least a week with them. Maybe next week she'd track him down. It wasn't as if he were going anywhere. Sounded as though he'd locked himself away. Good. She'd let him stew. Alex needed to find his own way. As much as she loved him, she couldn't be his reason for living, since she might die. And ... she had her own life to figure out.

Instead of wasting any more of the time she'd planned to spend on Saint Paul, she decided to go for a self-made tour, starting with the port. After several days of reuniting, her father had to get back to the church, her sister had to get back to work at the Aleut Heritage Museum, and her mother said she'd be busy running errands. Irene had resisted laughing. Errands on Saint Paul ... Instead of behaving rudely, though,

Irene bussed her mother's cheek. "Okay ... I'll go for a short hike while you're gone. Have a good day, *Ana-ana*. See you tonight."

Her mother followed her into the hallway. "You too, *panik*. Be careful. Don't exert yourself."

Irene offered her mother a smile and hug, then shrugged into her coat, draped a scarf around her neck, and topped off the winter ensemble with an ushanka-hat her mother insisted she wear when outside. She never should have told her family about her cancer diagnosis. Her mother was forever babying her and hadn't been pleased when she said she would return to San Fran next week.

She had to go back to California, though. While she had more than enough money, her soul was aching to create. She hadn't felt the need to research, let alone *create* something in more than a year. But now, that familiar excited feeling had returned. Especially at night, once her family retired for the evening, her brainwaves were firing on all cylinders. Whether it was because she finally felt healthier after months of feeling sickly, or the closure with Andrew, the passion with Alex, or the excitement of fighting for her life — literally — she felt more alive than she'd ever felt, and the creative side of her brain wanted to share her experience with others.

Irene left the small wood cottage and crossed the gravel street. It was a short hike from the church to the tidal lagoon. Heck, every building on the island was a short walk away. Even the airport was only a little over an hour's walk from her parents' tiny parsonage. While there were a few rolling hills on the island's volcanic landscape, she'd learned as a child to stick to the marked trails. Snow and vegetation easily hid deep crevasses and lava tubes.

Irene made her way to the beach, stopping and staring at the Bering Sea every few minutes, snapping pics of the plentiful fishing boats on the horizon, and watching for the occasional black fin. When she reached the cove, the tide was out, so she strolled along the soft sand.

Once upon a time, the lagoon served as a killing field, where hunters trapped unsuspecting seals in the low tide. Thankfully the barbaric act of clubbing seals no longer existed in this part of the world. She had never condemned her ancestors for killing animals, as they used everything and wasted nothing, unlike the fur traders who only wanted the seals' coats. She shivered at the gruesome pictures she'd seen as a child and was thankful for all the acts Congress had enacted to control senseless hunting.

Even today, as she walked the tidal flats, she saw remnants of seal bones and teeth. Many tourists registered to keep their treasures, but she just came here to watch the fog roll in. Even though the seals wouldn't migrate back to Saint Paul until May, she would likely spy the herd of free-roaming reindeer and the ever-present artic foxes that roamed the island year-round.

Irene breathed in the cold briny air. She'd miss her parents when she left, but no way could she live in this remote village more than a few weeks. No, San Fran was now her home. Although the thought of staying on Alaska's mainland held some appeal, there was nothing in Alaska for her but memories.

After a few hours, Irene made her way back to the three-bedroom cottage where she'd been born. The wood siding still bore the same rust-colored paint that it had always worn. It was as if one of the tribe members had decided long ago that all cottages would be rust-red, baby-blue, sable-brown, or dove-gray. And once chosen, each house had to maintain that color until the end of time. She had to admit, the staggered order of houses in different shades did give the fishing village a storybook-look. She snapped a couple more pictures with her phone as she made her way down the small knoll.

As soon as Irene entered the house, she knew something was wrong. The motivational scriptures set in frames and the old-rugged cross that hung in the foyer were crooked. And the house was too quiet. Her mother would have returned from her errands at the corner store and post office a while ago. And based on the aroma of fish stew wafting in from the kitchen, her mother had already started dinner, which meant that Irene should hear her puttering around. Even if she were in the washroom, she'd be talking to herself or humming a hymn; it's what her mother did.

Irene shoved her hands in her pockets, curled her fingers around the pocketknife that never left her side anymore.

"*I ... rene!*" Cal crooned in his saccharine-sweet voice. "We've been waiting for you, darling."

Of course her mother would have opened the door to Cal. Most of the crimes committed on Saint Paul were domestic violence, perpetrated behind closed doors. Since families were locked in closed quarters for months on end, many of the natives of Saint Paul experienced a sense of despair, so they drank to wash away their troubles. Drinking, of course, only made things worse. The cycle of abuse started from childhood, and many islanders continued the reckless life-style. Shortly after Irene had moved away, she'd read where her father had worked with authorities, setting up shelters, social workers, and programs to not only help the victims, but to educate the offenders. The paper had quoted her father as saying, *I will never give up on a lost soul. I believe with Christ at the helm, all persons can turn their life around.*

Because of her parents' instant attack and refusal to listen or forgive, Irene had been angry when she'd read that quote. Now all she felt was fear for her parents. She couldn't lose them now, not after all the years she'd wasted.

Cal smiled at her, waving her into the living area as if he owned the place. "Come in, my dear. I was just telling your mother how much I enjoyed our short time together."

Heat burned in her chest. "I swear to you, Cal —"

He raised an eyebrow, cutting off her threat, then nodded to her mother. "Your mother has been very hospitable. She even set out tea."

Irene gulped. Her eyes met her mother's knowing gaze. While her mother sat as still as a bird on the couch, forcing her soft round cheeks up in a closed-mouth smile, Irene could see the fear in her eyes. Her mother knew a bad man when she saw one. Her mother's father had been one of the natives who drank and abused his wife and kids. Irene's father had taken her mother away from that life.

Irene sat next to her mother and squeezed her cool hand. "It's okay, *Ana-ana*." She stared back up at Cal. If she could just get her mother out of the room, she'd do what she had to do, what she'd been preparing to do from the first time Cal shot Kevin in cold blood.

Cal strolled the length of the small room in two strides. Ignoring her father's tattered recliner, he pushed back the coffee table with his foot and perched on the edge. He scooped up Irene's hands in his. "Of course, everything is okay, Irene. Here's what's going to happen, love. You're going to say goodbye to your lovely mother and then come back with me. Your mother isn't going to worry or say anything to anyone because she knows how happy we are going to be."

Cal smiled down at her mother, and her mother returned his fake emotion with another quick raise of her closed lips. "Of course. If Irene is happy, I am happy too, and her *ata* will be happy."

"See." Cal shrugged. "Easy. Pack your bags, and we'll be off."

Irene stood, and Cal followed suit. "My bags are in the other room, Cal."

He excitedly wiggled his shoulders as if he were a teenage girl. "Oh, I know. I just missed you so much over the last few days that I don't want anything to separate us."

Irene walked toward the small room she and her sister had shared as children. Did Cal really think there was a chance that they could be together? Her fingers ached to attack him, but if there were any chance that she could get out of the house first, she'd take it. For that matter, she'd fly anywhere he wanted if it meant he wouldn't harm her mother.

Decided, Irene threw her suitcase up on the bed. If he started to do anything to her mother, she would fight, even to her death. But if he did as he said, she'd go willingly. No matter what happened to her after he took her away, at least her family would be safe.

Without concern of a sloppy suitcase, Irene hurriedly emptied the dresser and closet of all the clothes she'd bought before leaving Anchorage. She shoved everything into the new suitcase she'd purchased. She didn't bother going to the bathroom for her toiletries. The faster they got out of the house, the better. Her father would return home soon, and he wouldn't behave as passively as her mother.

Cal fingered the faded-blue light-blocking curtains that had hung in her room for thirty-some years. "So this is where the famous Irene Rose grew up. *Hmm.* I never would have guessed the woman of my dreams would have come from Saint Paul Island of all places."

Irene shook her head, then clicked the latches on the suitcase. She didn't need to pretend when her mother wasn't in the room. "All packed."

"Should we stop by the church and meet your father? Or the museum and meet your pregnant sister?"

Irene threw her hands up in front of her face. "I get it, Cal. You know everything about me. Why are you doing this? I haven't said a word to anyone."

He snatched up her bag with one hand, then squeezed his other hand around her arm. "Because Alex owes me a life ... and so much more." He forcefully escorted her out of the bedroom, back to the living area.

Her mother, God help her, stood. Irene saw the outline of the revolver in her mother's apron, but she shook her head when her mother started to reach for it. "No, *Ana-ana.* All is well. Cal will treat me well, I promise."

Tears snaked down her mother's cheeks, but she sank back to the sofa.

"Remember what I told you, Mrs. Rose," Cal offered in a low, demanding voice. "Irene will be safe as long as no one says anything. I am a man of my word, ma'am."

With that, Cal hauled Irene out of the house and dragged her down the driveway to the road. Irene glanced over her shoulder at the church that sat on the neighboring lot. More than likely, her father wouldn't be staring out the window. Still, she said a prayer that he wouldn't.

At his vehicle, Cal opened the passenger door and nudged her inside. One side of metal handcuffs was already strapped to the grab handle on the roof. He clicked the other cuff to her hand, then slammed the door.

Cal jumped in the driver's seat and sped toward the airstrip.

Irene stared around at the island of her birth, the place she couldn't wait to escape when she was a teenager, and only a few hours ago, she'd been planning to leave again. Now, Cal was forcing her to leave, which meant she might not see the island or her family ever again.

CHAPTER 23

~ Alex ~

Alex's knuckles were pure white as he landed. Last check, the winds were holding steady at thirty knots, and the cloud cover was thirty-five percent. The runway was only 150 feet wide on an island that was barely seven miles at its widest point. One wrong calculation, and he'd end up in the drink, the way Kevin had brought down that beautiful Kodiak.

After landing, Alex taxied to a designated space, and then charged toward the hangar, both duffle bags in tow.

He dropped the two sand-crusted fifty-pound bags in front of the man who'd been awaiting his arrival. "Truly, if I never see these bags again it will be too soon."

Wheelan nodded. "They're worth a lot of money. Glad you didn't take off with them."

Alex grimaced. "My integrity and Irene's safety are worth way more than two million dollars. Hell, I don't even like the way that sounds. Money might bring me to my knees, but it can't buy me."

"Glad to hear that, Alex."

The hangar remained quiet for a long while as they

waited. Neither of them were what you'd call verbose.

Once again, Alex prayed that he'd made the right decision. He'd know soon enough.

Wind battered the siding. Hard to believe the island could withstand the waves, let alone the constant wind. Although he was dressed for the weather, a shiver traveled through him.

"Here we go!" Wheelan said, pure adrenaline in his voice.

Alex knew the feeling all too well, but right now, all he felt was sick for what was about to go down.

"Please God, let this be the right decision." If it wasn't, it would certainly be his last decision.

~ Irene ~

Cal parked the SUV he'd borrowed — or rented — whatever Saint Paul now offered.

When she'd lived on Saint Paul, only a half-dozen or more people owned cars. Now, nearly half the population had some sort of beat-up and past-its-prime mode of transportation. Even her parents now owned some unidentifiable vehicle. She wasn't sure of the make or model, since the emblem on the hood had rusted down to nothing more than a nub, along with half the trunk and undercarriage.

As Cal plucked her luggage out of the cargo area, she dug for the knife in her pocket. Now that she wasn't near her mother, she'd use it. She wasn't sure how she would do it, but she knew damned well she wouldn't let him take off with her without a fight.

Cal tapped on the rear glass. "I'll get the plane readied and come back for you, my love."

Grrr ... If he called her *my love* one more time, she was pretty sure she'd have grounds for murder. Certainly, a jury of female peers would see it that way.

As Cal practically skipped to his waiting plane, Irene used the knife to gouge the grab handle. None of the screws that connected the handle to the roof were visible, so she pried at the plastic cover, which she assumed concealed the screws.

Frustrated, she tapped at the power window switch. She didn't want to endanger anyone's life, but while he was busy, maybe she could call out to anyone who passed to call authorities.

"Damn it!" She tapped the button again and again. "Freaking child-safety locks! Are you kidding me?" Irene stared back at Cal's plane. Too late. He was climbing out of the pilot's seat. "Daaammnnn it all to hell."

She tugged and tugged, but the stupid grab handle wouldn't budge. Frantic, she tried to wrench her wrist free, but all she managed to do was rip open her flesh. As thin as she was, her wrist bones were too pointy. Cal had tightened the cuff until it had clicked, then he'd clicked it again.

Tears streamed down her cheeks. Surely, he didn't plan to kill her. If he did, he certainly wouldn't have let her mother see his face. What then? Did he think he could keep her locked in his cellar forever and no one would come looking for her? Or was he so insane that he thought she'd actually fall in love with a murderous, drug-dealing thug?

Cal smiled widely as he approached the vehicle.

Oh, God, maybe he is that insane.

Irene gnawed on her lip and shoved the knife back in her pocket, wiping away the few tears that had escaped. If he saw the knife before he unlatched her, she wouldn't stand a chance.

Cal opened the passenger door. He unlocked the latch from the grab handle but didn't remove the one from her hand. Instead, he latched her hands together. His cold fingers brushed her neck as he loosened her scarf. Freeing it, he draped the scarf over the cuffs, masking them in the event anyone stepped out of the small control tower.

"Don't want you running off now that we're out of your mother's house, do we?" Cal crooned. "Don't worry, Irene. We're going to have a great life. We have a lot in common."

She stared up at him, doing her best not to spit in his face as she'd seen in so many movies. But no, she was better than him — or at least she was above doing something so grotesque.

This was her final moment, though. Planes didn't have child-safety locks. As soon as he buckled in and was taxiing down the runway, she'd jump out. If she jumped right before the plane lifted, she'd more than likely hit gravel or dried grass. He wouldn't be able to stop. He'd have to circle back around and land. By the time he caught up with her, she'd be in the tower, and she'd have whoever manned the station to call the police.

She'd just have to play nice until then. "Umm ... great ... plane," she hacked out the words, which made her statement less convincing. She cleared her throat and tried again, "Is this your largest plane?"

Cal escorted her up the steps and eased her into an overstuffed white leather swivel chair.

"It is. It's fully equipped with a master suite and

kitchen. Once we're in the air, I'll set the plane on auto-pilot and give you the grand tour."

Irene swallowed the lump in her throat. Apparently, he wasn't going to uncuff her until they were in the air. It'd be harder, but still, she'd manage. Heck, maybe she'd manage to not break a wrist, since she wouldn't be able to block her fall.

She stared at the door as Cal started to latch it shut. What if he locked it?

Realizing she had to act immediately, she jumped up and ran into Cal full force. The impact knocked him head-first out of the plane. His arms flailed as he tried to catch the door but found nothing but air. Irene, her hands shackled, was unable to stop her forward momentum or grab a handle, so she tumbled out after him.

Cal landed with a scream and then fell silent. Irene found Cal was good for one thing: a landing pad.

CLICK. CLICK. CLICK.

Irene stared up at a circle of men, some in uniform, some in plain-clothes. Some Aleut, some pale white. And Alex.

"Cal Landrum," a man in uniform shouted. "You're under arrest for the attempted abduction of Irene Rose."

"I think I knocked him out," Irene said to the man, then scowled at Alex. "You're late!"

Alex blinked. "Late for what? I brought the cavalry."

Irene struggled to get up, so Alex reached for her.

"I can manage," she groused. "I saved *myself* this time. So I suspect I can handle this little inconvenience." She righted herself, then dug in Cal's pocket for the keys. "On second thought, a little help, please."

Alex shook his head but reached for the keys and

freed her.

Cal groaned, tilting his head up to take in the group of law enforcement. "Son of a bitch!" He laid his head back on the runway.

"Cal Landrum," said the officer ... or agent, — whatever he was — a second time, "You're under arrest for attempting to abduct Irene Rose. We have a warrant for your estate and aircrafts, so we'll add all the rest of the charges later." The officer then proceeded to Mirandize Cal.

Irene turned back to Alex. "What the hell? How do they know who I am and what Cal was attempting to do?"

Alex lowered his lids. "You're right. I am late. And I'm sorry. I knew Cal would go after you the moment he knew you weren't with me, but I didn't expect him to go the same day."

Irene held up her hands. "You used me as bait?"

Alex licked his lips. "No, not really. I knew he'd come after you, so I made sure I was here when he did. I tracked his plane here, but then I had to convince the locals that he planned to go after you. By the time they arrived at your house, your mother said he'd just left with you. So, the officers waited for him to put you on the plane."

"So, you allowed them to use me as bait," Irene growled.

"I saved you, Irene. For the fourth or fifth time. I've lost count. And you used me."

"I saved myself this time, Alex. I delivered Cal to you and your team face-down on the tarmac." She planted her hands on her hips. "And ... used you? How on earth did I use you? I was nothing but a mistake to you. If it weren't for *my* plane crashing, you would have already offed yourself."

Alex huffed. "Well, that's just great! Thanks for throwing that in my face."

"I'm sorry. I shouldn't have said that. Besides, I understand why you were going to do what you planned, even if it was stupid."

Alex spurted out a laugh. "Is that an apology? At least I wasn't engaged and sleeping with the rescue worker!"

The circle of men gawked in their direction. "Oh, for crying out loud," Irene said. "We could do this all day." She turned and stormed toward Cal's SUV, clicking the fob as she approached. She called over her shoulder, "Tell them to put my bags in the terminal. I'll get them later. Bye, Alex!"

Yes, she was being stubborn, but she needed to calm down. And there was somewhere far more important for her to be. She had to go check on her mother.

When she was feeling more grateful, she'd seek out Alex. Until then, she had seventeen years to make up.

CHAPTER 24

~ Alex ~

Alex watched Irene storm off. Then turned for his plane.

He tossed a look over his shoulder at Sheriff Wheelan. "You coming with me, or you hanging out here for a while?"

Wheelan looked from Alex to Irene. "Aren't you going after her?"

"Nope!" he popped the word. "I promised to bring her home safely. I did my job."

Wheelan shook his head. "Damn, Alex. Here I thought some woman actually got her hooks in you, but you're still the same player you've always been."

Alex shrugged. "You coming?"

"Nah, man. This is the biggest bust in my life! I'll find my way back to Falcon Run. Thanks for the tip on Landrum. Imagine me, a small-town sheriff, taking down a major meth dealer."

Alex offered Wheelan a nod and headed off to his plane. He didn't care if anyone knew who really took down Cal, but he hoped Wheelan would give the Midnight Sons a thumbs-up. He may have gotten Cal off his back, but he still had money matters to think about.

Sam would be home next week, and Alex needed a

plan, something to offset the fact that they lost Old Betsy, along with all the other tales Sam would hear about.

Alex took off from Saint Paul and never looked back. Instead, he set his sight on the horizon. The weather would be nice soon. In four months, more than half a million people from around the globe would be visiting Denali.

Cal Landrum was not only out of the illegal drug trade, he was also out of the charter business, which meant there was an opening. A big opening.

Despite how Alex felt about Irene's clear, "Bye, Alex," she'd been right when she said people would pay for excursions. With Cal behind bars, there was a huge hole in the tourist trade.

"That's it, Dad!" Alex looked out at the heavens, at the clear skies now that he was away from Saint Paul and nearing Anchorage. Erik, Sam, and Daire needed official licensing, but they all knew how to fly. He'd taught them all. Vince had already taken all his courses and had his pilot's license.

We'll still run the search and rescue, but with Cal out of the picture, we can charter planes and helicopters. Glacier tours. Whale watching. Northern lights …

It would work.

"And how are we going to pay for the extra planes and helicopters, Alex?" They weren't the first words out of Sam's mouth, but it was the first real conversation they'd had. Sam had been home for a day, and after all the hugs and settling in, the team — all six of them with Nora now — sat down for a meeting.

Alex resisted sighing at Sam's negative reaction to his idea. "You don't think the bank will loan us the money with our track record? Who knows Alaska better than us? Who would tourists trust as much as a tried and true rescue team to take them on adventures?"

"I'm not saying it's not a great idea, Alex. But without collateral, the bank isn't handing over millions of dollars. Sure we'd have the aircraft as collateral, but they'd want a huge down payment, and there are a lot of other expenses to think about. The house is already mortgaged. What else do we have?"

Vince cleared his throat. "How 'bout my house? I can't see that I'll move back there any time soon. Since Karen left me high and dry, it would cost a fortune for me to replace all the furniture, appliances, and kitchen utensils. Hell, Mom cooks better anyway. Why would I want to live in an empty house when I have all of you?"

Sam shook his head. "That's how you were going to try to get your boat back, Vince. I won't allow that."

"Maybe ..." Nora started, but Sam lifted a hand, cutting her off.

"I know what you're going to say, Nora. And we appreciate it, but you can't stress yourself out. Not with being pregnant."

Nora sighed.

Alex smiled at Nora. She was always in his corner, even when Sam wasn't. "Thank you, Nora. It's okay. It was just a thought."

"It's a good thought, Alex," she said. "I like it, and I think it might be doable." Sam lifted his eyes instead of rolling them. And Nora smacked his arm. "Stop being so negative, Sam. It's a good idea. You mentioned the two of us leading hikes, so why couldn't we make an entire business out of it?"

"Because you're pregnant."

"Oh my God." Nora threw up her hands. "You can be so bullheaded sometimes. You were in the same office as the doctor and me. Weren't you listening? The doctor said I can continue the activity I already do. No, I can't go into a ring, but since I'm accustomed to exercise, he said I could keep going as long as I'm comfortable."

The table of men fell silent as Nora lectured Sam. No one ever stood up to Sam as Nora did. Alex tried not to smile, but he liked it … he liked her.

A pang stabbed his chest. He missed Irene. Determination and stubbornness were two of the qualities he liked most about Irene. She didn't fall at his feet. She didn't say what she *thought* he wanted to hear. She spoke her mind.

But it had been more than a week, and he hadn't heard from her —

"Okay, okay," Sam's words cut through Alex's meandering thoughts. "Fine! Alex, if you really want to do this, go for it. But … you're heading this up." Sam narrowed his eyes, drilling Alex with a fatherly stare. "I'll keep up with the rescues, so you can work 'round the clock on a proposal to present to the bank. If I need you for a rescue, I'll let you know. Otherwise, no messing around. If you want to do this, we're going all in."

Sam turned to Vince. "And no, we will not be touching your house. I'll talk to Mom, and if she's in, I'm sure we can get another loan."

Their mother Claire was still CEO. Even though she didn't get involved with day-to-day rescues, she kept her eyes on the books. Alex could only hope that she would be on his side.

The door creaked open. "I'm in!" Claire said. She approached the table, squeezed Alex's shoulders. "I love this idea. Alex, get with me when you're ready, and we'll work on a website design, tours, and prices. We'll take this to Dan, and he won't be able to say no. We've paid back every loan we ever took out. He's not going to say no."

Alex stared up at his mother, then his brothers, and then Nora. They had faith in him. More faith than he'd ever had in himself. But he had faith in himself now. And for whatever faith he lacked, he'd believe in his team. Believe in what his father had seen in him. What Irene had seen in him before she'd learned the truth about his weak spirit.

This would work. He would make it work. Along with his family, he would save the Midnight Sons, and more importantly, make his father, mother, and even the man in the mirror proud of him.

~ Irene ~

Irene stared down at the bound pages and the accompanying contract.

She'd done it. Well, she wasn't finished yet. She had to make one stop before she finalized the contract.

She shoved the document into her satchel, scooped up her purse and keys, and headed to the door.

After locking the front door of her condo, she inhaled the cool salty air. The weather was a perfect forty-eight and sunny. She loved sunny days in Anchorage.

Choosing to spend the last three months in Anchorage had been dangerous ... dangerously close to Alex, that is. So many days she'd wanted to drive the short two hours to Alex's house.

But she couldn't. Alex had needed this time. She had needed this time.

It'd worked — for her. She still wanted him as much — more — than she had on Middleton. Whether he still wanted her, she couldn't be sure, but he'd done other things. She'd been watching from afar, waiting to see if Alex would try to end his life or try to improve it. The Midnight Sons had been all over the news. And she hadn't heard of anything bad happening, so maybe the publicity had helped some.

She, of course, had needed the time to write. And write she had.

Irene uploaded the e-file her agent had sent, and then used her text-to-speech app to listen for any changes. She could listen to at least a third of the story during her drive.

Two hours later, she pulled onto a side road. Even in April, plowed snow still lined the streets in Falcon Run. She checked the address on the mailbox, then pulled into the long circular driveway and hopped out of her SUV.

The two-story house sat on several acres, with a barn off to the side. Multiple mini cabins sat behind the house, next to a lake.

For just a moment, Irene closed her eyes, imagined five young boys playing hide 'n' seek, dirt biking, sledding ... She imagined Alex as a twenty-something, sneaking young women into the cabins after dark. Then an expression she didn't want to see bombarded her thoughts. Alex coming home after losing his father. Having to tell his mother and brothers that he was gone.

No, she didn't hold any ill will against Alex for considering suicide to make up for the wrong he felt he'd done to his family. What she did hold against him was his inability to understand her situation ...

Still, she had to do this.

Irene rolled her shoulders and walked up the front stoop. She knocked on the door, waiting patiently.

Dogs barked. A "hang on" sounded behind the door, along with a "stay." The door cracked open and a familiar face poked out. "I said, stay!" Vince, the fair-haired brother inched his way out of the front door, shoving two furry heads back in the process. "Irene!" He stuck out his hand. "Um ... what brings you to Falcon Run?"

Irene accepted his hand. "Hi, Vince." She stared down at the envelope in her hand. "Is ... Alex home?"

"He's at a meeting."

Irene bobbed her head. "Of course. I just thought that maybe on a Sunday ... he might be available."

Vince sighed. "I'm sorry."

Irene handed him the envelope. "Well, when he returns, will you give him this?"

Vince took the large envelope. "Sure."

Irene shrugged. "I guess that's it, then."

"I'm sorry, Irene. If it's any consolation, Alex is doing really well. He's just super busy with the new business."

New business? "I'm glad. Just give him that please. He can call me if he has any questions."

Vince nodded and Irene turned to leave. She stared up at the house one last time, then shrugged and walked down the steps.

She opened her car door at the same second the house door swung open with a *thwack*, hitting the iron railing.

"What the hell is this?" Alex asked as he charged down the steps.

"Oh, you're home?" Irene offered sarcastically.

Alex stopped two feet from her, then shoved the manila folder at her. "I don't need your charity."

"It's not charity, Alex. It's yours. If you sign off on the book, that is. If you don't, my publisher will just change the name of the Midnight Sons to something else."

Irene moved to enter her car again, and he stopped her. "And the check just happens to be for 1.8 million?"

Irene stared down at his hand latched around her arm, and he removed it. "It's what I asked for. What you needed, right?"

Alex shook his head and blew out a breath. "I don't need anything from you, Irene. We're making it. I actually came up with a great idea that's helping the business. Actually, you gave me the idea."

"I did? Well, I'm glad I could be of some help." She waved him off. "So, read it if you want or not, and the check is yours if you sign off. If not, like I said, we'll still publish it. It's a good story. It's my story. And I don't care if you wanted anything from me. You did save my life, and for that, I will be forever grateful. Even if you turned out to be the world's biggest jerk! I stupidly thought that if you knew the truth you might accept me."

Irene yanked the car door open so she could get out of there before she did something stupid. Like cry in front of an uncaring ... un ... everything. How could she have fallen in love with him?

Alex threw the folder down and turned her to look at him. "I'm a jerk? I saved you ... several times. And you did nothing but give me a hard time, made me fall in love with you, and then broke my heart by not telling me you were engaged to someone else. How am I supposed to accept that you're engaged?"

Irene bit down on her lip. "I'm not engaged, Alex. I haven't been engaged for more than a year."

Alex's eyes narrowed. "Then why ... why did that man say that? Why did you turn down my suggestion that we get together once we were back on the mainland?"

"When you called the local news and gave them my name, the first thing they did was contact my station — the news station my ex owns. He said that because he's a publicity hound. He would never miss a chance to get his name on the news." Irene shook her head. "And I turned down your suggestion because of the cancer ..."

Alex shook his head. "What do you mean? What about it? I saw the scar on the back of your head. I read in the news how you took a sabbatical after your operation. I don't understand."

Irene heaved a breath. "Even after surgery, the survival rate is only fifty percent over the next five years, Alex. That's why I couldn't commit to you, to a life —"

Alex pulled her to him and pressed his lips to hers.

In seconds, she felt lightheaded and weightless, as if she might drift away if he weren't holding her so tightly. Without breaking the kiss, he ran his hands through her hair, down her back, over her arms.

All the hurt she'd felt minutes earlier melted away. She lifted her hands to Alex's chest, pulled him closer.

Alex finally slowed his lips. Instead of just kissing her, his lips moved against hers, forming words. "I love you, Irene. I haven't stopped. Please tell me you love me, too."

"I love you, too, Alex, but —"

He pulled back to look at her. "No buts. If I only have five years with you, I want to make every second count. How dare you steal the last three months from us, making me think you were engaged?"

"Alex." Irene stared up at him. He was even more handsome than she'd remembered. "There's more, Alex. I can't have kids. I can't —"

"Irene," he smiled, "you can't talk me out of loving you no matter how hard you try. Whatever road we have together, fine, as long as we're heading in the same direction, I'm all in!"

Irene smiled through happy tears. "Okay then. I'm all in too."

Alex wrapped his arm around her waist and turned her to the house. "Good. Come meet the family."

Irene leaned against him, feeling completely at ease. He wanted her … just as she was. She stopped. "Alex, the manuscript! That's still 1.8 million dollars."

Alex waved his hands. "Meh! It's just money. We'll get it later. My mom is probably drooling behind the window, begging to come out and meet you."

As they approached the house, first two dogs, then several people, a woman about fifty-something, Alex's mother she presumed, and a face she knew well, Nora Molina, stepped onto the front porch. Then several men followed the women outside.

Irene smiled. A year ago, she had no one at her hospital bedside. Now she had reunited with her family and possibly gained Alex's large family.

At first, she'd thought that she lost her life when she'd received her cancer diagnosis. But it turned out that she'd not only gotten her life back, but she'd gained a new life in the process.

EPILOGUE

~ Vince ~

Vince Kolya rested a hand on his brother's shoulder as he raised his mug. Alex's officially announced fiancée, Irene Rose, stood on Alex's other side, an arm around his waist.

Daire hopped off his barstool and tapped his glass, signaling it was time to get the party started. "Yo! Listen up!" He tapped a few more times, waiting as the drunken chatter diminished.

Vince waited as his other brothers, mother, and nearly everyone else at Grizz's followed suit, lifting their mugs. "To Alex and Irene!" Vince announced in a sing-song voice.

"*To Alex and Irene!*" The chorus of congrats circled the bar like a human wave at a football stadium, reminding Vince why he loved his small town. No matter what was going down, his fellow dive-bar devotees would ban together.

Vince draped his arm around Alex's shoulders. "An

engagement party... Why didn't I think of that? I thought your drinking buddies and woman only shared wine and song at a wedding reception. Now you get two parties."

Alex stared up at him. "Is that why you got married at nineteen, Vince? For the party? I thought you just couldn't stand being alone even for one night."

Vince cracked his neck. His family—Alex included —knew damn well why he'd married Karen. Karen had been wild and crazy, the first woman who'd challenged him since his high school sweetheart. The night he'd met her had been the first time in fourteen months that he hadn't drunk himself to sleep. Yeah, he and Valery —his first and only love—had been young, but they'd made plans. He'd truly thought that they would be together after high school. Valery had ripped out his heart when she'd left him high and dry, no explanation. But then, Karen had taken what little was left of his soul. Not so much his heart, as he'd never given Karen his heart, but she'd taken everything else he owned, right down to his tattered undershorts.

Refusing to ever let a woman—or his brother for that matter—get to him, Vince wagged a finger at Alex. "Oh, that's right...you never experienced the challenge of sleeping alone. Unlike you, if I wanted a woman in my bed nightly, I had to put a ring on her finger."

"It's gonna be like that, is it?" Alex grumbled good-humoredly, a smile lifting his cheeks. It was all part of the act they'd rehearsed. Alex had ad-libbed the married-at-nineteen part, though, initiating Vince's counterattack. "Not that you *have* a woman I can reveal all your secrets to," Alex continued, "but I'll make sure I remember your antics for the day you do. As for me, my past is behind me." He tugged Irene closer, planting a kiss on the top of her head. "My lady already knows my deep, dark secrets. So nice try, brother, but she's all mine."

Vince leaned behind Alex, scooping up Irene's hand from around his brother's waist. "You sure, honey. He's a wild one, that one. It's not too late. You haven't said *I do*."

Irene laughed, then stood on her tiptoes, kissing Alex on the cheek. "Thanks for the warning, Vince, but it's way past too late. Besides," she winked, "I'm not so tame either."

"*Really?*" Vince wiggled his brows. "Then while you're still single...how 'bout you and I get a little *wild*?" He lifted her hand over Alex's head and led her to the dance floor.

Alex set down his full mug and followed noisily, his heavy boots shuffling on the scuffed planks. "I know women are scarce in Falcon Run, Vince, but come on...

Don't show Irene how great you are. She might not want me," he teased.

Vince glanced back and winked. "A little challenge never hurt no one. Good to keep Alex on his toes, huh, Irene?" He gently squeezed her dainty hand, zigzagging his way.

At the framed section of wood floor designated as the dance floor, Sam pulled up a chair and nudged Irene down. "Have a seat, honey. You're gonna love this."

"Oh!" Irene giggled. "What's going on?"

Vince stepped onto the floor and started clapping a 2/4 meter. The crowd quickly followed suit, maintaining a perfect marching beat. It wasn't the first time the town had cheered him on. The DJ started the CD Vince had given him earlier. Ukrainian folk music flooded the usual honky-tonk bar, and more drunk locals joined in, clapping, stomping, and tapping their mugs.

"As most of you know..." Vince intoned, voice booming. He'd never needed a microphone. He *classically* walked, center stage, with steps that would make many a ballerino jealous. "...my father was a good-for-nothing son of a bitch who never gave me anything but a black eye. But that bastard could dance." Vince bowed, held Irene's enthusiastic grin. "Alex said the night you met...you had to persuade him to dance. Before you commit to my spider-monkey brother, let me assure you that *I'm* the dancer in the family."

Vince started slowly with his father's version of the *Gopak* dance. Arms crossed, he crossed the dance floor with low squats and high kicks, then spun into a pirouette.

Irene cheered. Barflies stomped. The rhythm of the claps increased as Vince dropped into deep squats, kicking his legs out repeatedly. Between each kick, he clapped, spread his arms wide, pointed his toes. For his grand finale, he jumped up, literally doing what his brothers called the Russian, as he touched his toes with outstretched arms.

Vince bowed in front of Irene, leaning over to kiss her hand when Erik tapped him on the shoulder. The music changed to a *popping* beat.

Erik, the wiriest of his brothers, began what he called *Locking*. With fast and exaggerated movements, he kicked and popped his arms, jumped, landing in a hurdle stance. The dance reminded Vince of a cross between a Native American ritual dance and hip hop.

Sam stepped onto the floor, sliding Erik out of the way as a rock version of *Smooth Criminal* started. "Not sure what they're trying to prove, Irene. Everyone knows I'm the dancer in the family." Sam shifted his ball cap low on his head, then did his version of the moonwalk. The crowd screamed. Irene hooted, punching her fists to the moderate tempo.

Daire marched onto the floor with high steps, knocking Sam back with a fake shove as a hip-hop beat pounded through the speakers, the bass rattling the hanging glassware. He hopped in front of Irene, fake-licked his hand, drew his fingers down his eyebrows, then stepped forward with one foot, pushing his hands up and out. He knocked out his right knee, rolled back, and knocked out his left knee.

Alex mean-mugged his brothers as he stepped in front of Daire. He waved his hands, speaking to the crowd, "Uh-uh. Ain't happening, brothers."

On cue, the music changed, and Alex sang, changing the words of the 1930s song to: "I *will* dance...just ask me. I *will* dance, Irene, with you." The track segued into *Dancing Queen*, and Alex sidestepped backward, shifting his arms as if he were repeatedly pulling a cross-bow, and wiggling his hips to the beat. He and Alex had worked on the three simple moves for days. Alex definitely wasn't a born dancer.

Irene hopped up, rocking her hips back and forth, blowing kisses at Alex. Thankfully, she didn't care that Alex couldn't dance. Irene loved his brother for everything he was, not his shortcomings.

The music transformed into a lively folk tune again, and Vince and his brothers joined Alex on the floor, clasped arms, and continued Vince's *Gopak* dance, kicking in perfect rhythm. They unlocked arms, and Alex reached for Irene, pulling her onto the dance floor, wrapping his arm across her waist, showing her where to place her arm, and then spinning her in a circle, arms up.

"Oh, my God!" Irene howled. "You guys are crazy! I love it! Another checkmark on my bucket list."

Alex laughed as he spun his fiancée around, smacking Vince on the back mid-rotation. "Vince really is the dancer in the family. He's been working on this for weeks, as an engagement gift to us."

Irene blew Vince a kiss. "Thank you, Vince!"

Vince laughed and returned the air kiss. "Just be grateful I drink too much, Alex. If I hadn't been passed out drunk after Sam and Nora's reception, I would have been the one keeping Irene company, and believe me, I wouldn't have questioned her dance request."

"I'm thankful *every* day, Vince!" Alex called, twirling Irene away.

Nora, her baby bump clearly pronounced at seven months, joined Sam. Erik and Daire reached for the closest women; there were always eager women waiting for men who were willing to dance in the dive bar.

Vince danced his way toward his quasi-adopted mother, Claire Belgarde. He had no desire to lead on local women by dancing with them. Too many desperate singletons in Falcon Run, and he was too jaded. It'd be a cold day in hell before he let another woman sink her claws into him. Sure, he liked to play, but like Alex used to do, he now only dated tourists.

Nope, his only goal was buying a new fishing boat and heading back out to sea, away from all the reminders of his *biological* family.

Just as he neared his mother, a woman stepped into his path. His legs locked in place, refusing to move.

Valery Yura, the woman he hadn't seen since their high school graduation, smiled and stepped into his arms with practiced precision. She turned him back toward the dance floor, pressing her body against his as though she hadn't left Alaska twelve years ago without even a *Dear John* letter.

"Hello, Vikentiy."

Thank you for reading *Alex's Atonement*. I hope you enjoyed Alex and Irene's story and will want to jump right into *Vince's Chance*.

Also, if you enjoyed reading Alex's Atonement, please consider posting a review on Amazon.com, BookBub.com, and/or Goodreads.com.

Find links to continue the Midnight Sons series on www.CarmenDeSousBooks.com/MidnightSons.

VINCE'S CHANCE

Vince Kolya inherited only one trait from his biological father: a need to be on the sea. The rest of his life
he has tried to emulate what he learned from his unoffi-
cial adopted family, the Belgardes: dedicating his life to
helping others instead of abusing them. Unfortunately,
he's yet to find a woman who wants the same things
he does in life. It's bad enough that his wife left him,
but she also failed to make his boat payments while he
was on a three-month stint. Giving up on relationships,
Vince throws himself into working with his family's
search & rescue team. Highest on his to-do list, though,
is saving money to buy another boat so he can get back
on the water, away from the reminders of his abusive
past.

Now that her father is dead and buried, Valery Yura is
coming home to her beloved state of Alaska in hopes
that moving her troubled son to the place where she
grew up will transform him into the loving young man
he once was. The last thing she needs is a distraction,
especially when it comes in the form of the gorgeous
man she's loved her entire life—Vince. A few too many
drinks and sexy dancing on the dock, and she's repeat-

ing ancient history, a situation she can't allow, so she runs from his bed. When her son goes missing after a fishing excursion, Valery feels that the authorities aren't doing everything possible. Although she's resigned herself to never seeing Vince again, she needs his help.

As much as Vince tries to hold onto his feelings of anger and abandonment, knowing it's paramount to protecting his heart, he finds himself falling deeper and deeper for Valery as they search for her lost son. The only way to win her love is to be her hero and find her son, but that hope fades when the authorities call off the search. Determined to give Valery closure and win back her heart, Vince embarks on an all-out manhunt for the missing boy. What he discovers, though, might be a death warrant for him and the woman he can't lose again.

Find links for *Vince's Chance* on
www.CarmenDeSousaBooks.com/MidnightSons

THANK YOU!

Dear friend, thank you so much for taking the time to read *Alex's Atonement*. I hope you enjoyed Alex and Irene's journey. They will return in the other Midnight Sons books, as I know readers love to see what happens after the story ends.

All the books in the Midnight Sons series are stand-alone stories — NO CLIFFHANGERS — but I hope you'll want to read them all, so you can personally meet each member of the team.

Find links to continue the series on
www.CarmenDeSousaBooks.com/MidnightSons

Midnight Sons Series
Sam's Folly
Alex's Atonement
Vince's Chance
Erik's Revelation
Daire's Resolution

ABOUT THE AUTHOR

I love writing. As far back as I can remember I created stories — no, not to my parents — with my best friend. We would sit for hours playing with Barbie dolls, creating new adventures with the iconic toy. Then when I was eight, I actually wrote my first story. A horror story about gigantic fleas of all things; I guess I had a fear of fleas. Who knew I'd grow up to be a romantic suspense writer?

When I was in college, I wrote my first novella. My professor wanted something that entailed drinking and fishing — he was a huge Hemingway fan. Well, he sure received a surprise when he read my short story. It entailed drinking and fishing all right, but there was nothing funny about it. It was sad; it was real life. Luckily, he enjoyed it, even admitted I was the first student who'd ever made him cry and that I had potential.

Unfortunately, it wasn't in my future at the time. After all, I needed a roof over my head and food on my plate. I was on my own and a career as an author wasn't feasible at that juncture in my life. At that time, if you didn't live in the Mecca — aka New York — you didn't stand a chance, or at least that is what my peers insisted. So, I shelved my dreams and set out for a career. I spent the next twenty-five years in the business world, rising to the top of a Fortune 500 company.

Now I'm back, seeking my dream. And guess what, it's a new world where dreams really do come true. My first novel, *She Belongs to Me*, was first published in December 2011. Since then, I've shared many of the stories I'd been writing, and I have many more to come. I waited twenty-some years to share my love of the written word, so I hope you will want to read all my stories.

Until next time, happy reading!

Carmen

ACKNOWLEDGMENTS

My journey as a writer has been a long one. Although my first book took two years to write and publish, the story took twenty-five years to compile, as life tends to get in the way of dreams.

If it weren't for my wonderful, supportive husband, my writing would not be possible. He truly made me believe in a happily-ever-after. Without my husband and two wonderful sons, there would be no reason to write.

I would also like to thank a friend who has cheered me on from the beginning, Tina Wainscott. Tina's books were an inspiration, but more so, her words of encouragement kept me going.

A big thank you to my best friend and cousin, who endure the first drafts of all my books and provide much-needed feedback. Without their insight and support, my novels never would see the light of day.

A thank you to my biggest fan — my youngest son — he has stood by me longer than any other person, championing me constantly through every rough turn in the road. And now, nearly ten years after I wrote my first book, my son is now writing his first series. I can't wait to introduce him to the world. SOON!!!

And lastly, a heartfelt thank you to my avid-reading friends who continually cheer me on and encourage me to finish my stories. You can never know how much it means to me when I read your reviews and see your wonderful comments on Facebook, Twitter, and Instagram. I truly enjoy are fun conversations.

A warm thank you again to everyone! I love you all.

Made in the USA
Columbia, SC
04 May 2020